WILDEST OF ALL

The Donnelly family are a tight-knit bunch. But when one of their own dies without warning, the mother, daughter-in-law and daughter, despite being united in grief, are each sent hurtling in wildly different directions. From the churches of Glasgow to the nightclubs of London, can they find their way back to each other before it's too late? And in the wake of a parent's death, who exactly is responsible for looking after whom?

P. K. LYNCH

WILDEST OF ALL

Complete and Unabridged

CHARNWOOD
Leicester

First published in Great Britain in 2017 by
Legend Press Ltd
London

First Charnwood Edition
published 2018
by arrangement with
Legend Press Ltd
London

A catalogue record for this book is available
from the British Library.

ISBN 978–1–4448–3678–3

Published by
F. A. Thorpe (Publishing)
Anstey, Leicestershire

Set by Words & Graphics Ltd.
Anstey, Leicestershire
Printed and bound in Great Britain by
T. J. International Ltd., Padstow, Cornwall

This book is printed on acid-free paper

Remembering Rana. She loved us.

Peter Donnelly was not a celebrity or a politician. In fact, he was rather insignificant in the grand scheme of things. Even so, his sudden death was akin to a bomb going off in the Donnelly family, and all life after nothing more than a series of aftershocks, the effects of which would be felt far and wide for years to come.

Millions of Peter Donnellys die every single day, of course: unfamous, unremarkable, unconditionally adored, or not, by spouses, children, lovers. This one lived in a modest three-bedroomed house in a neat modern estate in an area of north Glasgow deemed reputable by his mother, Anne, who had never fully recovered from her son's shock decision to abandon a promising law career in order to focus on his musical aspirations. The blame for this decision was laid firmly at the foot of his wife, Jude, who was in fact not his wife, but his life partner — another shameful decision forever tarnishing the family's good name. Jude felt Peter's loss so profoundly she almost dropped out of the world altogether, only clinging on for their daughter, who was seventeen when her father died. Truth be told, she, Sissy, may never recover. The pillars, the giants of her childhood, were all mortally wounded that day when the bomb went off. Nobody knew who was looking after whom.

1

Monstrous

They called her Sissy because her red hair made
them think of the actress in that movie they'd
both loved where pretty much the whole town
winds up dead. But names are a big deal in
Catholic families, so it was agreed the birth
certificate should say Cecilia. That way, Anne
could tell everyone that her first granddaughter
was named after the patron saint of music.
Everyone was happy. No one anticipated any
problems. Of course, the baby didn't have much
of a say in anything, though she became very
clear she preferred Sissy to Cecilia, no matter
what the kids in the playground had to say about
it.

Despite the shock of the first grandchild being
born out of wedlock, Anne took comfort from
the fact that Sissy's arrival was sure to bring
Peter back to his senses. He'd return to the law,
and in time she was sure Peter and Jude would
marry. The baby, like all babies, was a marvellous
opportunity to put everything back on track.

But seventeen years later, none of that had
come to pass, and now the family were gathered
in Peter's hallway awaiting the arrival of the cars
for his funeral. His sister, Susan, had travelled
from Manchester with her three boisterous sons
and unfaithful husband, from whom she would

3

never be parted, because that is the Catholic way. His brother, Danny, was there with his two well-behaved daughters, but not their mother because she — the vixen — had left him, and although Lauren had wanted to attend the funeral, Danny had forbidden it because you don't get to pick and choose your loyalties; you're either with the Donnellys or you're not, and if you're not, then you might as well be against them.

The assembled family looked to the top of the stairs where Sissy stood, wearing a dress for a thirteen-year-old child that she'd found in M&S a couple of days previously. Her dad would have laughed at that. On her feet were a pair of navy blue cowboy boots he'd brought back from a tour around the States. He'd made a mistake with the sizes and bought a couple of sizes too large.

'You're not wearing *those*, are you?' said Anne, as Sissy clumped down the stairs, fascinated by the strangeness of her own feet. When she reached the bottom, she smiled widely and clicked her heels together: *there's no place like home there's no place like home there's no place like home*. Nobody laughed, but Lucy, who was the youngest of Danny's girls, gave a watery smile and whispered to her that they were awesome.

Danny leaned over and kissed Lucy on the head. 'Good girl,' he said, and Sissy experienced it as a stab to the heart. No more daddy kisses for her.

She searched for her mother and found her

leaning against the wall behind Grammy. Red-eyed and vacant, Jude was no longer the mother she'd always known. It remained to be seen who she was now, indeed, who they were, and what they would become together.

'The cars are here,' said Susan, from her look-out post at the living room window.

A barely perceptible pause followed, then Danny said, 'Right. Everyone move out.'

The front door opened and everyone began to shuffle out. The three youngest cousins darted through the grown-ups, desperate for exercise.

'Wait,' said Susan, catching Sissy by the arm.

She brought her into the downstairs bathroom. Taking the corner of the hand towel, she soaked it, squeezed it, and wiped Sissy's face. Then she reached into her handbag and retrieved a comb with which she teased out the tangles in Sissy's hair and twisted it into a low ponytail.

'It'll be windy at the cemetery,' Susan said.

How clever she is to know that, Sissy thought.

'And here,' said Susan, pulling out a pair of tights from her bag. 'Your feet'll get sore in those boots otherwise.'

Susan knelt down and tapped on Sissy's knee, triggering a long forgotten morning routine. Sissy raised first one foot and then the other to allow Susan to pull her boots off.

'Right,' said Susan, running her fingers down the leg of the tights and stretching out the foot. Sissy wiggled her toes into the little cave Susan had created. So many times she had done this with Jude, holding onto her head to keep

5

balanced, always forgetting her mother preferred her to use her shoulders.

But today Sissy held onto the sink for balance, and studied her aunt's head, which she didn't think she'd seen from this angle before. Susan's roots were an inch long and greying. Something about this moved Sissy. She felt sorry for her aunt who'd be seeing absolutely everyone in the whole extended family today. It was the sort of day you'd normally want to make an effort for.

★ ★ ★

Three stretch limousines carried them to the church because Anne said it had to be done properly. Even among the principal mourners there was a hierarchy: Sissy and Jude travelled in the first car, Anne, Danny and Susan in the second, and all five cousins in the car behind, with Susan's husband their reluctant chaperone.

Sissy and Jude took a window seat each. Jude wondered later if perhaps it was the car being so big that put all that space between them. And perhaps it was Anne's tiny stature that made Susan and Danny sit so close, as though their presence was required merely to keep the old lady propped up. And Susan's husband, Phillip, stared at his phone the whole way, while the eldest girls, Lucy and Emma, kept his three boys entertained with a series of games ranging from I Spy to Yellow Car Touch in an effort to keep them calm.

'There's glasses in here!' shrieked the youngest, Andrew, having pressed a button to reveal a drinks cabinet hidden in the door. Lucy and Emma shared a look, a silent agreement to tolerate this now, but tell all to their dad afterwards about how inappropriate the boys had been in the funeral car, knowing already that Danny would nod, then shake his head, and say what else could you expect from boys as wild as they?

Jude had some pills from the doctor, one of which she had swallowed an hour before with one of her special teas, Earl Grey laced with vodka. Her journey to the church passed in a pleasant fuzz, although she was acutely aware of all the edges of her reality, and somewhat amused by the expanding hole at the centre of her which seemed to creep closer and closer to the boundary of her existence. She deliberately let her right arm trail into the centre of the back seat in case Sissy needed something to hold onto. She would always be there for Sissy. Sissy was the most important thing. For Sissy, her hand would always be open, lying between them like a half-built bridge.

★ ★ ★

The service was different things to different people. Sissy was insulted by it. Her dad hadn't been to Mass in years, he didn't believe in Catholic teachings, he'd never met Father whatever-his-name was, standing up there, bald and spitty, acting like some sort of authority over their family. She grasped the pew in front of her and her knuckles whitened. She wanted to use

7

them to smash that stupid man to pieces, especially when he said the words 'cerebral haemorrhage' with that sad face on. Everyone listening knew fine he was the only person in the whole church who hadn't been affected at all.

To the left of Sissy was Anne, for whom every word from the priest was a balm carried on divine energy from God, seeking to find rest in her very soul. She allowed herself to be tangled and carried, his holy words wrapping around her, soothing the skirmish inside. She'd thought she was safe, that she'd seen the worst of everything. They say to lose a child goes against nature, but to lose anyone at her age was a resurrection of all past griefs. A tumult of mixed memories; the mother she barely remembered, her distant father, the childhood she'd never had, the life she should have lived, her husband's passing. All the grief was resurrected and catapulted her to a new world of wisdom, because now she knew how petty, how *insignificant*, each of those losses had been because this loss — *this* — was the truest grief she'd ever experienced, and unless God sent an army to save her, she did not think she could endure it.

But she cleaved to the priest's words. He said all the right things, having been thoroughly briefed in the days between then and now. God would see her through. He always had.

Sissy, offended by the stranger's display of familiarity with her father, looked to her mother for comfort, but Jude's eyes remained closed throughout, her whole being numb with medication, barely hearing anything at all.

When it came time for Communion, the priest came along the front row and offered everyone the Body of Christ. Sissy clamped her lips together and shook her head. She soon regretted her decision when everyone else took it and kneeled down to give thanks. She sat conspicuously upright, like a creature in that game — What was it? Whack-a-Mole — and thought this probably wasn't the time or place for making statements, so she left her pew and joined the line at the back of the church.

She'd never seen so much black before. So many old-looking faces. Were the faces really old, or did grief just make them like that temporarily? She moved slowly down the aisle, unable to look anyone in the eye, anxiety building as she neared the front. She wasn't supposed to take Communion without having made confession, and by refusing Communion the first time hadn't she pretty much declared she wasn't ready to receive it? What if the priest turned her away? In the end, he didn't even recognise her. The bread stuck stubbornly to the roof of her mouth, refusing to enter her undeserving body. She battled it down with her tongue and swallowed it, then hurried to her seat and waited in silence for everything to end, fearing that to join everyone in hymn and prayer would dismantle her fury. If that went, she didn't know what she would have left.

They followed the coffin out but Sissy was the only one who followed it all the way to the car. She watched in disbelief as two grey-haired men in mourning suits settled the coffin inside. Feeling stupid, but unable to restrain herself, Sissy kissed her fingers and darted forward to place them onto the wood, her heart bursting with gratitude that she'd had the foresight to place a small cream envelope in his inside pocket.

She, Jude and Anne had gone to view the body together, and while she'd known writing him a letter didn't make much sense, it had been their thing to leave little notes around the place for each other. It was an absolutely crucial thing to do and if her mother or grandmother thought she was mad, well, she didn't care because she was not ready to stop loving him.

The men closed the doors and she was stranded on the other side of the glass. She knew she'd never be this close again, that he didn't belong to her any more, that he would be transported from here to the cemetery and that hundreds of people would see him pass and not understand what a spectacular human being he had been. They'd see the box, the flowers saying SON and DAD, and the cars following behind, and they'd know for a moment that something awful had happened, but then they'd move on, untouched, never to think of it again. It was just another hearse to slow down for. Something intriguing to sneak glances at from the safety of the sidelines.

She turned around, looking for someone to hold onto, and was surprised to see she'd put considerable distance between herself and her family. Everyone else had stopped at the bottom of the church steps, slowing the exit of those in the back rows. Her mother was already smoking. Her littlest cousins were running around in circles on the church lawn.

She looked for Cam and Rik. She hadn't expected them to be there but as she'd followed the coffin out of the church she'd spotted them squeezed in at the back. They'd probably never understand how grateful she was to see them.

She walked back up the path and joined the fringes of her family, feeling like an intruder. The rest of the congregation gradually escaped the church and drifted off in groups to smoke and talk, probably reluctant to complete proceedings. Then there was a flurry of activity. *Do you know where it is? Can I follow you? You'll get a lift with them if you're quick. I'll see you up there.*

Back in the limousines. People on the other side gawking as they passed. The walk up the hill. That rectangular shape dug out in the ground. The heap of dirt beside it. The green fabric marking the place. Was that to make it look better? Was it something to do with health and safety? The priest standing by the grave, as though he was the head of the dinner table and they all his guests. The red ropes that allowed the coffin to slip into place. Handfuls of dirt to scatter *rat-a-tat-tat* across the box.

The day was grey and dry with a light wind. Unremarkable, really.

⋆　⋆　⋆

The wake was held at the hotel Jude worked at. For some reason she'd reacted strongly against holding it there, but Danny had stepped in when she became hysterical, and her boss, Aleks, said he would take care of everything. It was easier to give in. Platters of sandwiches and sausage rolls came out in their hundreds. There was so much food left over, Father Murphy took a doggy bag home. Waste not, want not.

Sissy, Jude and Anne each sat in three different corners of the room, like boxers, each with their own entourage. Sissy greedily welcomed the vodka Cam had stolen from home. He splashed it into her lemonade beneath the table, making sure she got the biggest measures of the three of them.

Jude also had a long line of drinks before her, and in a short while she'd transformed herself. No longer the zombie of the past few days, she found these people enlivened her. At one point someone said something and she shrieked with laughter, causing the whole room to turn around.

She's sparkly, thought Sissy. How fucking dare she? A week of silence, locked away in her bedroom, unreachable, thinking of nothing and no one but herself, and now look at her.

Anne, on the other hand, maintained a dignified exterior, passing quiet conversation with people who had waited reverentially in line to pass on condolences, sometimes with a soft pat on Anne's hand or arm. If Sissy hadn't been worried about the smell of drink on her breath she might have sat down with Anne and held her hand. He'd been her son, after all. It hadn't occurred to Sissy that her grandmother was affected at all until she'd overheard a stranger in the bathroom talking about it. 'Goes against nature, so it does,' the voice said. 'A terrible thing.' Sissy had remained in the cubicle until she was sure she was alone, reluctant to rejoin a world where, as well as surviving her own grief, she had to think about someone else's too.

★ ★ ★

On the way out, she met Uncle Danny. He greeted her like a long-lost friend, rather than someone with whom he'd spent the past few days in close proximity. 'Sissy!' he exclaimed, and wrapped an arm around her. They shuffled their way along the corridor, he trying to loosen his tie with his free hand.

'He was some man, your dad. My big brother. He was! We didn't always see eye to eye, mind you, but he was my big brother and I loved him. Always looked out for me. See when that bitch . . . sorry, sorry, I know I shouldn't talk like that. See when your Auntie Lauren left me, I was in bits. I don't mind saying it. I was on the floor. You're too young to remember, but look, right, everyone was blown away by this. Ask your mother. Everything had been completely fine. No problems. No nothing. And then out of nowhere . . . bam! She screwed me. And your dad, Sissy, your dad brought me in. Do you remember that? Into his house. Me and the girls living with you? It wasn't for too long. She got the lawyers on me quick-smart. We're bastards, us lawyers.'

'I think I do remember, right enough.'

'Hi Daddy!' said a sing-song voice. Sissy was relieved to see Emma coming down the corridor towards them, the expression in her eyes a sharp contrast to the sweetness of her voice.

'Sweetheart,' said Danny, his breath wet and beery. 'I was just saying about your Uncle Peter. Did I tell you about the time he took on the Gillespie twins for me? Battered them both. They never looked at me again after that. That's the Donnelly way. Stick together. I hope you and your sister remember that. He was my hero. My big brother and my hero.'

Emma had slipped beneath his free arm and, with Sissy's help, began walking him back to the main room.

'Okay, Daddy,' she coaxed, bright and breezy. 'Grandma's just right round this corner, so maybe tone it down a wee bit. We'll sit you here and get you a coffee. Sissy, will you wait with him till I come back?'

Without waiting for a reply, Emma darted off to the bar. Sissy sat beside her uncle and wished for Rik or Cam to make an appearance. Maybe they'd gone into the garden for a smoke. A succession of strangers came by with commiserations. She nodded and bared her teeth in an approximation of a smile and gave thanks to each of them. So much gratitude required.

'Ah, here's my girl,' said Danny, as Emma made her way back to them with a coffee. 'Talk about your alpha females, eh, Sissy? No messing with this one. She keeps me in line, don't you, honey?'

14

Emma smiled blandly as she placed the cup down.

'Has she told you what she's up to, Sissy?' asked Danny. 'Has she? Have you?'

'Daddy, I don't think this is the place,' murmured Emma with a sigh, sweeping her hair behind her ear and securing it with a clasp.

'Don't be daft,' Danny reached across and gripped her knee. 'She wants to know, don't you, Sissy?'

Emma rolled her eyes and shook her head to signal her embarrassment, then confessed she'd been cast in a television drama.

'It's just a small part,' she said. 'It's no big deal.'

'No big deal,' said Danny. 'It's massive! It'll be seen all across the US. She's in two episodes.'

'Wow,' said Sissy. 'That's . . . surreal.'

'Your Uncle Peter would have been proud.'

'No doubt,' Sissy continued to smile and nod, like one of those toy dogs you get in the back of cars. 'Well done, cuz.'

★　★　★

Later, she found Rik and Cam smoking at the back of the hotel gardens beside the pond, and Cam advised her to get herself some normal relatives.

'Yeah,' agreed Rik. 'It's your dad's funeral. You should be everyone's focus, not her. What a knob.'

The sun was about to slip behind a cluster of trees. The day would soon be over. Suddenly

Sissy realised her feet were throbbing. She kicked off the boots and removed her tights. In the function suite, overhead lights came on, prompting people to rise and gather their belongings. She shuffled herself to the water's edge and lowered her feet into the pond. The coldness of the water was soothing, distracting.

'He looks just like him though,' she said. 'I never noticed before.'

They had no idea what to say, so they removed their socks and shoes and rolled up their trouser legs and joined her in the pond. They smoked and drank and laughed, revelling in the oddity of the situation, and gentle ripples on the water marred their dark reflections.

★　★　★

No one wanted to leave, surprisingly even Jude. As the place gradually emptied, the presence of Susan's three energetic boys became overwhelming.

'Come and sit by your grandma,' Anne urged them, but they could only bear to sit for a moment before the urge to slide across the function suite's dance floor overtook them.

'Oh, Phil, take them away,' Susan sighed, and he began the business of rounding them up.

The family members were at last sitting around the same table, forced together as more and more people left. Lauren had collected Emma and Lucy from the hotel and that, more than anything else all day, had pushed Danny into an unrivalled moroseness. If it weren't for the fact that his mother needed him to be strong, he might have allowed himself the luxury of tipping over the edge.

'Where's Sissy?' Anne asked, but no one knew. Anne rattled her nails against the table. She didn't enjoy one of her brood being unaccounted for now that the place was so empty. She didn't enjoy either that Jude, mother of the missing child, seemed not to mind. She clicked her tongue, only too aware that everyone around her had moved into a state of uncaring exhaustion, and that soon she would be deposited in her house and left alone with her thoughts and grief.

'Andrew, come here!' Phil's voice put paid to the giggling that had grown steadily louder and more manic.

'For God's sake, Susan, can't you do something about that?' asked Danny, pinching the bridge of his nose between thumb and forefinger.

'He's five, Danny. What do you expect?' said Susan, who rose anyway and went to assist her husband.

Danny rolled his eyes in Anne's direction but she was looking past him out into the garden. Out of the shadows emerged three swaying figures. They were all bare-foot and soaking wet up to the waist.

They struggled with the sliding door, and when they finally managed it, they tumbled laughing into the room, too drunk to notice their audience.

'Cecilia Donnelly!' said Anne, whose voice had barely risen above a whisper all day but now, powered by indignation, could be heard clearly by everyone. Even the woman drying glasses behind the bar turned around to stare.

'Sissy!' a young voice cried.

Sissy whipped herself round in time to see her littlest cousin running and throwing himself at her. She tried to catch him but the surprise of his enthusiasm, combined with her drunkenness on the wet, slippery floor, conspired to knock her over. She landed flat on her back.

There was a stunned silence, and then a wailing from Andrew, and then came laughter from Rik and Cam, and before she could help herself, she was laughing too. Phil plucked Andrew from the floor and carried him out, and Cam and Rik each took one of Sissy's hands and pulled her up. The room whirled unpleasantly around her.

'You are a disgrace, young lady. Have you forgotten where you are?'

Anne had crossed the room and stood now, tiny and ram-rod straight before her grand-daughter. Sissy felt herself shrinking beneath her glare. The room was so bright and hot after the cool darkness of the gardens. She closed her eyes and was greeted by a wave of nausea. She immediately buckled and vomited, narrowly missing her grandmother's pointy shoes. She was distantly aware of voices around her, expressing their dismay.

Jude and Aleks swooped in and carried her through to their office, while Susan and Danny steered Anne in the direction of a waiting taxi.

'I'm sorry,' Sissy mumbled. 'Is Andrew okay?'

18

'What did he think he was doing running at you like that?' said Jude, wiping Sissy's chin.

'He's just a kid,' Aleks said. 'Take it easy.'

'Easy for you to say,' Jude snapped, and then, 'Sorry. I'm sorry. You're right. I don't know what I was thinking.'

'Don't worry about it,' he replied. 'It's a difficult day.'

Jude poured water from a jug on her desk and gave it to Sissy. Then she turned to Aleks and said, 'I need to pay you.' She reached into her bag for her cheque book.

Aleks frowned and held his hands up. 'No. Jude, come on. You don't pay.'

'Please, Aleks. I must.'

He stepped towards her and covered her hands with his. He spoke softly. 'No. No way. Let's not have this.'

She leaned back from him, twisting her head round to check on Sissy. A timid knock came on the door and Cam peeked his head in.

'I brought this,' he said, holding out a red plastic bucket.

'I think that ship has sailed, but thank you,' said Aleks, taking it from him.

'Sorry,' Cam said. 'I should have been watching her.'

A derisive snort came from Jude, who was leaning against the desk, feeling none too steady herself. 'None of us are in best shape, Cam. Not your fault. Come on, Sissy, time to go.'

She stretched her hand out for Sissy to take and succeeded only in knocking her handbag off the desk. The contents spilled over the floor.

'I will drive you,' said Aleks. 'You can't manage on your own.'

His words instantly dismantled Jude's already fragile authority. She collapsed into herself, her shoulders heaving as huge sobs raced out of her. Aleks apologised profusely, taking her in his arms, telling her he hadn't meant she wouldn't be able to cope without Peter. Of course she would, she was strong, she was a good mother — all of this in his gentle, Polish-accented, near-perfect English. Neither of them noticed Sissy slide off her chair to gather up the contents of Jude's bag.

Cam remained at the door, unsure of what to do. He looked back down the corridor to the reception area where Rik waited for him. Rik's mother was due to pick them both up and drop Cam home. He took one last look at the tableaux in the office and decided Jude's boss could manage without him.

Aleks sat Jude down and urged her to breathe deeply. She tried to catch hold of his words, nodding as she gulped down huge pockets of air. Like a tent in a storm, all her ropes were untethering. She gripped his hands as he knelt on the floor before her, coaxing her back to calmness. When the panic subsided, she looked into his eyes: hazel, flecked through with amber, and brimming with concern. He was asking nothing of her, and yet she had a driving need to get away from him, couldn't face his kindness. She had no choice but to accept his offer to drive them home. Only thirty more minutes in his company. Count it down.

Kneeling on the floor behind her was Sissy. She'd packed up the bits and pieces that had fallen out of her mother's purse and thrown into the wastepaper basket a series of crumpled tissues. Now she stared down at the collection of cards and envelopes that had slipped out along with everything else. One cream-coloured envelope in particular caught her eye. Her brain told her it couldn't be, but her hand reached forward and picked it up. It was as real as all the others. The rest of the room fell into insignificance as she turned it over with trembling hands. There, in her own forward-sloping handwriting, was the word *Daddy*, and what came crashing down harder than the monstrous sense of betrayal, was the certain sad knowledge that it was now too late for it ever to be delivered.

2

A Moment in Time

Peter hadn't owned a suit, so he'd been buried in one of Danny's. Anne stayed with him in the funeral home for as long as they would allow, and prayed over his body, while trying to resist the disturbing double effect of seeing both her sons lying dead before her.

She felt hollow inside. So many people had been lost over the years, she had barely noticed the loneliness creeping in. Even after her husband Patrick died, Peter and Danny were both such gregarious characters, they papered over the cracks in her existence. She was nearing the end of her seventies, if she wasn't there already. It was quite possible she'd turned eighty without realising. There had been so many deaths. But surely there could be no future beyond this one.

She banished the thought as soon as it arrived. Life was a gift. She was blessed, even in her darkest hour. She must not forget this. Hadn't the Almighty himself sacrificed his own Son so she might live? There was a reason the Good Lord had left her so long and taken the others. There was a plan. There had to be.

Jude had taken Sissy outside to wait in the car but left behind the scent of alcohol that had followed her like a cloud over the past few days.

Anne tried not to judge, but already it was clear their situation was precarious. She worried for Sissy. Jude was in no state to take care of her. Seventeen was such an important age.

She prayed, and gradually a picture began to emerge, a plan that made sense of everything. She stood up and rested her hand on the chest of her first-born. She leaned over and placed a kiss on his forehead, so strange and stiff now his soul had departed. Then she slipped her hand into his inside pocket and took out the letter Sissy had deposited just moments ago. To save her granddaughter, she had to know everything about her granddaughter. She weaselled her thumb into the corner of the envelope and opened its secrets, then, remembering where she was, she slipped it into her coat pocket to read elsewhere. Peter deserved all of her attention. She prayed for him, and vowed she would take care of his family in his absence. She did not allow the part that was her own grief to overwhelm her. Dignity. Gratitude. He was in the arms of the Lord. No doubt he had found his father in Heaven and they looked down on her now. But what would they see?

Stifling a cry, she left the room. All the solemn certainty she'd had moments ago vanished in the very ordinary little corridor she now stood in. She might have stepped straight back into the visitation room and returned the letter had the funeral home's director not greeted her. They'd already stayed open for her long past their regular hours. The only thing she could do was say thank you and leave.

Danny had waited to drive her home. She felt the letter in her pocket and was appalled with herself. She wouldn't read its contents. But she'd felt such assurance as she'd taken it, there could be no denying it was God's hand that had guided hers. She would pass it on to Jude. After all, a mother needed to know what was going on in their teenager's mind, even at the best of times.

3

Into the Woods

Sunlight streamed in through the window and pulled Jude in from the dark. Disorientated, she turned over on the sofa and saw the lava lamp in full flow on the sideboard; the melted wax, transformed by heat into a bubbling liquid of green and violet, had spent the whole night rising and falling for no one's entertainment. On the coffee table, the empty bottle and dirty ashtray; in her mouth her tongue, dry and rough as sandpaper. Then the headache, thick and loud and persistent, followed by the crushing recollection of what life was now.

On the wall above the fireplace hung the family portrait Anne had organised for Peter's fortieth a few years earlier. They all looked so young, sitting behind each other on the photographer's white rug, looking down on her inappropriately like a bunch of loons. She'd squirmed through the entire experience, hating every moment of it, but in this one picture the photographer had somehow captured a moment of genuine glee. She wished she could remember what they were laughing at.

The clink and clatter of mugs and bowls told her Sissy was already in the kitchen. She rubbed her face, stretched out and groaned. The first day of the rest of their lives. Then she heard Sissy coming down the hall towards her; her lightness, her gait, even her breath, all things familiar and customary, learned through the everyday intimacies of having shared a house for years.

At first she didn't realise it was a door slam. The noise was so sudden and invasive it jangled her into a protective pose with her arms over her head. But when the walls didn't fall down and she realised there was a vacancy where Sissy had just been, she moved quickly to the window to see her daughter, dressed in school uniform, moving along the pavement at speed.

She ran to the front door and down the garden path, the cold hard ground a shock to her stockinged soles. She called out, but Sissy didn't respond or even look back, and Jude was left in the street wondering what to do. She'd anticipated them having some time alone after the intensity of the past week. So many people coming and going, so much to prepare — she was exhausted. Returning to work was a distant prospect for Jude and she'd assumed the same of Sissy, but she'd always had trouble predicting what her daughter would do or say or think in any given situation. Unlike Peter. Peter and Sissy had a bond she could only envy. He was the bridge between them. Without him, she feared they'd be rendered two little islands, floating in opposite directions until they lost sight of each other completely.

★ ★ ★

As Sissy burned her way down the street, her passion was interrupted by the practical notion

26

that she should have worn trainers because her smooth-soled school shoes threatened to steal her feet away from under her. Regardless, she picked up her pace, the only objective to put distance between herself and her mother's voice.

She caught the earlier bus and sat at the front, away from the other kids, who were already hyped up on sugar, judging by the amount of noise coming from them.

When they reached their stop, Sissy found herself trapped in her seat, unable to stand, or look them in the eye, much less walk with them the remaining distance to school. They gathered in the aisle beside her, bags jostling, bumping her head and shoulder, and then — was it her imagination? — a hush fell over them as they passed her. Only when the last kid passed the driver did she follow them off.

Two girls in fourth year had waited for her. They nudged each other until one found the courage to step forward. 'Sorry to hear about your dad.' The other one: 'Me too. Sorry. It's shit.'

She hadn't anticipated this. It made no sense. She'd woken up with such fury and yet now she felt like a fly on a sticky trap. She had no clue how to bring these two separate versions of herself together. She mustered a nod and picked up her pace.

The Head stopped his morning round of school corridors when he saw her. She'd never actually noticed someone's jaw drop before. Partly amused to learn it was a real thing, she followed him into his office and listened to his concerns with detached politeness, feigning indifference to his brazen scrutiny. He spoke carefully, studying her for signs of a breakdown. At long last he sighed and let her go to class 'against his better judgement'.

She would have had more respect for him if he'd had the courage of his convictions.

'You should be at home with your mother at a time like this,' he'd said, but home with her mother was the last place she wanted to be. Sissy and her dad had exchanged notes almost since she'd learned to write. Her last, final letter to him was more important than she could convey. She couldn't fathom why her mother would watch her slip it into his inside pocket, only to remove it as soon as Sissy left the room. Jealousy. Her mother had always been jealous. Even as a little girl, Sissy sensed the power she had over her father.

'Marry me, Daddy,' she'd urged him.

'But I'm married to Mummy.'

'But I want you to marry *me*, Daddy!'

His distinctive laugh that made heads turn, as opposed to her mother's bashful smile and embarrassed eye roll. Floating beneath her rage, Sissy felt something like sympathy, but then she thought again of the letter, and the burning started up again. She welcomed it. She could live like this forever, she thought, taking no shit and getting shit done, but half an hour into her first lesson the flames began to burn low. She squirmed in her chair, trying to resist the heavy settling sensation in her stomach. At break she ran to the shop and bought herself one of those energy drinks the boys liked to drink. She spent the lessons before lunch in a state of anxiety, twisting and turning at her desk, wrapping her ankles around her chair legs in an effort to sit still, the drone of Mr McGonagle's voice like a dentist's drill driving through her soul. She pulled her mobile out and texted Cam.

Whr r u?

His reply was instant.

Wrk. U?

McGonagle is killing me.

U back so soon? Wtf?????

Need out.

Gotcha see u lunchtime @b/house.

The boathouse in the park had hosted several misspent summer evenings between Sissy, Cam and Rik.

She folded her phone over, packed up her books and left, leaving the class in an uproar because McGonagle didn't even notice it happen. She should have signed out in the office, but instinct told her she could get away with anything at the moment, and besides, she didn't care who she pissed off.

'You do know I'm here illegally, don't you? Like, trying not to get noticed?' she said, in reference to his luminous yellow safety vest.

'Aye, and you do know I'm meant to be at work, don't you?' he replied, mimicking her tone. He took out a pack of cigarettes and offered one, which she took, leaning in to catch a light from him, an intimate move she'd learned from her parents and which had become normal between them. They began to walk around the pond, the site of many cider-fuelled Friday nights, the worst of which had resulted in them all falling in, then having to run away and hide from the police.

'Won't you get in trouble from work?' Sissy asked.

'Nah, doubt they'll miss me. Not had time to make myself indispensable yet.'

Cam held his cigarette between his thumb and middle finger, while Sissy took a more classic between two fingers approach. They'd helped each other decide on their style and now they moved quietly alongside each other, the giddy heights of the previous summer a distant memory.

She searched for something, anything, to say. Yesterday had been fine. The people and the alcohol and the structure of the day had carried them through, but today was different. Suddenly Sissy had a huge and heavy sense of the journey that lay before her. She longed to tell him about the letter. It lay in her bag, which was the entirely wrong place for it. She felt it straining against the confines of the book she'd slipped it into: *How to Pass Higher Human Biology*. She felt the words all jumbled up in her mouth, pushing against her lips, begging for escape. She clamped her teeth together, frightened of what they might become if she were to let them out. She felt Cam looking at her and had the sensation of shrinking, becoming less than. Her eyes were still puffy from a week's crying.

'What?' she snapped.

'You should get out of that,' he said, nodding

at her uniform. 'You know what folk are like round here.'

Grateful for something to do, she pulled off her tie and put it in her bag.

'I've an empty,' Cam said. 'We could go there.'

Cam's mum and stepdad dealt in bric-a-brac. They travelled up and down the country to various car boot sales, and when they were gone the teenagers commandeered the place, and smoked the pot Cam's stepdad kept in his bedroom drawer.

'Fine,' she said, slipping her bag from one shoulder to the other. 'Let's go.'

Cam's part of town held a fascination for Sissy and Rik that they would never admit to. Rik described it as 'real' and 'authentic'. Rows of three-storey closes, lots of boarded-up windows, empty roads with cars jacked up on bricks, and usually a lone police car patrolling the area. Occasionally, large groups of teenage boys skulked on street corners and whistled as they went past; Cam would shout over a generic greeting while Sissy and Rik followed his lead and picked up their pace. It was always a relief when they made it into the flat.

It was the last in the block and had been recently refurbished. Laminate flooring through-out, glossy surfaces in the kitchen, purple-framed flower prints on the wall in the living room. Sissy liked to sort through the boxes of seventies junk stacked up in the kitchen: wire pictures, glass swans, ceramic bunny rabbits — the list was endless and unpredictable, but today the flat was empty.

'They took everything. They'll be away till Sunday night.'

Sissy's eyes grew wide. The solution to all her problems — namely how to avoid her mother — had presented itself. They pooled their money. There was enough to get drunk with.

'Party,' said Cam, rubbing his hands together in glee.

Later, when they were drunk and Rik had joined them, Sissy's phone buzzed. She groaned when she saw the message, a stark reminder of reality.

Where are you? Mum x

'What? What is it?' said Cam, deep into a two-person shooter game with Rik.

Cam's. Staying over.

A two-minute delay then: *Ok. Take Care. Mum x*

Sissy hurled the phone across the room. It bounced off the wall, and startled the boys.

'What the fuck was that?' said Rik.

Overcome with remorse, she told them, 'Sorry, sorry, it's nothing, sorry.'

She reached for a cushion and pulled it to her, kneading it with her fists. A huge gaping maw had opened inside. It needed to be blocked up.

'Jesus, Sis. What the fuck?'

She threw the cushion aside, stood up and shook herself like an athlete preparing for a race.

'I need to get out of here,' she exclaimed. 'Who's up for it?'

They headed into the woods across from Cam's house, Sissy leading the way to the collection of empty cider bottles that marked their territory. They felt such ownership of this little patch that abandoning the remnants of their evenings here didn't feel like littering so much as decoration.

Cam, as usual, darted straight up his regular tree, an ash. The King of Trees, the Vikings used to say. Roots in hell and branches reaching towards the heavens. One of the few anecdotes retained from school, though no one could agree if it was Mr Mann in history, or Miss Leech in science that had passed it on.

High in the tree, Cam tipped his head back and yowled like a wolf.

'I can't fucking look at him,' Rik muttered to Sissy. 'Tell me when it's safe.'

'Get up here, ya pair of pussies!'

Rik flinched as half a can of beer landed close by him, splashing his jeans. Sissy picked it up and gulped it down, the bitter taste a long-accepted necessary evil.

'Get to fuck!' called Rik, wiping his trousers with his hand and then drying the hand on his chest. 'These are new.'

'Some view from up here,' Cam called, and then Sissy was on her way, wordlessly scaling the tree. She wanted to be off the ground. She wanted to be where Cam was, high and wild and not giving a shit.

'Oh Sissy, don't,' moaned Rik, but she was already doing it.

'I can see your knickers, you know,' called Rik, as her school skirt flapped around her. 'It's not decent.'

Her wet-soled shoes threatened to slip against the damp wood, but she found spaces to dig and cling and she hauled herself up with unusual ease. Soon she was level with Cam, breathless and irritated but unsure of the reason why. She straddled the branch he was on and shuffled her way towards him, raising herself on her hands and bumping along.

'Not bothered about splinters, then, no?' Cam said with a smirk.

She grinned. 'Do I look like I'm bothered?'

'Please be careful up there,' called Rik. 'I don't want to look like the lone survivor of some forest homicide.'

Another can hurtled through the air and landed beside Rik. He grabbed it and swallowed the white foam spurting out of the top.

'That's right, just keep chucking all your beer at me. I hate that!'

'You all right, Sis?' Cam said in a low voice, conscious of the potential eavesdropper below, but Sissy was rendered speechless by the view of Glasgow behind him: cars twinkling north and south over the far-distant Kingston Bridge, little black birds swooping with grace over the Clyde, and darkness slowly encroaching upon all of it. It was the world without Peter Donnelly, and it was carrying on as normal.

Cam dropped heavily into a sitting position opposite Sissy, jolting her back to the moment. The branch they were on bounced with his weight, his eyes mischievous or malevolent, Sissy couldn't decide and didn't care either way. The bark was somehow both rough and soft with

34

dampness beneath her hands.

'You're going to break that,' warned Rik from below. 'Then you'll be sorry.'

'You scared, Sis?' said Cam, grinning like a villain in one of his comics. 'Wooh, we're going to fall, Sissy, we're going to fall!'

He spread his arms like an aeroplane and tilted side to side, her cue to squeal and beg him to stop, but tonight she met him move for move until his laughing stopped and he gripped her arms with real fear in his eyes.

'Fuck,' he said. This wasn't the Sissy he knew.

'You okay, baby Cam?' smiled Sissy, and her eyes gleamed brighter than the moon as it sailed above her.

'You're fucking mental,' said Cam.

'Have you forgotten my dad just died?' she slapped back.

'What? No! I — '

Keen to push past the moment, Sissy leaned over and called down to Rik.

'You can come up now. We won't do it any more.'

'Nah, you're all right.'

Cam appeared to be still reeling from her harsh words.

'Sissy,' he said, 'I'm sorry. I . . . what's that?'

She'd reached into her skirt pocket and pulled out her dad's letter.

'This,' she said, 'this is something I wrote for my dad. I left it in his suit pocket. It should have gone with him.'

She smoothed the cream envelope across her thigh. Already it looked old. Fit for the bin.

'My fucking mum took it off him. Why would she do that?'

Hoping against hope that he could give her a real answer, she repeated the question, but she should have known he'd be no use. Still, it wasn't his fault he was so immature. She wished she were the same. She wished she hadn't been catapulted into adulthood with no warning. She wished she and her friends were still on the same plane, but it was unavoidable. She'd left them behind on the day Uncle Danny had come to the school. If only she could make it clear to them.

'I don't know,' she said, in a very small, tightly controlled voice that trembled nevertheless. 'I don't know how to live with her now. I don't even know who she is any more. Who is she? I've always looked at her as one half of him. Now he's gone. Who is she? And why would she steal his letter from him? My last letter to him? My letter that rounds everything off. That says goodbye. How am I supposed to say goodbye now? It's too late.'

She clambered to her feet and stamped on the branch.

'Jesus, Sissy, stop that!' Cam stretched a hand towards her, but she continued to bounce up and down. The leaves above them rustled and let loose a mini monsoon of trapped rain. Cam's panicked expression was so comical it made her laugh. 'If you're not going to stop then you need to move so I can get past!' Cam said, clinging onto the branch.

'Why's that? You're okay being a big shot up here as long as you're in charge?'

'Just move, Sissy.'

'Well, you don't get to be in charge all the time, all right? I'm in charge too,' she yelled.

'Sissy, will you move?'

As Cam manoeuvred his way around her, she shook the overhanging branch so the last of the drips fell over them both, and laughed into the night as she did so.

'It's not fucking funny, Sissy. No fucking need for that. None at all.'

But it must have been funny because she continued to laugh as Cam hurriedly fumbled his way to the ground, shaken by the power shift between them. She laughed even more when he and Rik begged her to come back down, and by the time they'd given up on her and were heading home, her peals of laughter were so loud she thought they might bring down the night sky. Neither Rik nor Cam could admit it was a relief when at last they couldn't hear her any more.

4

Butterflies Clinging to Plants on a Windy Day

As the days crept forward on Peter's housing estate, everything and nothing had changed. His street's gentle curve of pale modern houses swept beneath a canopy of rustling green; cars continued to bring people back and forth; children occasionally played out; the same postman came by every morning between eleven and eleven thirty, offloading the usual mix of bills and junk.

For the past few days the postman's bag had been bulkier than normal, thanks to the increase in mail to Ms Jude Corrigan at number twenty-four. It was easy to tell the difference between a birthday and a bereavement. Deaths attracted far more cards than any celebration. The postman felt for the family. Was it a daughter they had? For some reason, he thought so. P. Donnelly had been one of the few faces he saw regularly on this street, someone who always raised a hand in greeting or called hello across the road. He'd never been able to pinpoint his job, exactly. Normally, people who work from home reveal their profession in the mail they receive, but not P. Donnelly. Still, he wasn't a slacker, you could tell. Carried himself well. People like that made his day a little easier. Yes, he thought, as he reached into his bag for today's bundle of cards, P. Donnelly would be missed.

As he approached the letter box, a thought occurred to him. What if, instead of taking the elastic band off and slipping the cards in a few at a time, he just rang the bell and handed them over? He could pass on his condolences. People liked to hear good things about their loved ones, after all, and he'd like to tell them P. Donnelly always had a smile for him, always made delivering in this street a little lift in his day. It was a tiny thing but he was overcome with the urge to share his feelings, and really, who else would understand but the inhabitants of this house? Without thinking about it a second longer, he pressed down on the round brass button and heard the ridiculous sound of the kazoo doorbell carry within. He'd forgotten about that. It made him chuckle, but then it died away and silence fell again, thicker than before. To break it felt wrong. A few houses down, Mrs Conn was heading out with the baby. He caught her eye and nodded. Still no one answered the door. Feeling suddenly foolish, he bowed his head, took the elastic band from the pile and slipped the cards through the letter box, a few at a time. There was always tomorrow.

By minuscule degrees the bricks of the house creaked their way deeper into the earth, as the cards landed on the mat with a soft shuffling thwump. Sissy waited for the shadowy figure behind the glass to retreat before coming forward. Despite knowing what they were, there was still a small thrill to be had in gathering them up, all the tasteful pastel envelopes of various shades, sitting down to see who was thinking of them at this time, if there was any new information to be gleaned from all these strangers, some of whom had known her father longer than she.

'That doesn't mean they knew him better,' Jude said, finding Sissy poring over them.

'But don't you want to see them?' asked Sissy. 'I don't know half these people. Who's Andrea, John and Kevin, for instance? And this one,' she said, holding up a different card. 'Mark, Sandra and kids? Edinburgh postmark. There's so many.'

'Maybe later,' Jude replied, no room in her head for memories of these people. She squeezed behind Sissy's chair and made for the stairs, but before she could climb them Sissy's sharp voice rang out.

'I forgot you only like letters that aren't addressed to you.'

Jude flinched. It had taken over a week to realise Sissy's anger was more than an understandable reaction to Peter's death, and by the time Jude finally discovered the true cause, her memory of receiving the letter from Anne was so hazy, Sissy had interpreted her obfuscation as lying. The false reality they had inadvertently created had taken root, and anything Jude had to say about it sounded fake, even to her. After all, why *had* Anne taken the letter? It really made no sense. 'You need to know what's going on with her,' she'd said. 'You need to keep her safe.' But how could Jude hope to keep her daughter safe when Sissy's default approach was to punish her for something she hadn't even done?

Too tired to attempt another explanation, Jude turned her back on Sissy's rage and climbed the stairs to her bedroom with a heaviness that creaked almost to the very foundations of the house.

Sissy stood the cards on all available surfaces, giving them their rightful place as memory monuments to her dad. Day after day they came, until shelves, unit tops and tables overflowed and there was nowhere else for them to go. They perched precariously over everything like butterflies clinging to plants on a windy day. She returned to them over and over, finding comfort in the words of people she'd never met, words that weren't even addressed to her, but she took them anyway because Jude didn't want them and somehow that made it all the more important to read them:

Dear Jude, so terribly sorry to hear your sad news.

You must be devastated, Jude. Thinking of you and the little one.

We were so shocked to hear of Peter's passing. Keeping you in our prayers.

What a wonderful man he was. I'm sure you will miss him greatly.

Hoping you find comfort in the arms of your family at this tragic time.

But there was no comfort to be found within the family. Jude was disturbed by the cards propped up everywhere. Seeing them only made her think of birthdays, or babies being born. Even the flowers were wholly inappropriate and better suited for weddings. Perhaps she might

41

give them to a hospital or old folks' home, but before she finished that thought another came fast upon it — the certain knowledge she wouldn't take them anywhere, they'd lie exactly where they were until they turned brown and dropped their petals and the sharp tang of decay scented the air. Her apathy turned to self-loathing and she took to her room to hide her awfulness from the world.

Cigarette smoke curled beneath the gap between Jude's door and the carpet. It crept downstairs and reminded Sissy she wasn't alone. On the occasions Jude made it out of her room, they accepted each other's presence in silence, and took a sofa each, watching game shows or soaps, Jude brushing her hair absent-mindedly, peeling tufts from her brush, burning them like tiny hay bales in her ashtray, creating a smell no one thought to mention or open a window for. They lived on take away food: Italian Monday, Chinese Tuesday, chip shop Wednesday, Indian Thursday, KFC Friday, and so it rolled. The lasagnes and casseroles brought round by friends and neighbours went into the freezer and were forgotten. Defrosting anything was unthinkable, turning a dial on the oven impossible. Tinfoil boxes gathered by the back door, the bin overflowed, junk mail and bills piled up along the skirting in the hallway, and the phone went unanswered, causing the red light to blink angrily. In the darkness of the long nights, Jude crept down the stairs and pressed the play button over and over again, simply to hear Peter's voice telling her to leave a message. Sissy, lying awake in bed, stared at her bedroom ceiling. If she looked away, something might collapse.

5

The Sheer Goodness of Children

Anne's tiredness was a thick cloak with weights stitched into the lining. Every person she knew was a drain on her. There was literally no one she couldn't worry about. Her two remaining children oozed misery, but what could she do? Over the years, they'd built up a resistance to her methods of helping. And even in death, her eldest remained a source of anxiety. Sissy had said enough to raise her suspicions about her son's faith, or lack thereof, and now Anne was compelled to take the bus every day to attend Mass at the cathedral, where she prayed that Peter's soul would be freed from Purgatory and ascend into the arms of the Lord. But when would she know her prayers had been answered? *Lord, forgive me. I don't wish to seem ungrateful.* The fear of stopping too soon, and also the guilt at not having noticed her son had strayed from the path, spurred her on. Soon she was praying on the bus, on the short walk between the bus stop and the cathedral, and the whole way home and half way down her second cup of tea.

Anne wasn't as fond of the cathedral Mass as she was her Sunday service at St Martin's. Too many tourists and not enough familiar faces. Even the priest gave no indication that he recognised her after so many trips, and what with the effort required to take the bus in and out of town on a daily basis, the whole experience was proving to be a rather unsatisfactory one. Shocked by this realisation, she bowed her head and began muttering decades of the rosary in an attempt to chase the illegal thought away before it counted — a Catholic version of the child's five-second rule.

Out of the Cathedral, into the mizzling rain, she kept her beads in hand. At the bus stop she stared fixedly up the street and prayed until the bus came. She showed her pass without otherwise acknowledging the driver, took the first available seat and resumed her prayers. She tried not to think of how she failed to lose herself in the service, but as the bus trundled away from the Cathedral her sense of anxiety only deepened.

On the empty seat beside her, someone had left a newspaper. The words jumped off the page: *Explosion in Reports of Historical Sex Offences.* She tutted and averted her eyes; all these people these days, all their complaining. She didn't understand the modern desire to make such a song and dance about everything. In her day, they just got on with it. Threading the brown beads through her fingers brought no peace. '*Lord help me*,' she whispered

Her tailbone seemed to want to drill through the hard plastic back of her seat. Pain shot up her spine, spread through her pelvis, beneath her ribs. She closed her eyes and breathed deeply. One of the few benefits of being a woman: the acquired ability to breathe through pain. The ride was bumpy. At one point the driver hit a pothole and the bus shook so violently Anne was forced to grab the pole by her seat.

'That's *it*,' she announced to the largely empty bus. She pressed the button and alighted at the next stop. It took a moment to get her bearings, but actually she hadn't travelled far at all. The city was in full swing around her: couriers, police cars, shoppers, taxis, delivery trucks. She felt out of place. The chill air and drizzling rain wrapped itself around her, and slid down the collar of her coat, causing her to shiver.

'Out the way, Granny,' a harsh voice said. Unsure of which direction she should move in, Anne stepped uselessly on the spot as a young woman with a cigarette in her hand swerved a buggy around her. She watched her hurry off, a long straggle of bleached hair, a blur of neon trainers, shoulders hunching over the top of the pram as she pushed into the wind.

'Excuse me, excuse me!' Anne called, but a bus pulled alongside her, all whining brakes and loud splashes in the roadside water. The woman and her baby disappeared around the corner.

Anne loved children. She especially loved babies. Always had. Even as a teen she'd loved to babysit for any of the neighbours. She'd always thought it was just the sheer goodness of babies that she loved so much, but she'd come to understand it was also their vulnerability. Their complete and utter reliance on whoever was there. Their trust. When a baby looked at you, he saw someone on whom his life depended, and what was so marvellous about it was that he never for a moment doubted you'd be there for him. She always thought of babies as male, even before Peter was born. When it looked for a while that she and Patrick might not have their own family, she'd experienced a kind of madness. Yes, it was a madness, she thought. She could admit it now the years had passed and Patrick was no longer with her.

She took the underground, amazed at how little it had changed in all that time. Even the dusty carriage smell was familiar. The people had changed of course. Strange-looking girls with heavy make-up and huge black art folders. Tall skinny boys (men, she supposed) wearing oversized coats and reading thick books. Patrick had been tall and skinny. Funny to think what he might have looked like if this had been his time. Funny to think they most likely would never have married at all, their children never existed. What a world. Such pain she could have avoided. But such joys too, she corrected herself.

Back on the street, the grey had been temporarily banished by a weak sun. The wet pavement gleamed almost enough to blind her. She leaned against a wall while she gathered herself together. It was years since she'd been in this part of town. She had a vague idea that Danny lived somewhere close by. Perhaps she could prevail on him to take her home later. Her tummy was beginning to ache and the idea of another bus ride today was too much.

She pushed off from the wall and headed in the direction of Kelvingrove Park. She couldn't think where else she'd be guaranteed to find what she was looking for. Ignoring the *Big Issue* seller (but making a promise to herself to buy a copy later), she put one foot after the other, wandered over the bridge into the gardens, admired the imposing red sandstone buildings, and marvelled again at how unchanged everything was. To think, while she was running the shop, bringing up children and all the rest of it, to think that this was still here, still as it was, thoroughly unchanged, while she . . . she had changed so much, almost beyond recognition. But didn't everyone do that?, she thought. Isn't that just life? What life might have been. She shook her head. There was no point in these thoughts. There never had been any point. She stopped and looked up at the university, almost a confrontation. Despite herself, she laughed. It was still there. Not just the building, but the envy, the resentment, the desire. Oh well. At least she knew she was still alive.

An overweight girl in a hi-vis jacket overtook her.

'Come along boys and girls,' she trilled. 'Nearly there.'

A crocodile of children ambled past. Anne viewed them in bemusement, all chained up to each other, attached to some plastic contraption running down the centre of their group. She'd never seen anything like it. There was maybe a dozen of them, ranging in age from two to four, and they followed their leader without hesitation, each completely lost in their own experience. This was what she had come for.

She could hardly bear to walk so slowly, but she had to. Twelve little children so compelling in their variety. The confident leaders, the reticent listeners, the special one who was completely at ease with himself and showed no interest in the others. The nursery workers didn't even notice, so engrossed were they in their own conversations. She doubted they noticed anything, but then one of them held open the gate to the play area for her to enter, so she supposed they had at least a modicum of awareness. Her feet were beginning to ache and so she sat down on the nearest bench, not noticing the wetness soaking through her skirt and jacket. One by one, the children were set free and they swarmed the play area with an infectious energy, climbing various wooden structures, digging in the bark laid beneath the apparatus, investigating drips, cracks and graffiti with the same gusto as they approached the slide and swings. Gusto, she smiled. There was a word. Peter definitely had gusto.

A tear trickled down her cheek and she bristled with annoyance. It often happened these days, especially in the cold. Today she was feeling particularly choked up. She leaned over and wiggled a hand into her coat pocket. Her rosary beads came out entangled with a crumpled old tissue and some indigestion tablets. She took one and closed her eyes to stem the tears. Squeals of laughter made her smile in spite of herself. She couldn't resist looking.

She loved children so much. It wasn't just their trust, or their goodness, she realised. It was their potential. Their ability to be anything. She loved this time, this stage, this little window before life got its hands on them and turned them spoiled and rotten. This little stage when you had to do everything you could to tie them to you, before they got old and turned away from you, even if that meant being a bit tough with them. It was for their own good. She'd been lucky she'd had three. Three little humans to play off against each other. She'd long thought that was the key to her success — the discovery that even if a child doesn't care about pleasing you, they'll always want to pip their siblings. So a little word here, a calculated compliment there . . . whatever it took to get them striving. By and large, it had been a successful strategy. She regretted none of it.

Later, standing at the mouth of Danny's close, she looked up and steeled herself for the four-storey climb. She remained appalled by the disintegration of her son's private life. First, the divorce. The only consolation was that Danny hadn't instigated it. Anne still felt a bloom of anger whenever she thought of her ex-daughter-in-law — one of those tall, beautiful women of privilege with no idea of anything outside their soft, pampered world. The type of woman who thinks nothing of uprooting children and keeping them from their father, a fine father, in this instance. The problem today was everybody wanted everything. The house, the family, the job. No sacrifice. Really, Lauren should have cut back at work. Not that Anne was comfortable coming to that conclusion. She was aware of

50

women's rights and all that, in fact, she'd barely been typical for her time herself. But, really, once children are in the frame, someone has to be prepared to step back, and in that relationship no one had been, least of all Danny, who had watched his older brother do exactly that.

This was one area Anne almost thought she might have played differently. If she hadn't been so scathing of Peter's decision, Danny might have compromised more with Lauren. It was a sneaking, almost-thought, that frequently tried to breach the walls of Anne's subconscious, but by and large it was kept in check by her penchant for busyness. Another motto: the devil finds work for idle hands.

She entered the close and gripped the hand rail and began to pull herself up the grey stone stairs, her head full of memories of when the tenements were slums, when twelve people lived in a room and a kitchen, when several families shared an outside toilet, and the rats had the run of everything.

It was a close like this she'd been left at after her mother died in childbirth. The baby had died too, so there was no one left to blame. Men couldn't be expected to look after a family on their own so the two younger boys were put into a home and the eldest joined up. She never saw her brothers again, though she heard years later that one of them had made it to Canada. She'd never been able to verify it.

As she passed the first-floor doors, a child's plastic trike on the landing caught her eye. It was ludicrous anyone would choose to bring a family up in a place like this when a house with a garden could be found for a fraction of the cost elsewhere. A house with a garden was all anyone wanted in her day.

She'd been placed with a woman called Auntie Margaret. It wasn't immediately clear to Anne that there was no actual blood between them. Margaret had a daughter of her own, born out of wedlock, and so her entire existence was dependent on the benevolence of the local priest from whom the wider community took their social cues. Father Murphy was a regular caller to the flat.

'You're being good girls now, aren't you?' he'd say, in his Irish accent, and he wasn't just talking to the children when he said it.

Anne enjoyed his visits, sensing his sympathy for her situation, which, after all, was not of her doing, and at least she hadn't been born a bastard like Nettie — a truth which, in the absence of a mother of her own, she held onto and nursed.

One of the doors on the second floor had a selection of plants outside it, which looked nice enough, but again begged the question: why live without a garden? Why surround yourself with stone and concrete if what you truly desired was freedom and nature?

She was quite breathless by the time she rounded the corner and pulled herself up to the third floor. Her back and feet were sore, and her indigestion was playing up again. She used all of it as a spur. She could stop when she reached Danny's door, and not before.

At last she reached the fourth floor and, of course, he wasn't home. It was a Tuesday afternoon, after all. What had she been thinking? Still, she was here now. Going all the way back down was unthinkable. She reached into her handbag and pulled out the gadget Peter had bought as a joke, but which she secretly found to be invaluable. It was a telescopic walking stick that turned into a chair. Ingenious really. No one in her family had seen her use it and that's how she liked it. It was safe enough to use it here. She'd have four flights of warning footsteps in which to tuck it back into her bag. She took an indigestion tablet and settled down to wait.

Sometime later, a hand touched her shoulder.

'Mum! Is everything okay? What are you doing here?'

Uncomfortable as she'd become, she'd still managed to doze off. Annoyed, she held her hand out and Danny helped her to stand. She pushed down on his arm, letting out a small groan as she straightened up.

'Have you seen my new toy? Very clever,' she said casually, as she folded it back into its miniature state.

'Mum, you're shivering. Let's get you inside. How long have you been waiting?'

She couldn't miss the faint annoyance in his tone, which was hardly fair. She hadn't known he wouldn't be here.

'I wanted to see you. There was no point going home after Mass this morning only to come all the way back out.'

'You've been here since this morning?'

'No, no. I had an afternoon . . . some lunch, you know, and then . . . I must say I thought you'd be here earlier.'

'I went for a couple of drinks after work.'

'On a Tuesday? All right for some.'

He opened the door and dived through. She watched as he scanned the flat for incriminating items and wondered how bad it could be. Then, remembering he was an adult and his elderly mother had sat outside his front door waiting on him for hours, he turned back around with an expression of relief.

'Give us your coat, Ma,' he said. She hung her handbag over the end of a radiator and began to unbutton her jacket, eyes already making a sweep of the place. He went behind her to close the door.

'I thought you had a cleaner,' she said.

'I do,' he replied, blinking in that surprised way he used to as a child when he thought he was in trouble.

She wrinkled her nose. 'There's a smell.'

'Really?'

Anne wafted the air around her face like a perfumer trying to analyse a scent. If Lauren had been there, she would have called the display 'theatrical'. There were at least some benefits to the separation.

'Sorry, Ma. I'll open a window.'

'Are you trying to kill me? Let me warm up first.'

He sighed and took her coat, though he asked if she wouldn't like to hold onto it while she was warming up, but no, she wouldn't. She would, however, like a cup of tea, if it weren't too much trouble.

'And what about food, Ma? It must be a while since you've eaten.'

'Maybe a biscuit, son. I don't have much of an appetite these days.'

'You should have rung the office,' he called from the kitchen. 'I'd have come home.'

'If I just had a key, you know,' she replied, without much hope. Not that Danny would begrudge her a key, she was sure, just that he was so preoccupied with other matters.

'Here we are,' he said, carrying a tray through. He placed it on the small table between two couches and poured from the teapot. 'Now then. What's this all about?'

'All about? I need a reason to see my son?'

'You know that's not what I meant.'

'My *only* son now?'

'Mum.'

She examined the biscuits on offer. She took one and bit in. 'Oh, these are delicious! What are they?'

He shrugged. 'Just biscuits from the supermarket, Ma.'

'You'll need to show me the packet. Are they from Waitrose?'

'Probably.'

'That's you all over. No scrimping on style. A suit or a biscuit — I always know you'll choose well. How are the girls?'

'Aye, they're all right, Mammy.' He leaned back on the couch and rubbed his face before snapping forward and announcing his decision

55

to have a drink. 'Will you have a wee sherry or something?'

'No, no, I'm fine with tea but you go ahead. You've been at work all day.'

He sighed and shook his head, and slapped his thighs with alarming purpose, before looking straight into her eyes. For one horrible second she thought he was about to cry.

'Go on then, go on.' She waved her hand, moving hurriedly past the moment. 'Have your drink,' she urged. 'You've been working hard. You've earned it.'

Danny poured himself a finger of Scotch while Anne nibbled her biscuit.

'So has Emma done her wee filming bit then?' she said. 'That was marvellous, wasn't it?'

Her eyes flew around the room, anywhere but her son. She felt she had no reason to be there, and was further discomfited by the notion that she *needed* a reason to be there.

'Aye, I think so. Seemed to go all right from what I can gather.'

'Doesn't surprise me in the least. Such a talented girl. She was so good in all her school plays, wasn't she? But going on television! Did she enjoy it? She hasn't been over to tell me about it.'

'Sorry, Ma. They're with me this weekend. I'll take a run out on Sunday afternoon, if you like?'

'That would be nice.' She cut off the sentence too neatly, creating a space in which something was left unsaid. Both sensed it, but neither could guess at the missing words, or even say if they would be kind or cruel.

'Maybe we'll take a run out to Loch Lomond or something like that,' said Danny.

'Or how about a wee visit to Jude? I don't get over as often as I'd like, you know. We need to keep her close. I don't think she's coping very well.'

A small bitter laugh puffed from his lips. 'Who *is?*' He drained his glass and stood up for another. 'Sure I can't persuade you?'

'Aye, a wee tot. Go on.'

Bottles clinked as Danny rummaged in the back of the cupboard and pulled out a bottle of sherry.

'Don't open it just for me,' she called.

'Don't be daft, Ma. I don't mind.'

'Thanks, son,' she said, taking the glass. She sipped and felt herself relax a little. This would warm her up better than the tea would. The damp from the afternoon, followed by the cold hours waiting in the concrete hallway, had taken their toll.

'To Peter.' Danny raised his glass and drank it down quickly. Anne was taken aback. It was not like him to dive head first into serious matters. By the time she'd taken in what he'd said, he'd turned away from her and was refilling his glass.

'Yes,' she said, hearing a crack in her voice. A biscuit crumb caught in her throat, no doubt. She coughed and raised her glass. 'To Peter.'

He sat down heavily.

'I'm sorry, Ma. Losing a child. I should have said it sooner. I'm sorry.'

The sight of him slouching over like that, with his elbows resting on his knees propping the rest of his body up, his eyes pointing towards the floor like someone defeated . . . it angered her.

'It's hard for all of us,' she said, and was relieved to notice the earlier brokenness had been replaced by a cold, warning tone. 'But you know, I think Jude will be finding it harder than us. No family of her own to fall back on.'

As long as there was someone else worse off.

Danny glanced up and quickly looked away. His guilty face told Anne he'd barely thought of Jude and Sissy since the day of the funeral.

'She's always been a bit . . . well, ungrounded,' Anne continued, her sense of purpose returning. 'All those foster homes, no idea of anything. The way she tied herself to him.'

Danny looked uncomfortable, but before he could speak, she continued.

'Peter gave her a sense of herself. And then Sissy, of course. But without him, what is she?'

It was true, she realised. She was only discovering it as the words left her mouth. Jude had been barely into her twenties when Peter brought her to visit. A little waif of a thing, the kind of person you hoped your children would keep a distance from. Not that there was anything *wrong* with them, just that you knew time spent with them would ultimately prove difficult because, perhaps through no fault of their own, life had been hard and created for them a pile of baggage you'd always prayed your own child would avoid.

She tipped back the last of her sherry, placed the glass onto the table beside her tea cup, and looked at him, bright little eyes gleaming from between wrinkled folds.

'Sissy's the biggest concern, of course. The age she's at. So easy to go off the rails. She needs a strong mother, Danny. It's up to us to make sure she's got one. It's what Peter would expect of us.'

Danny had been looking forward to spending the upcoming weekend with his daughters, but it was clear now he'd been selfish, thinking only of himself.

'Of course, Ma. It'll be good for the girls to see their cousin. Check in on Jude. That's a plan. That's a good plan.'

They said a decade of the rosary together, and then Danny called a taxi and walked Anne down the stairs. Holding an umbrella over her, he helped her into the cab and made sure her seat belt was fastened. Sometimes the arthritis in her fingers was so bad she couldn't do it herself. Not that she would admit it, of course. You had to keep an eye on her.

'I told you I'd be fine on the bus,' she said.

'Mammy, I don't want you on the bus. I'm only sorry I can't drive you myself.'

'Yes, well.' Anne raised her eyebrows.

Danny paid the driver — 'thanks very much, mate' — and closed the door. The small prickle of pride she felt whenever any of her children took their wallets out softened her as he stepped back onto the pavement and waved as the cab pulled away. In the darkness she could have been a child peeping out of the window, whereas she only saw him grow smaller as the cab pulled away. He stood, shoulders hunched futilely against the rain that came down in sheets. She wanted to scream at him to use the damn umbrella for himself.

6

The Visit

On Sunday, Danny's car pulled up sleek and stealthy as a panther. Sissy only noticed it because she'd been thinking of calling on Cam and looked out the window to check the weather. When she saw the car with its private plate turn into the street, her tummy flipped twice in guilty panic: once for the ostentatious display of wealth which was out of place on their estate, and twice because the house was a disgusting mess.

'Mum! Uncle Danny's here!'

She ran through to the kitchen and grabbed a black bin bag. Everything went into it: all the takeaway boxes and junk mail, ashtrays, empty bottles, newspapers. The dishwasher was full, so she tidied the dirty dishes as best she could, sitting plates on top of plates, and cups in cups on top of plates, not noticing the clack and clatter as they chipped and broke against each other. The kitchen floor was littered with crumbs and scraps of food that had missed the bin, and brown splash marks where teabags had fallen. Transfixed by the horror of it, she couldn't avoid the knowledge of how she hated herself. She was rank and rotten and now everyone else would know. The thought forced her to the ground. Using her hands, she gathered up the worst of the mess, shouting for Jude to get up, but quietly, lest the visitor on the street should hear.

Outside, Danny walked round to open the passenger-door. Emma and Lucy hovered in case they could help in any way, and because they dreaded this visit and wanted to put off the moment of again coming face to face with their aunt and cousin's misery, and the inevitable sensation of discomfort that would follow.

Sissy dropped the mess she'd gathered into the bin, pushing the rubbish so far down it would split the bag and spill everywhere when she finally got round to emptying it. A dart through to the living room to check their guest's progress told her Danny wasn't alone. It was far more serious than she'd realised. She took the steps two at a time and pushed Jude's door open. Her mother appeared to be nothing more than a small hill in the bed.

'Mum, you have to get up,' she said, breathless from her cleaning burst. The shape moaned and shifted. Sissy sat on the bed, recognising a pale yellow blanket she thought had been thrown away years ago. It made her go easier. Gently, she patted in the general area of Jude's shoulder.

'Mum. Grammy's here. She's brought Uncle Danny and Emma and Lucy.'

No response came but she thought she detected a shift from beneath the cover.

'Mum, please get up. Please.'

The kazoo sounded and Sissy sighed. The bloody doorbell had become an axe over their heads. They couldn't change it because it reminded them of Peter and happy arguments over how great or awful it was, but much as she and her father had giggled about Jude's objections to it, there was no denying how wholly inappropriate it was for their new world. Why couldn't people just leave them alone? Then she wouldn't have to think about the doorbell at all.

Upon opening the door, Sissy said, 'What a lovely surprise!' and then wondered why she sounded like an old lady. Anne was at the front, of course, presented as the main event, an offering. Sissy opened her arms wide, allowing Anne to step forward and kiss her. Danny stood behind her, a towering giant, awkward as a badly placed skyscraper, uneasy in the company of females, even though they were his females, his mother and daughters. Unsure of himself now he couldn't fall into easy boy talk with his brother, he plastered a smile on his face and squeezed his niece. He ushered Anne inside, leaving Emma and Lucy to slink in behind him, which they did with a shy smile towards their cousin who, through sheer bad luck, had somehow been transformed into an alien creature, a stranger from another world. The space Peter had vacated was real and everywhere.

The guests gathered in the living room and Sissy offered tea, apologising for not having any biscuits. Danny seized his opportunity and was out the door before anyone realised what he was doing.

'He's a good boy,' said Anne. 'Picks a good biscuit. Where's your mum?'

'Uh . . . I think she'll be down later,' Sissy replied. 'She has stuff to do.'

The guilt of the lie was outweighed by loyalty to her mother, despite them not having spoken a friendly word to each other in days.

Anne sank back into her seat, pulling a cushion across her lap, making Sissy think of a small animal, like a squirrel or dormouse, burrowing into its hole to outlast winter. Once upon a time, her grandmother had seemed like a giant. On Saturdays and some afternoons after school, Sissy had dressed up in her grandmother's old nightgowns which were kept in a bag in the upstairs hall cupboard. In the majestic company of untouchable holy figurines and under the approving gaze from Jesus on the wall, seven-year-old Sissy traipsed up and down, scarcely believing her grandmother had once worn such items. The yellows, pale blues and pinks, all in sheer fabrics like chiffon, made Sissy feel like a princess, but later on, around the time Sissy began asking disturbing questions like: How can you prove God is real? and How is it fair that unbaptised babies don't get straight into Heaven? her father had hushed her, and she'd begun to realise that perhaps she had to look after her grandmother just as her grandmother looked after her.

Fifteen long minutes later, Danny returned laden with carrier bags of food, including Coke for the girls, even though their mother didn't like them to have drinks like that.

'No wonder you have spots,' Emma scolded, as Lucy helped herself.

Sissy made tea for Anne and Danny, and offered more every time they put their cups down. Danny drank his in three scalding gulps just so he could say, 'Yes, please,' next time she asked. They ate hastily cobbled-together ham sandwiches and marvelled at the multitude of sympathy cards and flowers.

'People are good,' said Anne.

When at long last Jude appeared in the doorway she was grey as a ghost, or, as Anne thought, some shell-shocked soldier returning from a terrible place. The guests paused over their sandwiches, lifted their heads in greeting, guilty at being caught in the act of eating, unable to rise easily to embrace their host. Jude sat down in the space clumsily vacated by Lucy and lit up a cigarette. Normally she refrained from smoking indoors when they had company, but today it didn't even occur to her and no one said she shouldn't.

Lucy reached to refill her glass.

'Should you?' said Emma, in a tone that clearly said she shouldn't.

'Just cos you can't,' said Lucy, sticky fingers around the neck of the bottle. She turned to the rest of the room and, in a very la-di-dah voice, announced, 'The camera adds ten pounds, don't you know.'

'I don't sound like that!' Emma playfully punched her sister's shoulder.

'Don't hit your sister,' said Anne. Emma immediately, curled into herself, eyes wounded, and Sissy was reminded of what it was to feel sympathy for someone other than herself. Danny munched on cupcake after cupcake, seemingly oblivious to events around him.

'I forgot about your telly job!' said Sissy brightly, desperate to lift the mood. 'How was it?'

'Oh my God, I loved it,' said Emma.

'Language, Emma.' It seemed Danny had half an ear on things after all.

'Sorry, Daddy,' Emma replied, before continuing. 'It. Was. Fab. I had to ride a horse! And my costume . . . '

As Emma told all about her brief television experience, Sissy had the sensation of moving back from the room. She tried to focus on her cousin's words but, although she could see her lips moving, she couldn't make sense of what she was saying. The whole situation had an element of farce about it. Uncle Danny sitting there on the footstool like some oversized toddler, the way his girls didn't stray too far from his side, how they watched his every move, ready to jump into action the instant he needed anything. Her mother seemed to be operated from afar by some separate entity. There was nothing alive about her. Her arm went up and down ferrying her cigarette between mouth and ashtray, but her eyes were void. She was like a black hole, sucking all the energy out the room, not even pretending to listen. Grammy, however, even though she had nestled herself so deeply down into the armchair, Sissy could tell was plugged into every little thing. In fact, Sissy was sure she could hear a high-pitched hum of energy coming from her. A gentle burp from Lucy, a crumb falling from Danny's cupcake, a stem of ash teetering on the end of Jude's cigarette, the number of Mass cards versus ordinary sympathy cards bought in the supermarket — nothing was overlooked — Anne took it all in, and more. It seemed to Sissy that even though she was on the opposite side of the room, somehow her grandmother had managed to crawl across the floor, slip beneath her skin, and read all her thoughts. As a child, she was aware of Grammy's ability to pinpoint a lie because 'The flames of Hell burn in your eyes,' so the sensation of her thoughts and feelings not being her own wasn't a new experience, just a forgotten one.

'Of course, you'll have had enough of all that now,' Anne's voice drowned out Emma's speech.

'What do you mean?' Emma frowned.

'It's all right to have a bit of fun, but you have your studies to think of. You'll be wanting to concentrate now on what's really important. Heaven knows we've all learned how short life can be. No time for mucking around.'

Emma turned wide-eyed to Danny, who persisted in remaining resolutely unengaged with the room.

'You're a bright girl,' continued Anne. 'I just don't want you getting distracted.'

Emma agreed emphatically.

'Of course, Grammy. I don't want that either.' She turned to the rest of the room and said, 'It was good fun. But not really a practical career choice.'

'Why's that?' asked Sissy, trying to be helpful when it became clear no one else would speak.

Emma's eyes flew to her grandmother.

'Let me tell you girls something,' Anne said. 'I had a friend called Nettie. A long time ago, before I was married. I lived with her and her mother after my father went off. Did I tell you about her?'

The three grandchildren remained silent, having been told about Nettie and 'Aunt' Margaret many times.

'Anyway, Nettie was younger than me by a year or two. Very beautiful. Blonde curls. Kept herself well, you know. Lipstick, stockings, the works. And Nettie was a performer, like you, Emma. A dancer. A great dancer by all accounts. But she had to give it up. Do you know why?'

The three girls shook their heads no.

Anne's gaze whipped round to catch Emma and hold her there. 'Because,' she said, 'she'd go to these auditions and what would she find? Some fella who didn't know a thing about dancing, who only wanted good-looking girls on his stage to keep his customers happy. 'Show us your legs,' he'd say. 'Why do I need to do that?' Nettie would reply. Oh, she wasn't daft. 'You can see I'm a good dancer,' she'd say.'

Anne leaned back and clasped her hands across her middle, satisfied she had her audience's full attention.

'I'm afraid that's how it is in the entertainment industry. Always someone waiting to take advantage. But Nettie was a good girl from a good family and she was smart enough to walk away. It cost her to do the right thing though. She had to give it up. I hear it's even worse these days. Casting couches and all that.'

Emma's face burned a furious red.

'Oh, it's nothing to do with talent, dear,' Anne

68

said. 'No one goes off talent these days. It's all about the casting couch. *You* need to watch — ' that last part directed at Danny who, upon hearing his name, was immediately reminded of all those occasions in the classroom when he'd been caught daydreaming.

'Sorry, Ma?'

'Your girls. If they fall off the track, it's hard to get them back on.'

Danny's eyes flicked quickly over to his daughters, who stared back in alarm, but Anne's gaze travelled to Jude, and from there to Sissy who, Anne realised with a jolt, was staring at her with eyes just like Peter's, angry, challenging, untamed. The shock caused her stomach to spasm and she grappled for her bag to find her heartburn tablets.

'Are you all right, Mammy?' Danny sprang forward, took her bag and found the tablets straight away.

She waved him off, yes, yes, everything's fine, no need to fuss. She turned her face away as she swallowed the pills and waited for the pain to subside. She tried to steady her breathing, but the intensity of Sissy's stare had disturbed her. It was as God told her. Without a doubt, there was work to be done here.

7

Blood and Raspberries

Her father's death had made her famous. Every corridor she walked down, every corner she turned, eyes were on her, a strange being, something other. In social sciences they'd been taught that the 'othering' of people was a step on the road to genocide. The thought darted around in her mind and she couldn't tell whether it was trying to escape, or if it was looking for a suitable space to nest. Grief flopped and twisted inside her like a divided worm from biology. It furrowed dark lines like charcoal on paper in art class. It wiped out any pretensions to the real thing in English poetry. It suffused her system and crawled beneath her skin like ants.

Sometimes she was dizzy with it and she ran to Cam, who always made himself available for her, losing two different jobs in the process. Rik, jealous of their closeness, began to bunk off too. They became comfortable with their freedom, revelling in mid-morning coffees or afternoon cinema trips, or first-person shooter games and a smoke when one of them knew their house would be empty.

One day, Sissy came in from a downpour to find Rik's parents drinking tea with her mother and grandmother. This had never happened before. Mr and Mrs Sutton were considered a pleasant enough, but slightly odd couple. Shy, they stayed away from social events, including school fetes and so on, so that Sissy didn't know much more about them than the little Rik told her. They were indulgent, a soft touch, they desired great things for their only child, though of course his happiness was really the only thing that mattered.

'Naive,' Anne had called them after meeting them at Parents' Night the previous year.

Mrs Sutton, a softly-spoken woman with caramel hair and watery blue eyes, sat with her hands neatly folded on the table. They fluttered up before her whenever she spoke, all her nerves fizzing up into the air around her.

'Sissy.' Up and down went the hands, over flashed the eyes to her husband, seeking reassurance, out came a dainty tinkle as she cleared her throat. 'Come and take a seat, dear.'

Mr Sutton rose and pulled the remaining empty chair back from the table. Sissy looked to her mother for a clue but her gaze was turned towards the garden. Her red eyes and puffy face were evident even from the side. Anne's face was furious. Resisting the urge to run away, Sissy approached the table.

'Is Rik okay?' she asked. He'd been in fine fettle when she'd left him half an hour earlier, stoned from an afternoon spent with Cam's home-made bong. She'd been feeling mildly fuzzy herself, but this unexpected welcome committee had flipped the switch on her paranoia.

'Yes, yes, dear,' said Mrs Sutton, patting the

table again. 'Come. Just a few questions. Nothing scary.'

The expression on Anne's face suggested otherwise.

Mrs Sutton explained in her breathy voice how worried she and Rik's father had become of late. Rik had been missing classes, it was quite unlike him, did she know of anything that may be upsetting him?

'No,' Sissy replied, feigning surprise, wondering how it was possible that she had somehow appeared to have slipped through the truant-catcher's net.

Mrs Sutton took Sissy's hand. It was soft and warm. Sissy was surprised at how repellent she found it.

'I know you have your own problems to deal with, Sissy, and you don't want to be worrying about Rik. But if there's anything you can think of, please let us know. We're so worried about him. You're one of his best friends.' She turned tearfully to Anne. 'We don't know what to do. He was doing so well. He's starting university in September.'

'Well,' said Mr Sutton, with a little shake of his head and a small laugh-like sigh. '*Supposedly*. The jury's out.'

Sissy became increasingly aware of her grandmother's thunderous stare and looked to her mother for assistance, but Jude remained captivated by the view from the kitchen window. She'd noticed lately that the garden needed attention. The weeds had run wild. The trouble was the garden had been Peter's domain. It was difficult to know what was worth keeping. What if she pulled up something precious? The preoccupation was as irritating to Sissy as Anne's stare was frightening.

'Goodbye, Jude,' Mrs Sutton was saying. 'I hope we haven't put you out. It's been lovely to see you,' and then in that low confidential tone people sometimes use when they're trying to indicate discretion, 'If there's anything we can do . . .'

Anne walked them down the hall and showed them out.

'Is everything all right, Mum?' Sissy whispered. Jude finally looked at her, and for the first time in a long while Sissy had the urge to climb into her lap and wrap her arms around her mother's neck.

'You, young lady.'

Sissy turned to see her grandmother's small figure in the doorway.

'You've got some explaining to do,' Anne said, pointing a finger.

In the time it took for Jude to look back out of the window, Anne had crossed to the kitchen drawer and taken out a white envelope which she thrust into Sissy's face.

'Letters from school! How could you do this to us?'

Sissy took it and spread it flat, blinking as she registered her school's headed notepaper. It had all caught up with her at last.

She was surprised by how little she actually cared. Perspective, as her father might have said, is a great thing.

'So what?' she said, determined to deflect Anne's fury.

'Where have you been going?' Anne demanded to know. 'Because you've *certainly* not been in school.'

'I'm seventeen,' said Sissy, proud that her voice came out so calm and measured, especially compared to her grandmother's. 'I don't *have* to go.'

'You've no idea how lucky you are. I didn't get half your chances, Cecilia Donnelly.'

'Please don't call me *Cecilia*. You know I don't like that.'

'Well, unfortunately, the world doesn't *care* what you like, young woman.'

Their voices fell away as Jude, who had been momentarily forgotten, took a bowl from the cupboard and stepped into the garden. Sissy was struck by what a mess her mother was. Bare feet sticking out from beneath Peter's old pinstripe pyjamas, a grey bobbly cardigan swaddling her top half, and her hair a frizzy mess. She walked over to the raspberry canes, bending beneath the weight of ripe fruit, and began to pick. Two for the bowl, one for her. She looked like she belonged in an asylum. A sudden swell of emotion caught in Sissy's throat.

'You see what you're doing to her,' Anne hissed. 'Think of someone other than yourself for a change.'

Sissy stared at her grandmother, open-mouthed. Even Anne seemed slightly taken aback by her harshness.

'Everything okay?' Jude smiled vacantly as she

stepped back indoors. 'Everything's settled anyway, I hope. The raspberries are perfect. Does anybody want some?'

Sissy turned to Jude, mouth still hanging open. Once upon a time, she would have been picked up and comforted.

'Well, they're here if you want them,' Jude said, putting them on the table as she trailed past and left them both momentarily united in surprise.

'The doctor's upped her dosage again,' Sissy said.

Anne sniffed. 'She misses your father, of course.'

'She wasn't even related to him,' Sissy said.

Anne frowned.

'By blood, I mean,' she explained. She knew she was being irrational but she didn't care, and then she began to panic about not caring. What kind of a monster was she? 'What about the rest of us?' she cried, tears threatening to overwhelm her.

'Pull yourself together,' Anne barely whispered. 'How dare you? How *dare* you? I'll not have this behaviour. I will not.'

The injustice was too much for Sissy, whose emotions breached her ability to hold them.

'He was my dad!' she burst forth, and left the room in such a furious hurry, Anne didn't know if it was the fact she hadn't eaten all day that caused her head to spin, or if it was just the power of Sissy's tailwind as she went. Whatever it was, she had to reach out and grasp the back of a chair to keep herself from falling.

8

Streamlining

The bungalow had been a mistake. Everyone had thought it, including Anne, but Patrick had insisted with uncharacteristic vigour, and so they'd sold the family home that had once belonged to Patrick's parents and moved to a newer part of the city.

'But you grew up here,' Susan had said.

He'd shaken his head.

'It's a money pit,' he'd replied, which was true.

'But *we* grew up here!' Susan had countered, which, in spite of wishing to remain in the house, irritated Anne enough to point out that as Susan had moved to Manchester, she was really in no position to comment.

The bungalow was north-west. 'Handy for Loch Lomond,' Patrick said, though their visits would always only be counted on the fingers of one hand, because not long after the move, Patrick had keeled over and died, leaving Anne alone in a tiny house bursting with too many mementos of the old place.

Gradually, she'd filtered their possessions into something more appropriate for her new home, but it had taken years, and she had to admit the streamlining still wasn't done. Black bin bags of clothes she had no use for lined the bedroom. Boxes of books were stacked against a wall. The old antique furniture was really too dark and too big for the bungalow's small rooms. Everything about the house irritated Anne, from the decision to buy it, which hadn't even been hers in the first place, to how she lived in it. The problem was she hated it all so much, she could hardly bear to think about how best to sort everything out. The junk hemmed her in and she began to see it as a metaphor for her whole life. Just typical of Patrick to do this to her. Thankfully, Peter and Danny were so good at getting her out and taking her places that over time she'd become practiced at not seeing what was right in front of her.

Peter's death, however.

Now the bungalow made her want to tear her eyes out. She emptied boxes, looking for items that had belonged to Peter when he was a boy. She turned up a Robert Burns certificate, given in recognition of excellent recitation. No mention of what the actual poem had been. It bugged her, and Susan and Danny were no help. It was unfair to expect them to remember when she herself couldn't, especially as they would have been so small at the time. Still, it rankled. Facts were slipping away, their family history being forgotten.

She found a tattered old teddy bear that Susan swore was hers, but Anne decided had belonged to Peter. She washed it by hand, using the fancy shampoo and conditioner she'd been given one Christmas and had been keeping for the right time. Years of grime washed away in just a few moments. She gave the bear a blow-dry and tied a green ribbon round his neck for Celtic, then she sat him on top of the bookcase in the living room, but when she realised she couldn't look at it without getting a crick in her neck, she put him on top of the television. He was better than most of the stuff that was on, anyway.

Ever since Patrick died, Anne had resisted all of Susan's attempts to help clear the place, but Anne's search for traces of Peter had re-opened the matter.

'You can't live like this, Mum.'

As in the weeks after Patrick's death, Susan was spending every free weekend in Glasgow, far from her family in Manchester. Heaven only knew what her husband made of it, Anne thought.

'I mean, look,' said Susan, holding up a pair of old brown trousers her father had tended the garden in, and that had been inadvertently set free from the confines of some old box or sack. 'There's absolutely no reason to have these now, Mum. I doubt even the charity shop would take them. Let me just take it all away for you. You'll be much happier, I promise.'

'I can do it myself. I'm not infirm and I'm not having strangers paw through my private things.'

'I'm hardly a stranger,' Susan said, looking hurt.

'Fine. If it'll keep you quiet.'

And that had been the mistake she had deep down known it was, because once they had moved past the clothes, the books, the knick-knacks, they had come across photographs going back a century, and Susan had wanted to know every detail about every one of them. A pot of tea was made, the radio went on, and they settled down to go through them.

'Incredible,' Susan said. 'Look at this. Even in black and white, it's like looking at Sissy.'

Anne took the photograph and peered at it. She remembered the occasion well because the photos had been done the week before Nettie and Margaret left for Australia. Even after all these years, Anne still felt embarrassment at the difference between them; Nettie, smiling and glamorous in her tight skirt and full make-up, and she in sensible brown lace-ups and her dowdy Sunday suit. She was working for Patrick's parents by that point, though she was still to meet their son.

Susan was right, Sissy *was* strong here. She'd never noticed a resemblance between them before, though everyone agreed Sissy was more like Peter than Jude, so it stood to reason. Anne felt an unexpected flush of warmth for her granddaughter, and began to sort through the old pictures with enjoyment until the news came on and Susan turned the radio up. The announcer was talking of unpleasant matters and Anne began to talk louder.

'Ssh, Mum, I need to hear this. It's in my catchment area. The kids will be talking about this on Monday.'

The story was of an alleged sexual assault involving a young footballer and a teenage girl in a hotel room.

'There's just so much of this stuff around at

the moment,' Susan said afterwards. 'It's frightening.'

'That poor lad though,' said Anne. 'Mud sticks. That's his career ruined.'

Susan was aghast. 'What about the girl?'

'She shouldn't have been in his hotel room to start with,' said Anne, surprised she had to explain such a thing.

'It doesn't matter, Mum,' Susan replied, in that annoying, condescending, school teacher way of hers that she never seemed able to leave at work. 'She has the right to say no at any time. And if he ignored her — well, I'm afraid it's rape. Oh look!'

She held up a photo of Anne and Patrick, walking, hand in hand, down the aisle on their wedding day. 'It's you and Daddy. See how happy you look. This one deserves a frame.'

Keeping her hands tightly clasped on her lap, Anne leaned over to see it more clearly. The truth of Susan's words landed like a chisel chipping into rock, causing a fracture somewhere beyond what was visible to the human eye. She felt it almost as a thaw, or a sudden opening right at the centre of her. Despite the chill their conversation had created, there was no denying the happiness bursting from her in that photograph.

9

A Little Thinking Space

Jude had covered all the mirrors in her bedroom and bathroom with towels and sheets. She didn't care that it was perceived as bizarre behaviour by her daughter and mother-in-law. The Jude in the mirror was a false one belonging to another time. The real Jude was in search of herself. She had no idea who she was any more. It had been years since she'd been alone. With the passage of time, she realised she'd been little more than a child when she met Peter. Without him, everything was new. She remained a mother, but she was a mother whose child didn't want her.

The doctor had upped her prescription again. A little thinking space, he'd called it.

★ ★ ★

Peter told everyone it was love at first sight. She'd liked that version of events. It gave them substance, something for people to *ooh* over, made them something concrete. Privately, she felt he'd simply worn her down, turning up at her work night after night until, at her boss's urging, she'd given in and agreed to a date.

The restaurant was a country house outside of the city, where silver cutlery lay in rows alongside white porcelain plates on white linen tablecloths. The wine list was expensive. He'd pointed to one and suggested they order it.

'That's almost four months' wages for me!' she'd exclaimed, as yet unused to his wicked sense of humour. He *did* ask for bottled water, which Jude considered to be an extravagance, but he also settled for the house red, which she found reassuring, and it disappeared more quickly than she anticipated. He said he was a man of appetites, and patted his rounded belly proudly. She told him he wore it well, he was lucky he was tall. He took her honesty on the chin. By the time they were on their second bottle, she'd forgotten to be intimidated by him.

'Go on then,' she said. 'What is it you do again?'

'I told you already. Corporate law.'

'Yeah, yeah, but what *is* that? What do you actually *do*?'

'I make sure big companies don't get into trouble,' he shrugged. 'I check their contracts for new business, make sure they don't accidentally break any laws.'

'Oh, *accidentally*,' she laughed.

'What do you mean?'

His sudden shift in tone made her uncomfortable.

'Oh, nothing.'

'You mean *something*.'

He'd held her gaze until it became clear she would have to offer something.

'It was a joke,' she said, after a long pause. 'It's no secret big businesses like to bend the rules to suit them.'

'So my work's a joke. Good to know.'

He reclined in his chair and sipped from his wine glass. His eyes, which hadn't left hers all evening, were now fixed on the carpeted floor.

'I'm sorry. I didn't mean to offend you.'

'You didn't offend me,' he said, shaking his head.

'Then what?'

He bared his teeth and wiped his mouth with the napkin.

'I didn't realise I was dining with such an expert, that's all,' he said, signalling for the bill. 'Oh, I'm sorry,' he said. 'Would you like dessert?'

'No, thank you.'

They sat in awkward silence while the waiter engaged in some deep conversation with the girl behind the bar. He was apologetic when he finally brought the bill over.

'I'm sorry, sir,' he said, with a thick French accent. 'New girl tonight. Very slow.'

'Ha,' Peter smiled at Jude. 'Maybe you could give her a few pointers.' And then, with a sharp smile to the waiter, he pointed at Jude and said, 'This one's a barmaid.'

The waiter smiled and nodded. 'Very good, mademoiselle.'

Heat spread across her face as Peter placed his card on the small silver plate.

'Thank you, sir. I'll be straight back.'

'Did you have to do that?' she asked, feeling embarrassingly close to tears.

'What?' he replied, eyes wide, eyebrows raised in mock surprise.

'This one's a barmaid,' she imitated.

'I didn't realise it was an issue for you.'

'It wasn't until you turned it into one.'

He made a point of sitting back in his chair. She realised she was leaning so far across the table, she was almost out of her seat. The waiter returned with the card.

'Very good, sir. I hope you have a pleasant evening.'

Jude had a strong sensation of being mocked by both of them. When Peter tried to help her on with her coat, she snatched it from him and shrugged it on herself. When he held the door for her, she didn't thank him. She walked the short distance to the car ashamed of her rudeness. When he opened the car door, she forced herself to look him in the eye, but his gaze remained determinedly focused somewhere above her head. Feeling like a child, she sank into the plush leather interior, hating the fact she enjoyed the unfamiliar luxury that wrapped itself around her. It wasn't until his weight fell into the driver's seat beside her that she thought about the amount of wine they'd had. But he was a lawyer, a serious person, someone who knew what they were doing, so it was a fleeting concern. When he leaned over and took her face in his hands and kissed her full on the mouth, she responded automatically, keen to put right her earlier mistakes. Somewhere, a voice in her head pointed out it wasn't right, but just like the drink-driving, that was a fleeting concern too.

★   ★   ★

Jude wasn't sure she liked this thinking space. In fact, she didn't think she'd ever been sure of anything. As a child, she'd floated through life, shunted from one foster carer to the next, too busy adapting to her changing realities to ever think she might make anything of herself. Now all she could do was drift along in the hazy cloud gifted by the pills, until something changed her path again.

When Aleks dropped by, she'd panicked. What if Sissy saw him? He said it was okay, there was nothing unusual in a boss showing concern for his second-in-command, and she'd responded by saying how dare he appear at her husband's house. Husband, husband, husband. This was how she thought of Peter now. Marriage was the one thing he'd been unable to change her mind on, though she could never explain why, even to herself. Husband, wife. That's what they were. Had been. Would never be.

'I'm not here for anything other than to see how you are,' Aleks said, but she couldn't believe him, and even if she could, his presence was nothing more than a reminder of her infidelity.

'You did nothing wrong. Nothing happened between us,' Aleks assured her.

But it almost had, and the certainty that it would have had Peter only stayed alive a little longer crippled her. Of course, Aleks was too diplomatic to remind her of all her complaints: Peter was loud, overbearing, drank too much, did too little, undermined her with their daughter, made it so that Jude was reluctant to offer an opinion on anything at all unless she knew what her partner's thinking on the subject was.

The truth was she didn't need reminding of how unhappy she'd been, but she couldn't remember if anything she'd told him was actually true, and even if it was, she didn't understand why it had once mattered. She'd loved Peter's huge, bear-like body, how she always felt safe around him. She loved his confidence, loved the way he wrapped his fingers around the neck of a guitar, loved how, when he sang, his eyes always sought her out.

Aleks tried to take her hand, as a friend does when their friend is grieving, but she refused him.

'I'm not asking anything of you, Jude. Take all the time you need. I understand.'

His kindness only made her feel worse.

Later, when Aleks had gone and the house lay in the dusky grey of twilight because Sissy was still out and she hadn't left her room to switch on the lamps, Jude decided the 'thinking time' prescribed by the doctor could be more accurately described as 'a pause', Everything in her life was behind her, there was no future, except, of course, she had a daughter. As long as she had a daughter, there had to be a future. She knew more than most that daughters need their mothers. What she hadn't realised until now was how much mothers need their daughters. Hold onto Sissy, hold onto life. That thought was a comfort, and she held to it as a child might clutch a soft toy as they spiralled into sleep.

10

The Miracle

By the time they arrived at the tea shop on Buchanan Street, Jude's senses were raw. She hadn't left the house since the funeral, and she'd barely passed an hour without an alcoholic drink of some sort to numb her day. But Anne had insisted on taking her out, therefore she was forced to drive. The day was fresh and bright and, compared to the dusty gloom of home, felt like an assault.

She hoped they'd have a chance to discuss Sissy — somehow, despite her best intentions, her daughter remained a far-off thing, uncatchable, unknowable — but the cafe was loud and busy and she didn't think she could find the energy to shout.

She surprised herself by stopping a passing waitress laden with trays and plates. *Is there anywhere quieter?* The waitress merely smirked. *We close at six. Quiet then.*

A couple were vacating a table by the window. 'We'll take that table!' Jude called. She cringed immediately, aware of other customers giving her the once-over, labelling her as some bossy woman with no social etiquette, but she failed to see what else she could have done in the presence of Anne's close-mouthed disapproval. She'd already commented on the smell of

87

cigarette smoke in the car, despite Jude driving the whole way to pick her up with the windows open.

They sat down and looked onto the street in an awkward silence, while the same waitress cleared the remains from the previous occupants, sighing because she really oughtn't to have to do this with people sitting right there watching. She piled the plates swiftly, no messing, then: *I'll bring you menus in just a moment.*

'Thank you for inviting me,' said Jude. 'I hope this place is okay for you.'

Anne gazed down at the passers-by and clicked her tongue, unsure of how to respond. Her task was to offer support, be a helpful guide — she just wasn't sure how best to approach it.

'I thought you'd like it here,' Jude carried on. 'I know you usually go to the big places on the edge of town if you need anything.'

'Danny's a good boy. He drives me.'

Anne continued to track the people below. 'That,' she said, craning her neck to peer down the street. 'What is that?'

'Princes Square. We can go there if you like. Sometimes they have concerts in the basement.'

'What on earth have they done to the front of it?' Anne said, referring to the iron-clad facade. 'It's hideous.'

Jude only just managed to stop herself apologising.

They ordered afternoon tea, which was impossible to enjoy because Anne was so taken aback by the amount of food that arrived: *sinful, would feed a family for a day, can a person not just get a simple cup of tea any more?*

After they'd eaten, Anne took a deep breath and placed her hand over Jude's.

'And how are you *actually*, dear?'

The sudden generosity of the question landed like a punch. Jude quickly ducked her head. She hadn't anticipated kindness. The urge to seize the moment, to tell everything, superseded any concerns she had about her daughter.

'I . . . ' said Jude. The words had arrived. She could feel them. They were sitting in a jagged pile in her mouth, requiring only that she push them out to give them life. She looked down at her bare fingers on the small table, felt Anne watching, missing nothing. Scattered remnants of cake and scone filled the space between them, and in the burble and clamour of the tearoom she might just as well have been a cork bobbing in the sea, directionless, powerless.

She worked her jaw back and forth until the words tipped out: *I wish I'd married him.*

She smiled foolishly at her blatant attempt to ingratiate herself with the woman who had urged them to do that very thing. She was also smiling because, despite the truth of her regret, she knew it actually didn't matter. They'd had their chance. Whether they were married or not made no difference to anything, yet the urge to climb back through time and drag him to the altar was overwhelming.

Anne didn't know what she was looking at. That silly smile of Jude's. The idea that their lack of marriage was something that could be laughed away, especially now there never *would* be a marriage, was utterly offensive. Peter had begged Jude to marry him, she knew he had, but for no reason Anne could fathom she'd turned him down, driven a wedge between him and his faith, brought a child into the world and, having encouraged Peter away from his sensible, secure job, they'd both failed to provide it with the necessary safeguards every child deserves. And now she was laughing about it!

'Well,' Anne said, and cleared her throat. 'How is Sissy?'

Thrown by Anne's lack of interest in her confession, Jude scrambled to reply, ashamed of her egotism.

'She's fine,' Jude blinked, picking up a teaspoon to stir the small amount of tea left in her cup. 'Back at school already. Doing well.'

'I know she's back,' Anne frowned. 'But is she going in?'

'Of course she's going in.' Jude tried to smile. It was her habit to always smooth the waters. She had a nagging feeling this wasn't the conversation she'd intended to have, but couldn't find her way back. 'Why do you ask?'

Any desire on Anne's part to lambast her daughter-in-law was quashed by Jude's odd demeanour. She decided to proceed carefully.

'And the letter I gave you? At the funeral? What did it say?'

A loud crashing sound from the kitchen startled Jude. She jumped and knocked her cup over. Tea splashed the table and swilled into her saucer. Anne dabbed at the mess irritably with napkins.

'The letter,' she repeated, her patience already gone. 'What did it say?'

'Ah, she found it before I had a chance to open it,' Jude confessed.

'You weren't supposed to let her see it,' Anne exclaimed.

'I know. I'm sorry.' She was so tired, she wanted to lay her head down on the table. She hated that letter, wished she'd never known a thing about it, wondered how something intended as a loving tribute could turn out to be so complicated. So much shame; the knowledge it wasn't where it ought to be, the fact that she hadn't even made the betrayal worthwhile by finding the information Anne said she needed before Sissy had taken it back from her. And then, of course, there was just the unavoidable giant failure of herself, succeeding nowhere, displeasing everyone.

By the time Anne looked up from wiping the spillage, Jude's face was wet with tears, though she gave no indication that she knew anything was amiss. Annoyed that she'd wasted all the napkins on the tea, all Anne could do was reach out and pat Jude's hand. She wondered if her family would ever grow its own backbone, or if everyone would just rely on her forever.

'You have to be firmer,' she said, in a manner she considered to be both kind and firm.

Jude picked up her fork and began to mash a small piece of Victoria sponge into her plate.

'Did you hear me?' asked Anne. 'She's walking

all over you. Bring her into line.'

'But she doesn't listen,' Jude said. She heard the whine in her voice but couldn't help herself. 'It's like she doesn't need me. Or even *like* me, actually, if I'm being honest. I know she's cut up about Peter, of course she is, but — '

Putting the fork back on her plate, Jude breathed in deeply. *Just say it, it's why you're here.*

'I think Sissy needs you, Anne. I'm not enough for her. I never have been.'

'I see,' said Anne. She began to gather the crumbs with her finger, sweeping them into a tidy little mountain, and then squashing them back down with her thumb. That sense of purpose she'd experienced while alone with Peter in the visitation room began to rise again.

'*Peter* was enough,' Jude continued, unable to bear the void in conversation. 'He was enough for both of us. So loud, and confident, and . . . and funny. You did such a great job with him, Anne. Sissy adored him. I hid behind him. Christ, I didn't even want a baby in the first place. Do you remember?'

Anne's shock at Jude's double offence of blasphemy and ingratitude, was quickly displaced by the oddness of Jude's question. Of course she remembered, but it was only now, years later, that she saw it. Peter had made sure everyone knew he wanted a baby. He'd even involved his younger sister and brother in the campaign to make Jude agree. Anne hadn't taken any of it seriously, they weren't married, after all.

'I remember you didn't seem too happy about it,' Anne offered her daughter-in-law.

'Not so much happy as determined not to repeat the mistakes of the past,' she admitted. 'Peter said I went into motherhood like I was going into battle. Ready for sabotage at any point, you know?'

She made a jokey one-two with her fists. Anne stared back at her, wondering how best to deal with such a creature.

'Motherhood *is* a battle,' she conceded at last. Her voice was low and direct and every word cut through the hubbub.

Jude sensed what Anne was saying was important.

'I'd never thought of it like that, but you're right,' she agreed.

'The difference between us,' said Anne, 'is I fought for it, while you fought against it.'

Choked with shame, Jude lifted her cup to drink. Finding it empty, she sighed and replaced it.

'Well. I didn't exactly have the best role models, did I?' she said, quietly.

'You know, it's interesting,' said Anne, twirling her cup on its saucer. 'It didn't even *occur* to me I couldn't do it. Not at any point. I was so desperate to have my own people, I would have done anything to make it happen. *Anything.*'

'You're a good mother,' said Jude, after a lengthy pause. It seemed to be the only thing *to* say.

Anne clicked her tongue and gave Jude's hand another pat. She was beginning to see some kind of sense emerge from this cataclysmic mess they were in.

'You and I both know how it is to grow up without parents,' she said. 'I know she's seventeen and not quite a child, but we know more than most what it's like, don't we? The unexpected difficulties. So to have us on her side . . . in that regard, she's fortunate.'

Surely it was all part of God's plan. Jude was weak. Anne would keep her close and that way she would be close to Sissy. That way she would guide Sissy.

'I hadn't thought of it like that,' admitted Jude.

Jude flushed with gratitude that she wouldn't have to do it on her own, while Anne revelled in the importance of the task she had been chosen to do. She didn't particularly like her daughter-in-law, but when it came to family, well, like didn't really come into it. Their eyes met and the connection pulsed and buzzed between them.

'Seventeen is a dangerous age,' Anne said, tapping on the table to drive home her point. 'But don't you worry. Together we'll see she's all right.'

* * *

Back on the street, Jude steered Anne through the meandering shoppers. 'Busy for a Tuesday, isn't it?' observed Anne, who stopped at every shop window but could not be enticed into any of them.

As they neared the car park, a male singing

94

voice weaved its way through the crowds, stopping Jude in her tracks. She stretched on tiptoe to hunt the source, while Anne carried on until she realised Jude wasn't behind her. Irritated, she found Jude watching a busker singing 'Unchained Melody' to a small audience.

The man had a rounded stomach which protruded over baggy blue jeans and scruffy white plimsolls. He clutched a baseball cap to his chest, which gave the impression the decision to perform had caught him unawares and this was his gesture of respect to the audience. His other arm he swung with abandon — the song had taken on a physical life and demanded his caress. His voice was deep and rich and gravelly, and soared from his mouth with the power of angels.

Buoyed by the music, Jude laughed at her overblown religious comparison, especially as Anne, the most religious person she knew, the woman who said God could be found in the most unexpected of places, stood resolutely unimpressed, preferring to look anywhere other than at this man who Jude believed was proof positive of a higher power.

Peter had sung the same song to her in a pub one night, but it hadn't been like this. The strength of this man's vibrato caused his head to nod in approval of the sounds he made, whereas Peter always sat back from a song, performing with a gentleness that belied his size. The busker grabbed the notes, almost seeming to attack and wrestle them into submission, beating them to the ground before raising them up again and presenting them to the audience as a new thing, familiar but strange and utterly captivating. His voice swooped and rose again with ease, and as he approached the song's highest point, Jude held her breath. There was no way he could possibly reach it. She wanted to look away, couldn't bear the car crash of noise that would inevitably be, but at the same time she was transfixed, sure there was a discovery to be made on the other side of that absurdly high top note, if only he could get there.

Somewhere off to her left, there was a commotion. Someone grabbed at her jacket, grasping fingers. Annoyed at the interruption, she pulled back, only to find Anne's wide eyes on hers, and then Anne falling backwards, headed straight for the ground. Jude threw her hand out to catch her, but it was too late. Anne's tiny form was prostrate on the pavement, her skirt flung up around her stick-like thighs. A stunned moment of silence and then an awful, throaty moan, frightened and fluttery.

Jude knelt down and gently, futilely patted Anne's shoulder, unwilling to touch anywhere else for fear of hurting her further. The singer's immaculate ascension went for nothing as his audience changed its focus. A medley of voices: *he went that way, I saw him, he had that look about him, someone call an ambulance, I'll be a witness, is she all right, she'll be all right, that's out of order, broad daylight as well, changed days so it is, changed days.*

★ ★ ★

Danny arrived at the hospital in blazes — what was she doing out, why was she in town, who was supposed to be looking after her?

'Goodness,' said Anne. 'To hear you talk, anyone would think I was some sort of recluse. Stop fussing.'

Jude was apologetic. She'd been distracted by a particularly good busker.

Not that good, Anne told Danny. He was scruffy to look at. He'd made no effort. Plain rude.

It was true, Jude thought. It was hard to imagine a person with talent like that could be so poor, but maybe that was part of his act. Maybe he got more money if he elicited sympathy. Perhaps he wasn't as good as she remembered. Maybe it was just the idea of a jaw-dropping voice like that coming from such an unexpected place that she'd been attracted to. The contrast between his talent and his poverty elevated him. Like Peter, she realised now. She shook her head and tried to concentrate on Danny, still bleating on about his fragile bloody mother, who Jude often thought would outlive the lot of them.

'What's she going to do with a fractured wrist?' Danny asked no one in particular. 'We'll need to get nurses in.'

'No, you will *not*,' said Anne, apoplectic with rage. 'I'm perfectly fit. Nurses! I ask you.'

Danny insisted she wouldn't be able to even make a cup of tea, and what about bathing and showers and all of that? What if she slipped and couldn't put her hand out to save herself? What if some unsavoury type saw her with her arm in a sling and followed her home? Was he the only one seeing the big picture here?

'She can stay with us,' Jude said, quietly. 'If you'd like to, that is.'

Danny stopped his speech mid-flow. 'What was that?'

Push on, just push on, thought Jude. Don't think about it, just do the right thing.

'I was saying your mum can stay with us if she'd like to.'

'I thought that's what you said,' replied Danny, with the look of someone who can't quite believe their luck. 'Well, what do you think of that, Mammy? Wouldn't it solve a lot of problems?'

Anne and Jude held each other's gaze for a long moment, Danny oblivious to the rich seam running between them now.

'I daresay it might solve a problem or two,' Anne said. Jude blinked and looked away. 'Just until things get a little better,' Anne continued, as Danny, who had no inkling they were talking about anything other than his mother's wrist, helped her into a wheelchair.

'Ah, what a day,' she sighed, feeling her spirits rise as she sank down into it. 'Fancy my purse being stolen with barely a penny in it, and now here I am, gifted the loan of a wheelchair — for a sore arm, mind you! — on the very day my back's playing up. The Lord really does work in mysterious ways.'

11

Wildness Coming on Hard

It started off well enough. Anne's presence breathed life into the house again. Sissy was sympathetic and fussed over her injured grandmother, while seeming more able to tolerate being in the same room as her mother. Conversation resumed, though wine bottles continued to empty almost as fast as the ashtrays filled up, but at least most of the smoking was done in Jude's bedroom now rather than elsewhere in the house. They began eating properly again, or at least reduced their reliance on takeaways to a couple of nights a week.

Anne used her fragility to persuade Jude to drive her to the cathedral. *You may as well get out of the house while you're not working,* she said. If there was an argument to that, Jude didn't know it. The car journeys were spent discussing Sissy's progress. Anne was critical of Jude's hands-off approach.

'You don't understand,' Jude said. 'I don't want to isolate her. I want her to be comfortable with me. There's been too much friction already.'

'She's a child crying out to be saved. You should be bringing her to church for starters.'

But one thing Sissy would not tolerate was mention of church, and she resented Jude opening the door to that conversation.

'You only go because you take *her*,' Sissy pointed out when Jude broached the subject. 'And anyway, have you seen what they've been up to? Paedophile priests and all that? You'll not get me in with a load of repressed sex offenders, no way.'

'How *dare* you, madam?' Anne could barely get her words out. 'Talking filthy like that. Have you no idea of the good work the church does every day throughout the world? How dare you!'

'You do what you like,' Sissy replied. 'But I'm not a hypocrite. I don't believe it. I won't go and you can't make me.'

'Under your mother's roof you'll follow your mother's rules, young lady!' raged Anne, but as the battle ground between Anne and Sissy expanded, Jude began to retreat.

Cam and Rik found themselves invited round with increasing frequency: *Do you remember Rik, Grammy? He's my gay friend. Your church wouldn't like him though, would they? Are you allowed to talk to him? And here's Cam. He's not going to uni or working or doing anything at all really, are you, Cam?*

Sissy, you remember Father Lyons from your father's funeral. Come and say hello.

No one escaped and everyone was embarrassed by their antics. Anne had Danny attach a holy water font onto the wall by the front door, apparently because she missed her own so much, but privately because she was sure Sissy wouldn't be able to resist dipping her fingers in every time she passed. *I assumed she'd okayed it*

100

with you, he said later, when it became clear Jude had known nothing about it.

'Mum, when is she moving out?'

'She's your grandma, Sissy.'

'There's nothing wrong with her though.'

'She's broken her arm!'

'No, she's fractured her wrist.'

'She's an old lady, Sissy,' and then the killer line: 'It's what your dad would have wanted,' which both of them understood to be a truth as well as a colossal cop-out.

The Virgin Mary statue appeared from the bungalow, along with the Jesus portrait that always seemed to be watching, no matter where in the room you stood.

'Don't be upset now,' Anne said, as she removed the sympathy cards to make way for her additions. 'We're not forgetting him. We're remembering him in a different way. It's maudlin to have these up all this time. No wonder your mother barely leaves her room. Maybe if you prayed with me. And your exams, are you sure you're studying enough? This is the rest of your life we're talking about.'

The effect of which caused Sissy to pile her books up in the woods one night and set them alight.

'That's mental,' said Cam, who, having left school a year earlier, was finding his initial enchantment with adulthood somewhat on the wane, although his friends' overt jealousy over his perceived freedom made it difficult for him to admit it was the case.

Sissy stood over the fire, her face wax-like by

the light of the burgeoning blaze, her eyes burning hotter.

'I won't be told what to do,' she bellowed, throwing another book onto the pile, not knowing if she was shouting at Cam, or the fire, or at the grey smoke as it unfurled through the trees.

'What *will* you do though?' asked Rik, who was simultaneously thrilled and appalled by Sissy's behaviour. 'Don't look at me like that. It's just a question.'

'Who cares?'

It was the most obvious thing in the world that what she might or might not do in the future had no bearing on anything. 'It doesn't fucking matter. I'll . . . I don't know . . . I'll do fuck all. I'll become a zoo keeper. I'll go somewhere. Edinburgh . . . or London, why not? I'll move to fucking London.'

Rik and Cam exchanged a look and burst out laughing.

'You think I won't?' Sissy snarled, circling round to shout in their faces. 'Do you think I won't do whatever I want?'

The boys backed down so quickly, Sissy saw her wildness reflected in their fear. She took it as a warning and reigned herself in, but everyone understood she was tightly coiled, ready to spring. Cam and Rik packed themselves around her like protective padding in the hope that their presence might do something to contain her when she did finally explode.

In a way, her grief branded itself onto their friendship. Cam and Rik had never been easy bed-fellows. Expelled from one of the city's private schools for smoking pot in the toilets, Rik had moved to St Martin's just as Cam left. He'd slotted into Cam's vacated space with ease. They each secretly harboured a jealousy over the other. Cam envied the easy way Sissy danced her fingers through Rik's hair, the way she let him cuddle her, knowing there was no danger of his misinterpreting their friendship. Meanwhile Rik felt he was the stranger in the group because Sissy and Cam's friendship went back years. Now Sissy was weak and had become the outsider, but she was the group's linchpin. They had to keep her on track.

One afternoon, when Sissy and Rik should have been in a double biology class, Cam produced a small bag of weed.

'Proper skunk. Gets you high as fuck.'

A swirly graphic looped along to music on the TV screen as he built the joint under close scrutiny from Sissy and Rik.

'It just looks like any other grass,' sniffed Sissy.

'Aye well, try that, then tell me it's like any other shit.'

The high came like a rocket. She was floating above herself, distantly aware of her hands holding the spliff a hundred miles away, clumsy and heavy. There was the sensation of thick fingers interlacing with her own, and the joint went to its next home. Then there came a cascade of giggles, even though she didn't know what was funny, but perhaps that's what was funny because then she was lying on her side, tears running down her face, stomach aching with laughter.

When the laughing stopped, a hush fell over them; real, tangible, solid. They looked at each other in amazement, eyes wide like children, mouths puckered into little expressions of wonder. Then mirth began to tug at the corner of their lips and their faces stretched into laughter once more.

Later, one of them was missing, but Sissy couldn't figure out who. Then Rik walked into the room and she realised she was holding Cam's hand and everything was perfect.

'You're doing it again,' Rik said, leaning against the door frame. He looked pale. Sissy knew she should respond, but she couldn't climb back up through the soft fug she found herself in.

'Doing what?' said Cam.

'Cutting me out. Look at the pair of you. Why don't you just get a room and be done with it?'

A snickering from Cam triggered an awakening in Sissy. She struggled to swing her thoughts into focus.

'It doesn't mean anything, Rik. We're just sitting here.'

Rik began to pace the short length of room behind the sofa.

'C'mon, man,' said Cam, in between giggles. 'Be chill, man.'

But Rik was in a different place to them, edgy and paranoid. He batted off Cam's words and stumbled back out the room. A moment later, the sound of vomiting carried through the small flat.

'Ah, shit,' said Cam, pulling himself to his feet.

Sissy followed him to the bathroom, where they found Rik hugging the toilet bowl. They cleaned him up, made him rinse his mouth out with toothpaste and water.

'I think I took a whitey,' Rik mumbled.

Cam snorted with laugher. 'You think so, Sherlock?'

'Stop fucking laughing at me,' Rik said, which only made them laugh harder, even though they knew it was wrong. Maybe it was the wrongness that made it so funny. They put him to bed in Cam's room and closed the door.

'You'll feel better soon,' crooned Sissy, who might have lain down with him had Cam not taken her hand and led her back to the living room.

Something was different when they returned, like someone had come in and subtly changed the colour scheme. They both felt it and each wondered if the other had too. Cam changed the music and pulled the sofa cushions onto the floor. They leaned against the couch, sleeves touching. Something other than childhood friendship crackled between them for the first time, and without knowing who made the first move, their lips touched, soft and right and feather-light. When they broke apart they were grinning.

'Are you alright, beauty?'

'Am alright. Are you alright?'

They kissed again, their breath coming on hard. Hands slipped beneath clothes, fingers insinuated themselves down waistbands, pushed through zips and buttons to caress warm, silky skin. They were amazed by themselves and each other, how everything just flowed; how real it all felt even as they spun in increasingly dizzy circles away from that room with the venetian blind and the living flame fire; the detritus on the table: fags, ashtrays, cardboard roaches, a scattering of shiny chocolate wrappers, even the sofa cushions beneath them were elevated into the most magical of magic carpets.

Afterwards, Cam was concerned about the slim dash of blood lying across Sissy's lower abdomen. Did it hurt, was it okay, did she feel all right? And she said yes, I'm fine, it was okay. I'm glad it was with you.

They couldn't tell Rik what had passed between them, which, in the clarifying light of day, they agreed was nothing more than friends being a bit extra friendly. It made sense at the time, no need to question it too deeply.

The following days passed in a fuggy comedown haze, both of them each in their own way quietly desperate for the next opportunity to drink and smoke and be rid of Rik as quickly as possible.

12

Ya Boo Sucks

Anne's wrist was slow to heal, though somehow she managed to hoover, cook and clean with more enthusiasm than if the house were her own. She'd never been particularly houseproud but it had occurred to her that perhaps one reason Sissy stayed away all the time was because her home wasn't welcoming enough. When it became clear that wasn't the case, she set rules that she had to stay in four nights a week in order to study. Sissy, unwilling to share that she no longer possessed such a thing as a school book, spent the evenings in her room, swapping messages with Cam and Rik, or poring over the few handwritten notes she had saved from her father. His small, forward slant pressed hard into wrinkled scraps of paper that had somehow avoided the wastepaper basket.

Dear daughters, at supermarket buying food to feed you. Be good!

Dear daughters, saved you cheesecake. It's in fridge. Aren't you the lucky one?

Dear daughters, sorry for you that it's exam time. Not for me though. Ya boo sucks!

They'd had no idea such throwaway comments would one day be so valuable as to be treasured more than anything else Sissy possessed, while her own final letter to him sat in a drawer alongside socks and knickers, forever redundant, impossible now to part with.

Nicknamed 'Hagrid' by Sissy's friends, Peter had been a vital, hairy, giant force of nature. As time passed, there came brief moments of forgetting he was gone, then she remembered and it hit her — the impossible, unfair nature of it. She longed to reach out to her mother or grandmother, but the devastation was too heavy and impermeable. It was alien as a sand storm. It had whipped across and lacerated them with its sharpness; it had covered and suffocated them; it had slipped down into all the spaces between them, and worked its way into all the wounds, so that when the time came that Anne accidentally erased Peter's voice from the answering machine, there was nothing for them to do but accept it. There was no shouting, no crying, just a solidifying of the grief that anchored them, yet sent them careening away from each other. It was as though they all felt they deserved nothing more. Nothing remained that was worth fighting for, and so when the postman, with an optimistic smile, rang the doorbell one day to hand-deliver the brown envelope containing Sissy's exam results, no one expressed surprise that they were far worse than anticipated. Rik's results were marginally better, but it was clear no one was going to university any time soon.

'So London it is then,' said Cam.

The other two looked at him blankly.

'That's what you said,' he reminded Sissy. 'Said you'd move to London. That night with the fire. What are you, chicken now?'

'No,' said Sissy, her tone and expression indicating the exact opposite.

'Come on then,' said Cam, who had toyed privately with the idea ever since it was mentioned. 'What else is there? Trust me, the jobs here are shit. What you gonna do instead? Go back to school? *College for Dummies?*'

'Of course not,' muttered Rik, who had been thinking that exact thing.

They were sitting on the bench by the boathouse in the park. The summer sky was low and the clouds were heavy with rain. The idea seemed to sparkle and glow as its feasibility grew.

'I've an uncle down there,' said Rik. 'So my parents might be all right with it.'

'Screw your parents,' said Cam. 'Are you a man or a mouse?'

'Yeah, screw your parents,' said Sissy, a smile breaking over her face. 'We're adults now.'

'Technically speaking, no, we're not. Not me and Sissy anyway,' said Rik.

'Shut up, you,' said Cam, wrapping an arm around Rik's neck and rubbing his knuckles into his hair.

'Yeah, Rik, shut up!' laughed Sissy. She dived on top of both of them and they rolled across the damp grass, exuberant with the wonder of their imminent independence.

*   *   *

It was a subdued leaving party that gathered one evening in the bus station, the lights of which created a halo that diluted the midnight murk of the sky above. Anne insisted that she and Danny be present to wave Sissy off, and spent the journey there peppering the conversation with hopeful contributions such as: 'It's never too late to change your mind,' and, 'London of *all* places.'

When they pulled in, Sissy jumped out and headed straight to Cam, who stood shivering in his thin jacket, having made his own way there.

While Danny offloaded the bags and went to park the car, Jude and Anne loitered, unsure of what to do with themselves. Only Rik's parents seemed to feel they deserved their space there, seeing their seventeen-year-old off on the night bus to London, showering him with enough affection to last him until Christmas when they assumed he'd be home. They would have preferred him to take a daytime train, but the bus was cheap and Cam in particular had to make the pennies last. He cut a lonely figure, only confessing once safely on the bus that he hadn't actually explained to his mother he was leaving — *just fucking hassle* — but he'd call in the morning before she had a chance to worry.

From his mother's arms, Rik cast a sheepish smile at Sissy and Cam, who skulked well away from the main group.

'Wee birdies flying the nest, eh?' Danny's voice seemed far too loud and jovial for the occasion. 'What d'you make of that then, eh?'

'Rik has a good head on his shoulders,' Mrs Sutton smiled tearfully.

'We're not worried,' said Mr Sutton, ruffling Rik's hair. 'Are we, son?'

'Not him you need to be worried about,' murmured Danny, taking a step towards them and nodding sideways towards Cam.

'Yes, well,' said Mrs Sutton, planting a last kiss on her son's cheek.

'Sissy, come and kiss your grandma,' called Danny.

Anne received her kiss in silence, neither able to look the other straight in the eye. Then Sissy turned to her mother.

'You've got your duvet,' Jude said, causing Sissy to raise the bin bag in mortified confirmation.

'Good luck getting that through morning rush hour,' joked Mr Sutton. Sissy scowled at the bin bag. Another of Anne's ideas forced upon her.

The driver boarded the bus and the engine growled into life. Jude peered into her daughter's eyes, hoping something familiar would resurrect before it was too late, but Sissy, disturbed by her mother's sudden intensity, couldn't return her gaze.

'All aboard!' called Danny, who couldn't rest while surrounded by all that potential for *emotion*.

Overcome by a desperate desire to pack into her daughter all possible drops of goodness before she left, Jude seized Sissy and whispered hoarsely into her ear: 'You're going to do so well. I wish your dad could see you now.'

Tears from Sissy now, and perhaps she would have replied if Danny hadn't inserted himself between them — *don't miss the bus now, hahaha* — and ushered her to the open door, away from her mother.

'Attagirl! Show them what you're made of. Donnelly through and through.'

He took the bin bag from her and shoved it into the belly of the bus, along with all the rucksacks and pull-alongs. Then he gave her a bear hug so fierce it took Sissy's breath away.

'I don't want you to worry about your mum,' Danny said in a low voice. 'We'll take care of her.'

His words landed like arrows; sharp, incisive, laced with insinuation.

'I think she can take care of herself,' Sissy said, pulling herself free of his vice-like embrace. 'She's a grown woman.'

Surprise rippled almost imperceptibly across Danny's face. Shocked by her own words, Sissy's mouth opened and closed. She tried to pass it off as a joke, laughing as though to say, 'I'm kidding! Everything's fine!' but as with everything else, the damage was already done. She hurried to the soft darkness of the bus and took her seat beside Cam and Rik, forcing herself to wave out of the window. She saw Danny walk back towards Jude, his slumped shoulders mirroring hers, his head moving regretfully from one side to the next. She saw her mother lift her hand to her lips and throw a kiss towards the departing bus. She saw Mr and Mrs Sutton, motionless, holding onto each other for support, and behind them, the tiny figure of her grandmother, whose power only seemed to grow as her frailty increased.

13

Flies in London

Their house was half way down a long line of terraces. Two-up, two-down, downstairs bathroom, decked courtyard for a garden. Sissy and Rik took the upstairs rooms, leaving the tiny living room with its worn sofa for Cam because 'That's what you get when you ain't on the contract, bro.'

Despite the Suttons' reservations, Rik had convinced them of the merit in allowing Cam to stay with them, despite his name not being on the contract. 'He'll paint everything, fix anything. You know how useless I am. Please, I need him,' he'd wheedled.

The kitchen was the largest room and had a table where they'd gather round to discuss their day, break open beer, share ideas, solve the world's problems. They were high on possibility and unpacked in a hurry, keen to start the urgent business of 'really living'. They ordered pizza and sent Cam to buy beer from the shop at the top of the road.

A gay couple in their forties lived one side, and a single woman called May on the other. It didn't take long for them to work out May was an alcoholic. They averted their eyes as they passed her in the street, her clothes dishevelled and her underwear on show, and sniggered about it later. Even streaks of black mascara staining her cheeks didn't provoke sympathy. She was old and a failure. They were young and bold. They would change everything.

May lived with three cats and a dog, until her Glaswegian boyfriend moved in, bringing with him a beautiful blonde husky that prompted Cam to knock on their door to offer dog-walking services. The answer was always an aggressive no. The boyfriend was the worst stereotype of a Glaswegian, the kind of guy normally only found on television. Small eyes, big belly, bad attitude, he drove a pickup truck for a living and drank super lager on his days off, judging by the number of empty tins that were thrown into the garden. Over time, little islands of dog shit began to appear in their garden along with the tins.

One day Cam and Sissy were playing cards at the table when a shriek from Rik called them upstairs. They ran up to find him perched on the end of his bed, looking out the window.

'He is so disgusting,' Rik said.

'We know that already,' said Sissy, joining him on the bed. 'What is it this time?'

Outside, the boyfriend was in the process of setting up a barbecue, using its metal legs to nudge aside any intrusive piles of faeces. Mesmerised by the horror of it, the three teenagers watched for an hour as the boyfriend navigated his way through the maze of shit, delivering coals, lighter fluid, meat, to his cooking point. Then he fired it up and, wearing a string vest, long shorts, white socks and Crocs, he flipped burgers with a fag hanging out his mouth, the ash falling or flicked into the burning coals. Occasionally he chucked a burger onto the ground for the two dogs who stepped among the mess with low tails and delicate paws.

'I honestly didn't think people like that existed,' Rik said.

'Those poor fucking dogs,' muttered Cam. 'I should report him.'

'I saw her out in the garden the other day,' said Sissy. 'She sprayed it with air freshener.'

'Fuck off did she,' said Rik.

'Or it could have been fly spray, I suppose.'

The flies paid no heed to the rickety wooden fence dividing the properties. Soon, the back garden was designated a no-go area. Not long after that, they agreed to keep the windows closed as well.

Sissy began to feel the walls close in on her. Rik's uncle had organised a sales job for him in a mobile phone shop. He was on a fast-track management programme, though the work was dull and the money didn't go far. His first pay cheque left him worrying he'd be sharing with Cam and Sis a little longer than he'd anticipated. To everyone's surprise, Cam found a job within the first week.

'But it's only labouring,' Sissy frowned. 'You hated that when you did it before.'

'The weather's better here,' Cam shrugged. 'You have any luck yet?'

She shook her head and glanced away, uncomfortable with Cam's soft scrutiny. Every morning, she was woken by the industrious sound of her housemates readying themselves for work. It wasn't until she was sure they'd both gone that she dragged herself downstairs and sat watching morning television, waiting for Phil and Holly to project their faux happiness onto the nation. Happiness on steroids, Cam had described them, but Sissy didn't see it. She stared blankly at the screen, drinking tea, eating toast, until the relentless barking from next door forced her into the shower and out the front door.

That moment of stepping outside gave her a lift every time. The heat, the light. She revelled in the crumbly newness of everything. At home, the estate was modern, clean, maintained. Here, nothing was uniform. Streets were a messy trail of pebble-dashing, or red brickwork, or fake wooden cladding, gardens might be green or paved, bins plain or painted, windows with blinds or nets or shutters or nothing at all. Pigeons pecked at rice left for them outside number 48. A pungent smell of skunk served as a gateway out of their road. 'Ah, Bisto!' became their catchphrase every time they walked through it.

She spent her days walking up and down the bustling length of the market, stopping at stalls, picking up items and turning them over, pretending she was actually interested in their fake designer gear, perfume, mobiles, paint, brushes, all manner of plastic toys, but she returned them all with an apologetic smile. The stallholders got to know her and dismissed her as an odd-ball, while all the time she was watching, waiting for something, she didn't know what.

She tried counting all the different languages she heard and quickly felt foolish and parochial. Huge flat breads in the Turkish shop drew her curiosity, but to actually enter the shop and deal with the gregarious owner remained a task beyond her. The insides of shops spilled out onto the street, unfamiliar fruits and food stuffs piled high in crates, cellophane-wrapped meats in lurid marinades glistened alarmingly in chill boxes beneath the sun. All of it — the smells, sounds, sights, the fizzing, aggressive energy of the place — fascinated her, but when the market thinned out and stallholders began to pack up, she would fall almost by accident into Sainsbury's and buy something microwavable from the yellow sticker section for that night's tea.

Sometimes she went to the tube to study the underground map. It was there she could make sense of where she was. Only eleven stops to Victoria. From there, only another nine hours or so home. The journey that had seemed so intimidating when they disembarked the bus that first morning now appeared eminently doable, tempting, in fact. She liked to stand close to the escalator and watch the steps as they disappeared downward, almost like falling off a cliff, she thought, or a wave returning to the sea.

Dear Sissy,

I feel I must alert you to the fact your mother has gone from bad to worse. She rarely leaves her bedroom. She misses your father terribly, as we all do. Father Lyons is

117

a regular visitor, however, and God willing, we will pull through.

Your cousins Lucy and Emma continue to excel. We are so proud of them and all their achievements. Emma has a difficult time ahead, deciding which university will best serve her interests. She's quite the catch, it seems, as several institutions vie for her attention. Uncle Danny, of course, will be lost without her, but Lucy will continue to be a source of comfort. I worry how he will cope when Lucy's time comes. Still, we have a couple of years before that dark day!

We had some unpleasant news. Your father's headstone had begun to tilt sideways, having not been secured properly in the first instance. It was quite the problem to rectify since all the paperwork is in your mother's name and she — well, she could not be provoked to care, it seems. You'd think the company would be more understanding, but no, they wanted nothing to do with it. Eventually Danny stepped in and they were persuaded to allow him to bring the paperwork to your mother for signing. To think they expected your mother to go into their office herself. They'd have waited a long time. In the meantime, your father's headstone sinking into the ground a little more each day.

I suppose this is getting a little morbid for your tastes. Sometimes I think it's my age, but then I think, no, it's real life and some of us have to deal with it.

I trust you're having a good time of it in London. I've never been, myself. Your grandfather could rarely be persuaded to travel anywhere, much less to London, a place full of foreigners! And that's before they started letting everyone in! Do please be careful, dear. We couldn't bear any more bad news.

I enclose a photograph of your father's gravestone for your perusal.

Love, Grammy

They came through the letter box on a regular basis, sometimes three a week. Your mother this, your mother that, your cousins this, your cousins that. She read them hungrily, desperate for news of home, to feel connected to something outside of herself, but between the lines of each letter she detected a stronger message: you have failed us, abandoned us, shamed us, you are therefore Not A Good Person. She found it was tolerable as long as there was proof they remembered who she was.

Sissy put the letter with the others, along with the letter she'd written for Peter, which remained stubbornly above ground, undelivered. Every day, she checked and it was still there. Of course it was. But how do you send a letter to a dead man? Its presence gnawed. The ragged paper edge where intrusive fingers had dug in and ripped out the secrets within. She didn't dare reread her words in case they revealed a person so infantile and selfish that no one in the world could love her again the way her dad had done.

14

Scattered Islands

With Sissy gone, Jude found even less reason to persist with a daily routine. She resided almost permanently in her room, trying to forget about the guilt-inducing presence of her mother-in-law downstairs, and the world waiting beyond. Every time the phone rang, she stopped breathing and stared at the flashing LED display until Anne picked up downstairs. In the days and weeks after Peter's death, they'd been inundated with calls. She'd ignored them all. Now the phone was a constant companion in case Sissy rang, which she rarely did. Thank God for Caller ID.

'You should get on Facebook,' Anne said, and she knew she ought to. One day soon she would. When she could face the rigmarole of passwords and account names and whatever else was required, she'd get on Facebook and Twitter and Snapchat and Instagram and all the ways people liked to communicate these days, or, more specifically, how Sissy liked to communicate these days, if she liked to communicate at all, which seemed unlikely given her lengthy silences between calls.

It's normal, Jude told herself, quelling the deep stirring of unease that came along with thoughts of Sissy. Normal for kids to branch out on their own. She'll be back.

But what if she wasn't and Jude had lost them both? She rolled over onto her front, burying herself deeper into the bed. Downstairs, Anne pottered in her usual loud style, sending pointed messages up the stairs with each new domestic task undertaken. Guilt upon guilt. Jude should be down there looking after her ageing mother-in-law, but she'd been up here so long now. She didn't have the energy to cope with Anne's vigour, and, no doubt, her delight and wonder at seeing Jude finally out of bed, like some modern-day Lazarus. If only she could re-enter the world by degrees, step by step, but she knew she'd been hiding too long for that. There had been too many ignored knocks on the door, too many untended visitors. She'd spun herself into a deep cocoon and, like some exotic butterfly, she couldn't emerge without putting on a show.

She loved this bed. For years, she and Peter had slept on an old sofa bed Patrick had redirected from St Vincent de Paul.

'No one else would have it,' Patrick had said, when asked if there weren't worthier recipients. So they'd received it, and spent many an uncomfortable night until they'd finally pulled the money together for a real bed. They'd done it properly. Paid off all the debts, worked hard for a deposit, got the house, looked after Sissy, made sure she was comfortable before even thinking about themselves. The trip to the bed shop had been a serious one. Did they want a soft mattress or firm? The salesperson tried to up sell them to a king-size. It was beyond their budget and

Peter, embarrassed, struggled to decline. It's a romantic decision, he told the saleswoman. They were used to each other's presence at night, they didn't want a huge space between them. Jude was glad of the smaller bed now Peter was gone. His empty space was so much closer to her than it might have been. If they'd still had the sofa bed, she knew she would never have folded it up ever again.

Anne's voice carried up the stairs. She had a habit of speaking in low tones so Jude couldn't actually hear what was being said, but could be sure she was the topic of conversation. If she wanted to be discreet, Jude wondered, why didn't she just go into the kitchen and close the door? The unease set off again, making its regular journey from the pit of her stomach to nestle in her jawbone. She stretched her mouth wide to disturb the tension residing there. More gossip flying from this house down the phone line to someone. What on earth could be so interesting to talk about? What was there still to say? Nothing changed. She couldn't have foreseen that by hiding away she was making herself the centre of attention. Everyone's worried about you, Anne said. Just show your face. But to show her face would be an admission that she had moved on, caught up with the rest of the world that had continued to move ruthlessly forward without Peter. She wasn't ready for that yet. She reached for a cigarette from the pack beside the bed. Here was a problem. Only three left. The prospect of asking Anne to bring her more made her wrap herself even tighter into the duvet. This was ridiculous. Trapped in her bedroom at her age? Scared to face her mother-in-law? Was she really such a teenager?

Her eye was drawn to the open wardrobe where Peter's shirts hung in a neat row, belying the chaos his leaving had caused. She had an association with all of them. The Hawaiian short-sleeve he'd worn on their first holiday years before; the Ted Baker she'd picked up in TK Maxx; the checked one from Burton Sissy had chosen for his fortieth. All of them. Strange how they needed someone to come along and give them life. Strange how they needed a body in order to fulfil their function.

She hadn't realised she was crying again. Her face and nightdress were soaked, the cigarette one long finger of ash teetering precariously over the bed clothes.

At the foot of the stairs listening was Anne, conversation finished. She clutched the phone to her chest, not realising she was bruising the skin beneath her wool-mix M&S cardigan. She did what she always did when faced with uncomfortable matters: she suppressed it with anger. Anger put her on top. Put her in control. It gave her the energy to climb the stairs.

'That's *it*. That's enough,' she said, pushing open the door to Jude's bedroom. 'You've hidden away in here long enough.'

She crossed the room and pulled back the curtains. Low winter sunlight streamed in to highlight the millions of dust particles floating in the air. The window flew open.

'It's so stuffy in here.'

She pulled the dressing table stool over and sat by the bed. When Jude didn't stir, Anne pulled the corner of duvet that was bunched up in Jude's fist until she had the whole thing and was lifting it clear off the bed. A foetal Jude screwed her eyes up against the light.

'You can't go on like this, Jude. Do you think you're the only person who misses him?'

That was such an unfair accusation, Jude opened her eyes.

'What would he think if he could see you now? Lying in bed all day like something broken. Something unclean. Not eating. It's a disgrace. Would he love you like this?'

'Please, don't,' her voice small and croaky.

'And Sissy. What about her? Do you have the slightest idea of what she's doing? Is she even alive? She doesn't reply to any of my letters. Don't you care?'

What was she saying about Sissy? Of course she was alive. She'd spoken to her recently, she was sure. Arranged money for rent. Somehow Jude knew she wasn't helping by bailing her out all the time, but at least it was a way of keeping in touch. What was she supposed to do? Call her bluff? Let her be evicted?

Her mother-in-law was in the en suite now, her voice rattling on. Then a cold dripping cloth covered Jude's face, shocking her into sitting up. So exposed, she felt naked. So this was it, was it? The time had come.

Anne busied herself around the overflowing laundry basket, emptying and gathering colours for a wash.

'Just leave it, Anne,' said Jude.

'It's been months now,' Anne said with a sigh, as she heaved herself back up to standing, arms full with her son's unwashed clothes.

Without understanding how she got there, Jude found herself blocking the doorway.

'Leave it,' she said, with force.

A flicker of alarm passed over Anne's face. She gawped for a moment, unprepared for the reality of Jude's re-emergence into her life.

'Oh fine, have it your way,' she said finally, throwing all she'd been cradling onto the floor. 'But this room is disgusting,' she snarled. 'Get it cleaned up. Now.'

Jude stood aside to let Anne pass. A damp December wind flowed through, making the curtains quiver, but it wasn't the cold that caused Jude to shake. Peter's unwashed clothes were little scattered islands across the floor. She gathered them up, his smell no longer detectable. There was no point to them any more. She should have let Anne do one more thing for her boy. The bed sheets were grey and rumpled and covered with ash and cigarette burns. Putting the clothes onto a chair, she stripped the bed for the first time in months. She was bored and disgusted with herself. It couldn't go on. Her gaze wandered to the phone lying on the bedside table. Surely someone she wanted to speak with would ring soon.

15

Gay

It was pay day and the urge to party was upon them with an unfamiliar fierceness. What had started out as a great adventure had been reduced in recent weeks to arguments over unwashed dishes and unflushed toilets. Cam and Rik's discovery that most of their pay cheque was swallowed up by such dull essentials as rent and bills had brought about a general household depression that over time focused into resentment towards Sissy, who, despite not having a job, seemed to have an invisible source of income. She sensed their animosity but remained unaware of the cause. Confused, she retreated further into herself, and without her, the hollowness of Cam and Rik's friendship was exposed.

But now it was Friday, which, in any language, translated into party night. Too pissed to contemplate a tube journey, Rik, Cam and Sissy took a cab across town to a new club Rik had heard of. The driver took them as close as he could but they had to cross a small park to reach the club which was operating out of a disused railway arch. Feeling like imposters, unused to and unworthy of such novelty, they cautiously joined the line. The deep throbbing bass of the DJ's decks rumbled beneath their feet.

'If you close your eyes you can imagine it's trains,' Sissy said, her voice slurring slightly. 'It's like going back in time.'

'Fuck off,' both boys told her, and they all laughed, giddy with relief to be away from their claustrophobic set-up in Walthamstow, happy with each other again.

'Well, hello,' a tall blonde man turned to Sissy. 'Aren't you a poppet?'

'Well, aren't you handsome?' replied Sissy, taking in his mashing jaws and pinprick eyes.

'Thank you, darling,' the man replied. 'I've been working at it.' He ran his hands across his midriff.

'Can I touch?' Sissy asked, thrilled by her newly discovered boldness.

'Of course, baby. Lap it up. Anyone else?' he called over the sea of heads, but he wasn't interesting enough to inspire the line of clubbers, most of whom were involved in their own eccentricities. Eye make-up, facial piercings, neck tattoos, glitter, high heels, neon jewellery.

'Is this a fucking gay place?' Cam said, as comprehension dawned.

'Chill, darling. They're very accepting,' quipped Rik.

Sissy laughed. 'Cam, have you met Rik? He's our gayest friend.'

'I'm fucking picking where we go next time,' scowled Cam.

The doorman lifted the red rope and they slipped through.

'Stick with me and they won't even notice you,' said Rik, handing notes to the teller behind the window. They followed the noise along the grubby grey corridor to the main dance room, which lay behind two swing doors and opened out into a cavernous universe laden with half-naked men bouncing and grinding to the beat.

Red and green lasers splice the darkness.

'Fucking *yes!*' yells Cam. They gather round and Rik pulls out a tiny bag of yellow pills. They each take one and hug, declaring love for each other. This is their own special, unique ritual, made to cement their friendship, to put them in a good place before giving themselves over to the drugs and music.

Cam is first to insert himself among the heaving mass of bodies, pulling Sissy and Rik behind him. They push through until they make a space for themselves. They stop and look at each other in wonder, feeling as though they've surely walked straight into the centre of sound. Energy from the men around them crackles through every tiny empty space before it finds them and plugs them into the same urgent pulse, an endless wave in an ever expanding web of music.

The beauty of it takes their breath away.

Sissy can tell the crowd loves her. She's so tiny. She attracts attention. A beautiful man with piercings all over his face caresses her head in a low, gentle motion that somehow seems to emerge from the mad driving beat of the music. He's fascinated at how Sissy's hair spreads through his curious fingers, before he's swallowed back into the crowd, but Sissy knows that no matter where he goes, they're still connected. An invisible silvery thread zig-zags its way through the maze of dancers, and will keep them connected all night long.

Rik's already snogging someone. This, too, is beautiful. Sissy feels a new wave of love rising in her, lifting her literally off the ground, and then she's being passed over heads, many hands touching her. Another guy laughs in her ear: *You're so tiny! You're like a little doll!* She recognises his delight in her. *You're gorgeous too,* she shouts over the noise as she's settled back onto the floor, a circle of hairless, tanned torsos around her now, guys in jeans or black leathers grinding against each other. She loves it as much as they love each other.

A flash of concern for Cam crosses her consciousness, but, perfectly, there he is, enveloping her from behind, his knees tuck in behind hers and he nuzzles her neck. She pushes herself round. His eyes are liquid gold, his lips softer than feathers. They sway together while, all around, the rest of the room jumps in unison to the DJ's command. They are the kernel of the room, the centre of love. Sissy folds her arms around Cam's long, slender neck, and they share the sweetest kiss there has ever been.

She loves this boy so much — from when he used to steal her schoolbag to force her to chase him in primary, to him being kicked out of school and hanging around the gates waiting for her to come out and improve his day, to their first bottle of cider together — she loves his whole fucked-up life. She loves that only she knows how much he hates his stepdad, that he thinks his mum's desperate. She loves that he trusts her so fucking much, which leads her involuntarily to think about her dad, and how Cam's been there for her since Peter died, how clever he is that he doesn't force her to talk about anything, how clever that he just *knows* her, knows what she needs, and how, somehow, he's silently communicated that he will always, always be there for her.

The drums are building a rhythm, picking up speed. It's impossible to kiss any longer. They hold on to each other and bounce up and down until the beat throws them apart. Joyfully, they rejoin the mad crush, the pure and true spiritual communion. They throw their arms up and thrash, separated now by bodies, but bound by that same silvery thread no one can see but everyone is aware of.

★　★　★

If managed properly, Cam says, the comedown is almost as good as the high. Rik always finds a boy to love and stays with him until late on Sunday, so Cam and Sissy have the house to themselves. They have spliffs rolled and waiting for them. The sun rising over their tiny garden turns it into a kind of paradise — it's the only time they use it. They drag duvets out over the warped decking and wrap themselves up with shades on to protect their eyes. They smoke and talk in voices low and languid. They are beautiful. They are strong and independent and

130

wise. They are in the beginning days of the miraculous journey that will constitute their lives. Everything is perfect. Everything is as it should be. Then they make love and sleep, their bodies curled perfectly into each other because of course they are designed with only this union in mind, and then they wake and smoke and make love and then sleep again, all day long.

Afterwards, they each retreat to their own rooms. Sissy tells him they are friends and there's no reason friends can't occasionally have sex with each other. He agrees. They congratulate themselves on their maturity. Sissy doesn't think deeply about it because that would be uncomfortable, though she expects it will keep on happening. No need to put a label on whatever passes between them. For Cam, it's a little more complicated than that, but he keeps his thoughts to himself and through the week he watches her from a distance.

16

The Neighbours

Cam was on his second job after falling foul of his building-site workmates. 'What can I say? It just didn't feel right,' he said. After a week of complaining about his new call centre job, he came home one Friday and announced: 'He's a fucking cunt. And his fucking job sucks balls.'

Sissy and Rik exchanged looks. They knew all about it. It wasn't just that the work was boring, but his boss was a French guy called Pascal who liked to monitor everyone's tea breaks and give public dressing-downs for minor misdemeanours. He also liked speaking in his own language, particularly when he knew people couldn't understand him. When he was with the French speakers of the office, he'd smile and speak in a confidential manner about a person as they approached and then laugh as they hurried past, nine times out of ten with their head bowed.

'Obnoxious,' said Sissy.

'It's life,' said Rik, pouring hot water into a Pot Noodle. 'It's called being a grown-up, darling.'

'It's called he's gonna get his fucking lights punched out, is what it's called.' Cam kicked a chair away from the table and sat down, glowering. He took out papers and tobacco, hunched over and began rolling. Much to Sissy's disappointment, he didn't sprinkle any grass into it, and she didn't like to ask. Rik continued to poke at his Pot Noodle with a fork, tilting his head to look at the garden next door. He'd become fascinated by the changing state of faeces according to the weather. As it got colder, somehow the foulness of it was less.

Cam pulled a rogue tobacco leaf from his mouth and flicked it onto the floor.

'What did you get up to then?' he asked through the smoke.

'Who, me?' said Sissy.

'Well, I'm not asking him, am I?' Cam said, nodding his head at Rik. 'I know what he's been doing. He's been at work all day, same as me.'

His tone was harsh and unexpected. For some time, Sissy had been experiencing a growing realisation that her lack of direction might be a problem, but it hadn't occurred to her that anyone else might care. Not that Cam appeared to be in an overly compassionate mood.

'Uh, nothing much,' she shrugged, trying to keep it casual.

'Must be nice not having to work.'

She recoiled from the spite in his words.

'I do have to work. I just haven't found anything yet. What?' she said, catching the look that passed between them.

Rik shrugged and turned back to the window, forking noodles into his mouth, impervious to a view that would turn an iron stomach. Cam shook his head. 'Nothing,' he said. 'You gonna be alright for the rent next week?'

'Of course.'

'How?'

'None of your fucking business is how.'

'Children, children,' Rik said, tipping the last of the Pot Noodle down his throat. 'It's Friday night. Now are we going out or what?'

Cam leaned his chair back on the radiator.

'Only if we go somewhere normal. I can't hack another night fending off pretty boys.'

Rik rolled his eyes.

'Charming. Okay then. Heteronormativity, here we come.'

Their destination was a large chain pub on the corner of Hoe Street whose regular clientele were commuters marching towards middle age, who popped in 'for a quick one', only to be found three hours later, prisoner of a pissed-up moroseness.

'Could this place be any more depressing?' said Rik.

'Mate, as long as they take our ID and serve us beer I will consider this a paradise,' said Cam, raising his glass and pouring the lager straight back.

Rik shuddered. 'Animal. Do you have to dislocate your jaw to do that? Eh up,' he said, having picked up a range of national colloquialisms since leaving home. 'Look who's here.'

They turned to see their neighbour, May, with her boorish Glaswegian boyfriend, sitting at a table on the other side of the room. Too late, they ducked their heads back down.

'Hello, chickens!' May called brightly. They groaned when she stood up and gathered her bag and coat, and urged the boyfriend to follow suit.

Soon, all five of them were crammed into a booth. The boyfriend's name was Jimmy, which prompted another eye roll from Rik: *Such a cliché*, he said later, keen to dissociate himself from anything tying him to a place they all now considered to be the epitome of parochialism.

May and Jimmy had a lot of advice to give. Live it up while you can, you're only young once, seize the day, or *tempus fugit*, as Jimmy said, sparking surprise among everyone apart from May. *He's actually pretty good with languages*, she said. *What country was that, love? Show them what else you can do*. And then followed a series of scattered phrases from all parts of the globe.

'That's really good. Sure it is?' Sissy urged Cam and Rik to agree.

They talked about the neighbours, learning who to avoid, and who didn't realise their blinds were transparent with the lights on, and they knocked back more drinks when May got her purse out. 'I'll get them. I want to. You're only young. Give us a hand, Jimmy.'

'I don't know how we kept a straight face,' whispered Rik, while May and Jimmy were at the bar.

'He's a nightmare,' Sissy agreed, 'but she's not as bad as I thought.'

'Aye, just a shame she doesn't take care of her dogs though,' muttered Cam, knocking back the last of his pint. 'Might ask them about that tonight.'

'Don't,' Sissy said. 'I don't want any trouble.'

'Plus,' said Rik, 'he's a big fuckin' bloke.'

'It's all fat,' said Cam, and then sniggered wetly into his empty glass. 'I could take him.'

Sissy and Rik exchanged a look. They'd seen this before from Cam, nights when he poured drink after drink down his neck as if he were trying to douse a fire. If they could get him home and shove a spliff in his hand he might be fine, but before they could move, May returned, carrying a tray of little glasses with a luminous green liquid in them, Jimmy carrying beers behind her. 'Drinkies for everyone!' she trilled as she sat down, bustling up against Cam, forcing Rik and Sissy to shift along. Jimmy perched awkwardly on the end while May distributed the shots by holding the glasses between a red manicured thumb and middle finger, her other fingers daintily splayed. 'This is what you young ones like, isn't it,' she said. 'See, Jimmy? What did I tell you? We're living it up tonight. Cheers!'

Jimmy grew quieter as May got louder and drunker. Cam seemed to relax as more drink was brought to the table. As the night wore on, Sissy and Rik forgot they'd ever been worried. Whenever they offered money, May told them to put it away.

'You're only littlies! What brings you down here anyway? I know what he's here for,' she nodded at Jimmy. 'He's old and big and ugly like me. But you lot are gorgeous and lovely and young, ain't they, Jimmy? Oh, I wish I was young like you again, I do.'

She leaned over and pinched Cam's cheek. 'Oh, what? You jealous?' she said to Rik, with a cackle. 'Here you go, you have one an' all.'

136

Turning to Sissy, in a low voice she said, 'I can tell I'm not his type, but boys do get jealous even so. It's a mum thing. They're all the same.'

Sissy smiled, feeling more than a little woozy. The pub had filled up and was noisy with chat and jukebox tunes from the eighties and nineties.

'So what about those dogs then?' Cam's voice cut through the blur.

'Oh, I love my dogs,' May said straight away. 'Well, only one's mine. The little brown one. Cha-cha. The big one's his. The husky. Bolt's his name.'

'Aye, cos whenever you call him, he bolts,' said Jimmy, spinning a beer mat around on the table. 'Daft mutt. Low intelligence. Probably the runt. I was ripped off. Still, what you going to do?'

'Give him to someone else if you don't like him,' said Cam.

Jimmy pulled his head back, revealing the wonder of his three chins stretched ear to ear.

'I never said I don't like him.'

'You just said he was a runt.'

'Aye, but I never said I don't like him,' said Jimmy, who looked increasingly perplexed by the direction of the conversation.

'You never take him for a walk or anything.'

'Aye, I do.'

'How come your back garden's covered in shit then?'

'Cam,' Sissy said, warningly.

'Cos you never walk him, that's why,' Cam continued. 'Or the other one. What's it called? Cha-cha? It's out of order to have dogs and not even walk them. That's like a basic human right,

137

know what I mean?'

Rik spluttered into his glass. Jimmy and May eyed Cam, their jaws slack with confusion.

'Know what else is a basic human right?' he continued. 'I'll tell you. To be able to walk into your garden and not eat flies because of the amount of shite lying about everywhere. Or to be able to walk into your garden without putting a hanky over half your face because of the smell. Man, it's fucking rank. Can you two not smell it?'

May turned to Jimmy. 'I've never heard the like, have you?' Then back to Cam. 'No, I can't smell it. You're talking rubbish.'

'No, he's not,' said Rik. 'We saw you out there one day with air freshener.'

Sissy's head rolled from Cam to Rik. Were they seriously doing this after the amount of free drink they'd just been given?

'Sorry,' said Rik in response to Sissy's horror-struck expression. 'I can't pretend. It's disgusting,' he said, leaning over the table and speaking straight into their faces. 'And do you know what else?' He stood up and his wagging finger came out. 'You two are too old for this. Seriously? Did you think for one second about the irony of trapping us in a corner so we can't go anywhere and telling us to *live our life* and we're *only young once*? Do you think we want to spend one of our precious Friday nights being badgered by a pair of old crones? No disrespect, but do you know what I mean? I've been working hard all week. I just want to relax and enjoy my night.'

Jimmy suddenly stood up and leaned over to grab Rik, but almost as quickly Cam stood and put his hand on the bigger man's chest.

'You want to take this outside, big man?'

'Cam! Jesus, no!' said Sissy, trying to pull him back to sitting.

Jimmy looked down at Cam and flicked his arm away, which hit some of the glasses on the table.

'Bloody hell, Jimmy, you've spilled me drink all down me,' wailed May, dabbing at her chest with some serviettes.

'Aye, well,' said Jimmy, sneering down at her. 'That's what you get for pouring money down these wee runts' throats. I fucking told you.'

Everyone was stunned by the sudden change.

'Stupid cow,' he continued. 'See what you've done. Can't even come out for a quiet drink, oh no, always got to turn it into a party. Am I not good enough for you on my own? Throwing yourself at other blokes. You fucking disgust me.'

And then he was gone, leaving May crying into her glass and the three teenagers aghast.

Hesitantly, Sissy put her arm around May and tried to console her, but it only seemed to make her cry harder. 'There, there, it's okay, it's okay,' Sissy crooned. 'Nothing to cry about.'

Rik hurriedly finished his drink and slipped off to the bathroom, while Cam remained on his feet, eyes trained on the door in case Jimmy might fly back in at any moment. He sucked his teeth and wiped his chin. Adrenaline flooded his system. His hands were shaking. He felt like maybe he should go for a run to try to shake off the energy. He scanned the room for Rik. Typical of him to start something and then disappear. A tanned woman with red lips and poker-straight blonde hair gave him a small pouty smile as she walked past. His eyes followed her distractedly, her rolling backside moulded on top of long muscular legs. She reached her table and was swallowed up by a middle-aged gang of raucous girlfriends. She threw a glance over her shoulder and smiled at him again. He'd begun to notice an increase in the attentions he received from older women. At first he'd imagined they were just being unusually friendly but gradually he was coming to the conclusion there might be more to it than that. Sissy and May were deep in conversation and there was still no sign of Rik. He'd probably ditched them in favour of the local gay club, which they'd discovered one night when Cam had ducked into what they thought was a deserted industrial estate to piss.

His eye was drawn again to the blonde. She'd pulled out a small mirror and was touching up her lipstick, but it seemed maybe the mirror served a higher purpose because when he looked at her she turned round to face him immediately. She dipped her head to the side and her hair fell in a long platinum swoop. She smiled at him quizzically, *are you up for this or not*, and he struggled, he really did, and then he nodded towards the door, and thirty seconds later she followed him out.

★　★　★

The smell in May's house wasn't as bad as Sissy had feared. More of a stale musk with a faint tinge of urine than the used toilet she'd half-expected. She could cope with it. The dogs barked and jumped crazily around them, ignoring May's orders to stay down. They quietened when she chucked some biscuits in their bowls. The cats curled and draped along the sofa but shifted themselves obligingly so Sissy could take a seat among the thick carpet of animal hair lying over everything.

The house was a similar layout to next door, but the front room had been knocked through, turning the downstairs into one long space that had the potential for elegance.

'This is great,' Sissy said, eager to please her new-found friend. 'We couldn't do this next door. Cam sleeps in the living room.' As she said it she realised that wasn't strictly true, that more often than not he slept in with her.

'Thought you was just renting?' May called over the sound of cupboard doors opening and closing.

'Yeah, but we couldn't do it even if we weren't. What's so funny?'

May staggered through from the kitchen with a bottle in her hand.

'Nothing, really. You're so young, that's all. To hear you talk about knocking down walls and all that. It's sweet.'

Sissy looked at the whiskey May plonked down between them and felt sick. All she really wanted was some water and a cup of tea. May poured them each a finger's width.

'There you go, sweetheart. This is Jimmy's but he won't mind. Make you feel at home.'

'Will he be all right about what happened earlier?'

May smiled, her eyes like wet glass. 'Oh yeah. He'll come round. Don't worry about him. He's probably crashed out upstairs already.'

'Does he act like that a lot?'

'Like what? Oh, *that*. No, he don't mean it. He's under a lot of stress, and, no offence, but your friends weren't very nice to me either. But that's just blokes for you. They can't help it. Ain't you got any brothers?'

'No. Only child.'

May nodded, sagely.

'Little princess, ain't ya? I bet you're the apple of your daddy's eye, ain't you? What? Have I said something wrong? Oh, I have, haven't I. I'm sorry, sweetheart. Oh my goodness, come here. Tell me all about it.'

Sometime later, when the flood reduced to a trickle, Sissy sat wrapped in May's arms and gratefully revelled in her attention, feeling it was a long time since she'd given herself over to someone else like that.

'Poor mite. And that's how you've ended up here, is it? And there's me talking about my troubles all night long. You must think me dreadful.'

'No, no, not at all. I'm sorry to go on like this.'

'What you got to be sorry for? Oh, that's us all over, innit? Women. Apologising for everything. Well, *some* women. I still can't believe your mum took that letter meant for your dad. What was

142

she thinking? Look, here, take a hanky.'

Sissy pulled one from the box May offered and blew her nose. 'Apparently my gran took it and gave it to her. But I don't even know if I believe her. She's so pathetic, she could say anything. Anyway, it doesn't matter, does it? Even if it's true, she still let her move in with us, like she condoned it, or like she could take his place or something. Like I wasn't enough. Anyway, the truth doesn't even come into it. The fact of the matter is the letter's still here, isn't it, above the ground, not down there with him.' Her voice broke again. 'Oh, hello,' she said in surprise to the husky who had come over to investigate.

'That's Bolt,' said May. 'Handsome boy.'

The dog nuzzled against Sissy, demanding to be stroked.

'His eyes are different colours,' said Sissy, blinking through her tears.

'Yeah, it's quite common with the breed. Jimmy thinks it's a defect. Shame.'

The dog curled up and lay on Sissy's feet, making her laugh. She ran her hands over his thick coat and ruffled the back of his neck. 'Cam's right, you know,' she said, made brave by drink and honest conversation. 'He should be getting out more. It's not fair.'

'I know,' May sighed. 'But tell me this, if I do it, right, then I'll always be doing it, won't I? And I already do enough for him.' She indicated upstairs where Jimmy presumably lay, snoring in a stupor. 'Why should I start doing even more?'

'How about I take them then? For a walk, I mean. I'd like that.'

She'd never walked a dog before, but suddenly it seemed like her life's purpose.

'I mean it. I love dogs. I'm free during the day. It'll do me good too. Oh, say yes. Please say yes.'

May chewed her lip. 'I dunno. Dunno what Jimmy'll make of it after tonight, to be honest.'

'Yeah, but it wasn't me. I didn't say anything bad, did I? He can't hold tonight against me. And anyway, dogs need to be walked, no matter what he thinks about it. He's lucky someone hasn't phoned the RSPCA by now.'

'Yeah, all right,' May replied, sharply. 'We love our dogs. We don't hurt them. Anyway, what about Cha-Cha? You can't take one and leave the other. It ain't fair.'

Sissy eyed the small sleeping dog on the couch beside May.

'Of course,' she said. 'I'll take them both.'

May agreed Sissy could walk the dogs on days Jimmy was working. She gave her a key, with the strict instruction not to enter if the truck was parked outside.

Having a reason at last to get out of bed boosted Sissy's mood. Most days she gave them two walks, timing it so they were back in the house by 5 p.m., thereby minimising the risk of running into May, who, in the sober light of day, might change her mind about a relative stranger popping in and out of her house. The dogs looked healthier and barked less. The shit in the garden dried up and shrank to the size of pebbles. Sissy struck up conversations with other dog walkers and, slowly, began to realise how isolated she'd been. She had the sensation of emerging from behind heavy curtains. She felt lighter and more positive.

'You do know it's not an actual job though, right?' said Rik one evening, after another soul-crushing day in sales.

'Hey, leave her alone,' said Cam. 'It's her business.'

Rik raised his eyebrows and gave a long low whistle. 'Someone's changed his tune.'

Sissy was relieved but confused by Cam's turnaround. She'd stayed so late at May's, she'd failed to realise he hadn't gone straight home from the pub. When she'd tiptoed in around 3 a.m., she'd found him asleep in the living room. Guiltily, she'd climbed the stairs, oblivious to the tension disappearing from his body as he heard her steps retreat.

In the darkness, Cam had sighed and stretched as best he could on the sofa that was his ill-fitting bed. When at last he fell asleep, it was with a deep sense of shame that mingled confusingly with his burgeoning teenage pride.

They skirted around each other on the Sunday. Sex and intimacy was so much harder when not prefaced with a night's worth of drug-induced dancing as foreplay. They cast thin jokes about Rik's whereabouts and wished separately for his return. It was one of the longest Sundays either of them had ever known.

17

Dismissed Notifications

One cold afternoon a few weeks later, Sissy was at the top of the nearby sports field trying to dissuade Bolt from eating another dog's shit when the distant figure of Cam appeared at the other end. It wasn't yet dusk so she knew she had time to return the dogs before May came home, but still she automatically checked the time on her phone. Mid-afternoon and another missed call from her mother, who had been calling more often of late. Sissy dismissed the notification, as usual, and headed towards Cam, leaving Bolt to do whatever disgusting thing he had to do.

The smell of freshly baked bread carried over from the nearby factory. 'I love that smell,' said Cam, when they met in the middle. 'Do you think they'd give me a job?'

'Oh, Cam. Not another one.'

'What could I do? I told you the French cunt's a bastard. Hello, boy!'

Cam scratched Bolt behind the ears. The dog jumped up and Cam allowed him to knock him down. They rolled on the cold ground together.

'He's just been eating shit, you know.'

Cam laughed. 'I know what that's like, don't I, boy? I know what that's like.'

They moved to the edge of the field and

continued their walk round. Cam threw a tennis ball for Bolt, while the little brown dog waddled resentfully by Sissy's side, picking up pace only when offered biscuits.

'So this is what you've been doing, is it?' said Cam. 'Just coming here every day?'

Sissy shrugged and looked off to Canary Wharf blinking in the distance. 'Pretty much.'

'Don't you get bored?'

'Is it any worse than going to work?'

'I don't know. Is it worse than having no money?'

Sissy sighed and shrugged again. She was bored of this conversation.

'You not going to tell me to mind my own business like usual?' Cam risked a cheeky grin, knowing he was in dangerous territory. Sissy knelt down and gave Cha-Cha another biscuit, feeling the weight of reality enclose her. She'd thought somehow everything would sort itself out, but as the weeks turned to months it was clear she was going nowhere. Rik had a whole life she knew nothing about. Even Cam had plugged himself into some social scene she wasn't part of. She wondered where he disappeared to but couldn't bring herself to ask. Instead she waited for the weekend when a pill would reliably dispel the week's worry and bring her to a place of elevation, where the truth revealed itself to her and she re-understood the point of her existence. The days between weekends were flotsam, a tedium to be endured so long as ecstatic transcendence was her weekly reward.

She steered the conversation towards their weekend plans and found Cam unwilling to commit to anything. 'Just don't fancy it, that's all,' he said, as he stepped away to play some more with Bolt.

'Do you want to do something else then?' she asked, doubtfully.

'Nah,' he replied, tossing the ball. The dog lunged after it, his long blonde hair frisking behind him. 'Gonna be a bit busy. Been invited to a party.'

'Cool,' said Sissy, lightly. 'Whose?'

Bolt came darting back and dropped the ball at Cam's feet, bouncing on his back legs ready to sprint again.

'No one you know,' said Cam, throwing the ball further than before.

That was the last word on the subject. Sissy understood she was no longer the only girl in Cam's life. She also knew she had no right to be upset because they'd never had *that* kind of relationship. Theirs was one fuelled by drink and drugs and familiarity. She was fine. Really fine. She was so fine, she failed to notice how Cam watched her on the way home, and how she missed her chance to let him know that it mattered.

Later, when they'd returned the dogs and had tea and home-made cheesecake, which consisted of digestive biscuits smothered with cream cheese and strawberry jam, Rik came home in a temper, having received a nasty phone call from their letting agent.

'The *rent*, Sissy. The fucking *rent*.'

Bulldozed by the twin assaults of the afternoon, Sissy could only stare open-mouthed as Rik focused months of pent-up frustration into one single, huge issue.

'How could you not pay the fucking rent?'

'I don't know anything about this,' she sputtered at last.

'That's fucking abundantly clear. In fact, do you know anything about anything? Well, do you? All you do is mope about all day like some old lady. You're about to be eighteen, for fuck's sake. What the fuck are you doing with your life?'

His words were vicious, but what blindsided her most was the revelation that the events of the day were linked directly to the day her father died. She thought she'd been moving on, but her best friends were giving up on her, and the worst part of it was she knew she deserved it. Her behaviours, her attitudes, had brought them to this, and her behaviours and attitudes were a direct result of the massive sinkhole that opened up in her life months before.

'I'm sorry, I don't know what happened. I'll sort it out, I promise.'

'It's the *rent*, Sissy. The fucking *rent*.'

She knew exactly what had happened. She had all the missed call notifications from her mother to prove it.

Later, she sat in her bedroom feeling a mixture of guilt, embarrassment, a need to punish, and a need to be punished. With nothing else to do, she took out the small pile of letters that had arrived from Glasgow over the past few months, most of them little missives of guilt from Anne

— your mother needs you, are you going to church, have you got a job yet, why are you hiding from us — and only a few from Jude. Those were short, often tear-stained and blotchy, clearly written while drunk and, Sissy thought, presumably posted drunk too. She'd replied to none of them, though each had been received with no small sense of satisfaction that while she was making a life in London, those she'd left behind languished after her. Her silence was the price they had to pay for being such crap adults in the aftermath of her father's death. She flipped through the envelopes until her fingers came to her father's letter. She separated that from the pile, the rest she bundled up and slipped into an envelope addressed to the inhabitants of 24 Shieldhill Close. She took it to the postbox and dropped it in before she could change her mind.

On Monday morning, Rik's alarm went off as usual, and, as usual, it woke Sissy up, but instead of blocking out his presence by pulling her pillow over her head, she waited until she heard him leave and then put on the dress she'd worn to her dad's funeral. It was the only smart thing she owned.

She took the train into town and one hour later was sitting in a small office waiting to speak to Cam's former boss. Self-conscious in her oh-so-pretty dress, she did her best to ignore the stream of tired, scruffy workers peering in at her through the glass. At last, the corridor outside fell into silence. The only sound was the loud tick of the clock on the wall. It reminded Sissy of school clocks, large, plain, industrial, the seconds hand juddering its way round the clock face. Five minutes passed, then ten, then anxiety gave way to irritation and she had to force herself to calm down. She'd turned up unannounced, after all.

Forty-five minutes later, a sour-looking man with long dark hair strode into the office. He did a double take when he saw her. Clearly, he'd forgotten he'd told her to wait there. Annoyance flickered across his face, but he swept his hair back and sat down opposite her.

She had her speech ready. She planned to throw herself on his mercy — if he saw how desperate she was to work, he couldn't possibly turn her down — but she needn't have worried. After a few blunt questions regarding her background, the answers to which she wasn't convinced he listened to, he slipped a piece of paper across the desk to her.

'Fill this in. Training normally is a Thursday but lucky for you we have a large survey beginning today. I'll run you through it this morning. It's not hard work.' He sighed, or groaned, and waved his hand dismissively. The lack of difficulty in the task ahead of them appeared to be a source of deep disappointment.

And so began Sissy's first paid job, calling people at home and running through page after page of questions, inputting data into the oldest-looking computers she'd ever seen, learning how to steer a rambling conversation, and when to adopt a strict tone forbidding waning respondents from hanging up the phone half way through an interview. At the end of her first week, Pascal called her back into his office to tell her how well she was doing. By now she was well exposed to the stupefying nature of the job, but she flushed with pleasure nevertheless. She returned home excited to share her news with the boys, who had been cold with her all week; Rik still furious with her for missing the rent and Cam resentful she had taken his old job.

Even standing on the crowded train with her face squashed against a stranger's armpit didn't dampen her enthusiasm. She skipped down the stairs at St James's Street and took further cheer from the Christmas lights beginning to appear in people's windows, a sight that previously only deepened her depression, but this afternoon's events had given her the boost she needed to confirm with herself that she wouldn't be going home to Glasgow, therefore she didn't have to face the daddy-shaped hole in her life. She was moving forward. London was home. Everything that came before would soon be only a distant memory.

As she turned into her street, blue flashing lights halfway down slowed her walk. Despite the urge to turn back, she was compelled forward as myriad different futures at once presented themselves and one question loomed larger in her mind than any other: Who's dead this time?

She broke into a run and arrived at her house breathless, not from exercise but panic. The police car was abandoned in the middle of the road right outside her house. She fumbled the key into the lock, telling herself they might be in any other house; just because they were parked outside hers didn't mean they'd come to see her. She pushed the door open and her brief hope was extinguished immediately by the presence of a large uniformed body blocking her way into the kitchen.

'Excuse me,' she said, ashamed to find herself on the brink of tears. The officer turned round and sized her up while keeping his head angled towards the chattering radio clipped to the front of his uniform. He moved aside to reveal another officer, a woman, sitting at the table opposite Cam. It took a few seconds for Sissy's brain to unscramble what she was seeing and downgrade the situation.

The table was littered with bloodied scruffs of toilet paper. Cam held a clump of paper to his nose. She noticed now the mild discolouration around one eye, how the skin seemed to be closing in around it, and she experienced a simultaneous wave of relief and fresh worry.

'This is her,' said Cam. 'Ask her.'

All eyes focused on Sissy. The female officer took her details and asked her to confirm whether she'd made arrangements to walk her neighbours' dogs.

'That's right,' said Sissy, her confusion growing.

'So you agreed with Mr James Thomson that you could enter his property with a view to taking his dogs out for a walk?' the woman asked, pen poised over her small notebook.

'Yes, uh, you mean Jimmy? No,' said Sissy. 'I

153

agreed it with May. His girlfriend. Why, what's happened?'

'I think we'll be asking the questions, alright?' the male officer said. 'Now why don't you go back to the beginning?'

Sissy explained the arrangement and how she was only supposed to go in when Jimmy wasn't there. A look passed between the officers.

'I didn't know that,' said Cam, his voice muffled and thick behind another sodden tissue.

'Are you sure you don't want us to call an ambulance, Mr Docherty?' the woman said.

'What? For a nosebleed? Nah, you're alright,' said Cam, picking up the rapidly dwindling toilet roll and wrapping a fresh batch around his hand. 'So you gonna charge him or what?'

'Technically speaking you didn't have permission to be in there, Mr Docherty. Your friend here did; you didn't.' The police officer's tone implied he had far more important matters to deal with.

'Aye, but I wasn't in there when he did this, was I? I was in the street.'

He took the tissue away from his face and looked at it with disdain before placing it on the table along with the rest.

The female officer took a conciliatory tone. 'Look, if you pursue this, then all that'll happen is he'll retaliate by trying to bring charges against you for trespass.'

'Bollocks,' said Cam. 'That's not how it works.'

'Listen to me,' the woman said, in a voice that suggested her patience was waning. 'What it comes down to is you took your neighbour's dogs by illegally entering his premises. I'd say you're lucky not to be getting yourself arrested for burglary. Take my advice, keep your head down and stay out of Mr Thomson's way. If we get called back here, it might be the custody officer you end up dealing with.'

'Fucking unbelievable,' said Cam.

She made him sign her pocketbook and turned to leave when the male officer had an afterthought and turned back.

'Still got the key, sir?'

'Fuck's sake,' muttered Cam, fumbling around in his jacket pocket until he found it and handed it over, the police man assuring him he'd hand it back to its owner. Sissy showed them out and returned to hover in the kitchen doorway, unsure of what to do or say.

'What are you looking at?' Cam said, furious and humiliated.

'I'm sorry, I — '

'You get a job,' he continued, in an accusing voice, 'and suddenly no one's walking those poor fucking dogs again. Is that right?'

Sissy shook her head and spoke quietly. 'It's not that, Cam. It's just . . . if I'd known what you were planning to do, I could have told you about the truck thing.'

'Wouldn't have made any difference anyway. The truck was gone when I went in. I'm not stupid, am I? He got me when I came back. Bastard.' He examined the tissue. The flow appeared to be stemming. He dabbed his nose gently and shook his head with a small, bitter

155

half-laugh. 'They were barking all fucking day. The key was sitting right there,' he said, nodding to the small bowl on the table before them. 'It was just spur of the moment. Bad luck.'

'You should probably put something on that,' she said, nodding at his eye. 'I don't know. Ice or something?'

She got up and found an empty ice cube tray in the freezer.

'It's better than nothing,' she said, attempting to hold it against his face. He shrugged her off, and the tray clattered to the floor.

'What's the fucking point?' he said. 'It's done now.'

He went through to the living room and closed the door. On cue, the dogs began to bark.

★　★　★

The call centre was a fifteen-minute walk from Liverpool Street station and occupied one floor of a six-storey block. The employees were mainly young, scruffy and miserable, with straggly hair, bad skin, and postures so neglected that their necks appeared to have been swallowed by their rounded shoulders. Women were outnumbered three to one. In the air hung a permanent tang, normally attributable to well-worn trainers. An older woman with dyed red hair and thick, green-framed spectacles would periodically do a circuit of the room with a can of air freshener, triggering a cascade of coughing.

'Pack it in, Hazel!'

'Wash your bloody feet then!'

Anything to break up the day.

Sissy consistently exceeded her targets, which gained her attention because Pascal had a whiteboard system that announced to the room who was flying and who was failing. She caught people looking at her as if she might have specialist knowledge she was keeping for herself. The truth was she had no idea why people on the other end of a phone line seemed to enjoy speaking to her. Whatever the reason, it made her popular with the management, who quickly moved her from domestic calls to business, which required extra training, and paid marginally more money with the possibility of bonuses.

She was plugged into the world at last, and Rik approved. When the weekend came, they hit it hard, leaving behind the boredom of the week, and also Cam, who hadn't yet found another job and refused Sissy's efforts to pay his way.

'Ignore him,' Rik said, as Sissy tried once again to persuade Cam to join them. 'He's just scared all those fit-as-fuck blokes will want to do things to him. Homophobe.'

'Fuck you,' Cam scowled.

'I don't understand why you won't just let me pay. It's my eighteenth, for fuck sake. It's only money. I don't give a shit about it. It just lets you do stuff. Come on,' she was wheedling now. 'I want you to. It's never the same without you. I miss you.'

'Charming,' sniffed Rik.

'Stay here if you miss me so much.'

'Yeah, very funny.'

'Don't see what's funny about a quiet night

157

chilling,' Cam shrugged.

'Cam, it's my birthday! I can't not go out on my eighteenth!'

'Suppose I'm no match for those wee pills you get hold of there, am I?'

Rik raised his hands and headed for the door. 'I'll leave you two love birds to it.'

Alone, they stared at each other, before Sissy pulled back a chair from the table and sat down opposite him, determined to clear the air.

'What you on about?' she asked. 'Are you okay?'

He raised his shoulders in approximation of a shrug, but remained hunched over his cigarette papers, unable to look her in the eye.

'This isn't like you, Cam. You used to be up for everything. Listen,' she reached over and placed her hand on his forearm, 'you'll get another job. It's not going to be like this forever. In the meantime, I've got money. Let me help you.'

He stared at her hand on his arm, and sat poised with his cigarette half-rolled. He put it on the table, shrugging her off in the process. His arms extended long and knobbly from his T-shirt. She thought she was getting through to him. All she had to do was bring him in.

'Mind I told you my dad burned a hundred-pound note once?

She was so proud of finding the courage to mention him, she didn't notice Cam's sharp intake of breath, or the way his lips curled over his teeth.

'He did it to prove it didn't mean anything,'

she continued. 'So, I swear, I don't mind giving you money. It doesn't mean anything to me. It's just a social construct.'

Cam's hands slapped the kitchen table, causing tea to splash over the rim of his mug. His chair screeched across the floor, knocking against the radiator, causing Sissy to startle.

'Woah, calm down! What did I say?'

He stood with his head bowed, hair falling across his eyes, unable to voice his feelings or understand how he'd come to the point of loathing his best friend. Except it wasn't quite as straight forward as that. He'd slept with a couple of different women, none of whom held any real interest for him, despite their experience. The way they cooed over his youth and laughed at themselves because they couldn't believe they were doing it with someone so young made him feel like a novelty act. Not to mention the bastard next door. Every time their paths crossed Jimmy puffed out his chest and acted the big guy, just because he'd managed to land a punch on him. Sissy didn't care about any of it. The fact she didn't know was irrelevant because she *should* know and she *should care* and the fact she was so damn uninterested in him and was moving on, working for that prick of a boss he'd had — well, it made him want to punch something, or himself. And there she was wittering on about money, so fucking clueless about everything that she thought burning money was a heroic act. He wouldn't say anything, of course, because it was her dad who had burned it and you couldn't speak ill of the dead. Instead he batted her away with one hand and left the room.

She didn't understand why he was being so distant until it occurred to her that she was practically begging him to come out and the fact that he wasn't meant he must have something, or someone else, to do. Swallowing her hurt, she hit the night with a vengeance. She and Rik marched to the tube station each with a single purpose: she to party until she forgot, and, he until he pulled. When that happened he would slink back to his new friend's flat. His disappearance barely ever registered with Sissy because she would have taken so many pills, and become soulmates with so many people, that by the time she was travelling home on the first tube, she'd be too numb to care very much about anything. And when Wednesday morning arrived, most of her comedown would be gone and she'd be itching for Friday night all over again.

'You look better,' Pascal told her one Friday morning. She was alone in the staff room making tea and he caught her by surprise. Pascal rarely made small talk. 'You've been sick, I think,' he said.

'Uh, no, not really,' she replied, confused. He frowned and stepped closer.

'But you've been . . . low, I think, these past few days. You think I don't notice?' he smiled, as she stepped round him to put the milk back in the fridge. 'I notice everything. It's my job. I'm the boss. Is everything okay? Anything you need to discuss?'

Sissy found his friendliness a disconcerting contrast to his usual sullen demeanour. Perpetually dressed in black and rarely seen without his coat, Pascal's shoulder-length dark hair was the only part of him that reflected any light. Sissy had been intrigued by him from day one and his aloofness meant she could watch from a distance. He had a way of repelling people and drawing them in at the same time, particularly the male workers, who gathered in groups to sulk and moan about his seemingly impossible-to-achieve targets, yet whenever he deigned to cast a word in their direction, they fell about in a fawning, joking manner, all boys together, safety in numbers.

'I'm okay.'

She flinched as he reached to tuck a loose strand of hair behind her ear.

'What?' he said. 'Oh, I forgot. You British girls are so uptight, aren't you. It's nothing. It's just a little touch, that's all. Your hair, it is better this way. These British boys, they don't notice these things, but I do.'

She touched her hair self-consciously. 'It's fine,' she replied, trying to hide her embarrassment. 'I don't mind.'

'Normally you are so . . . ' he waved his hand vaguely. ' . . . so well put together. Not this scruffy mess. Have you been — how you say — burning the candle at both ends?'

He was so close she could smell his aftershave, a faint musk that invited her to breathe in a little more deeply. She noticed the stitching on the lapel of his coat was beginning to unravel. She wondered what would happen if she were to pull on the thread.

'You like to party, I think,' he said, dragging her attention back to him. There was amusement now in his eyes, which transferred inexplicably to Sissy, despite her self-consciousness. She shrugged, tried to keep her face straight, remembering this was her boss talking.

'A bit,' she admitted. He flashed a grin at her, the first she'd seen.

'Me too,' he said, then writing on the back of a business card, he put down details of a club he would be at that evening. He held the card out, but before she could take it, he pulled it back.

'Just between you and me, understand? Otherwise all these . . . ' He indicated the world beyond the staff room. 'They will be coming too. I have enough of them through the week. And also, I am your boss so . . . careful, yes?'

She nodded, pleased and baffled. She took the card and slipped it in her jeans pocket, the argument in her head already starting up: she wouldn't go, he was her boss, how old was he anyway? At least ten years older. But on the other hand, why not? She presumed it was a straight club he'd given her the information for, so it was unlikely Rik would join her. Cam obviously couldn't be invited and wouldn't come even if he was. She returned to her booth and carried on with the day's new batch of calls, but through every conversation her thoughts were somewhere else.

Putting on her coat at the end of the day, she noticed Pascal lingering by the exit. People streamed past him in a hurry, excited for the weekend, while the evening shift trooped gloomily to the vacated office chairs for four hours of calling people at home. It was the grimmest shift on earth. No one wanted to answer surveys at the best of times, but Friday nights were particularly tough. A combination of tiredness and alcohol made the British public more belligerent than usual, it seemed. It was impossible to time the calls so you finished on the stroke of nine. You could finish a survey at 8.57 and have to keep dialling until the big hand hit the magic twelve. After an evening of hostility, it was plain bad luck if someone decided to answer your questions at two minutes to nine, but you had to keep on with it and suck up the mockery from your workmates on their way out the door.

As she approached, she realised he was trying to entice members of the dayshift to stay on for the evening. The occasional person about-turned, but the majority left with an extra spring in their step, knowing they'd put one over on their boss for once.

'Not you,' he said. 'You go home. Get ready.'

She ducked her head as she slipped past him and hoped he hadn't seen the smile spread across her face. That was it then. She had to go because she'd just passed up the opportunity to tell him she couldn't make it. He was expecting her. She couldn't risk pissing him off and losing her job. By the time she arrived home she'd made a pact with herself not to tell Cam or Rik where she was going. Cam had been bitter

163

enough towards her recently. He really didn't need to hear she was spending time outside work with his despicable ex-boss. Rik, however, had other ideas and badgered to be let in on the secret.

'Just some people from work,' she said, wondering why she hadn't said that in the first place.

'Who?' asked Cam. 'Some of them were alright. Maybe I'll come too.'

'You don't know them,' she replied, almost tripping over her words. 'They just started when I did. Anyway, thought you were skint?'

Cam flinched and Sissy experienced a wave of self-loathing as she saw his embarrassment. She pushed it aside. She'd offered to take him out on more than one occasion by now. It wasn't her fault he couldn't get along with people. As though sensing her disloyalty, the dogs next door began to bark. Grateful for the distraction, she seized her opportunity.

'For God's sake, those poor bloody mutts. They've just gone right back to their old ways, haven't they? Want me to try talking to May, Cam? See if they'll let you take them back out again?'

A derisive puff of air was all the reply he gave, which she was glad about, because the last time she'd seen May in the street the woman had picked up pace and hurried past without saying hello. Jimmy still spoke to her on the odd occasion their paths crossed but it was in a sneering, derogatory way that left her no doubt about her low status in his world. She suspected he was the reason May refused to talk to her any more.

'Anyway,' Rik was saying, as he prepared his evening meal of a chicken and mushroom Pot Noodle, 'I'll say the same to you as I said to her. Walking a dog is not the same thing as having a job. When are you going to sort yourself out? Sometimes I think I'm the only grown-up in this place.'

Sissy and Cam exchanged a look and then smiled in recognition of their chastisement. For a moment it was almost like the old days when their friendship surpassed everything, even their feelings for Rik, but almost as quickly as the light between them appeared, Cam's face darkened again and he recoiled from Sissy's smile.

'Well, despite the fact I have the means to join you because, you know, I *work*, I'm actually not going to,' Rik said, 'even if I *had* been invited, and by the way, I know I wasn't, which I actually find pretty rude, to be honest. Even if it's only some *yawn* place for straights, it's nice to feel included, you know? *Some* of us have money to spend, even if some others of us don't.' He nodded theatrically at Cam. 'But as I say, I will not be joining you because I have plans of my own.' A brief pause. 'Aren't you going to ask? Does no one care? I'll tell you anyway.' A pause for dramatic effect and then Rik swung his arms and pretended to skip on the spot. 'I have a date.'

'A date?' Sissy said. 'Like, a *date* date? With an actual person?'

'I can't shag around forever, can I? Or can I?'

165

Rik's smile ran from ear to ear as he pretended to weigh the benefits of monogamy against promiscuity. He carried on chattering in between mouthfuls of noodle, not noticing Cam's mood steadily sinking, or how Sissy stared at the kitchen clock and willed the hands to speed their way round to the point she could leave for her train back into town. Through the wall, the dogs' incessant barking seemed that little bit louder.

18

Various Brightly Coloured Wrappers

The club Pascal had directed her to was up a side street from Leicester Square. Unsure whether to go in or wait outside for him, she lingered self-consciously a few hundred yards from the entrance. As more people arrived and a queue began to form, she began to doubt she'd be allowed in. Wearing her usual clubbing mix of jeans and trainers, she felt distinctly under-dressed. Judging by the women in the line, heels, make-up and hair was the order of the day. She took out her lipstick and gave herself an extra coat, though she considered it akin to going into battle with a kid's plastic sword.

London was neon. The lights from advert hoardings almost turned night into day. Tourists snaked through and around each other, some on their way home, others just getting started. Sissy shivered in the cold night air and cursed her cowardice. She'd have brought a jacket if she'd known she'd be hanging round street corners like a wuss. If only she had a number to call. She checked her phone for messages — he had access to her file, after all — but there was nothing. She eyed the growing line, and the thick-set bouncers dressed in black at the end of it, and decided to go home.

She turned around and smacked straight into

Pascal who was rounding the corner just as she was leaving. She stepped back and apologised before she realised who he was. He caught her by the wrists and laughed.

'Where do you think you're going, *ma cherie*? Friends, allow me to introduce my new *compadre*. Her name is Sissy.'

It was only then she realised two other men were with him. They looked at her with bored expressions and sailed past her towards the venue. Pascal shrugged and said, 'Shall we?'

'Pascal, I'm sorry, I should have googled the club. I'm underdressed. They'll never let me in . . . '

He placed his arm around her shoulder and began to walk her towards the doors, all the time quietly nodding his head as she gabbled on about how woefully ill-prepared she was. He led her past the line, past the judgemental eyes of polished women, the non-seeing eyes of predatory men, and with a nod to security, he led her straight into the club, through a set of double doors, around an almost empty, circular dance floor, and sat her at a small table behind a roped area in a raised part of the room, before going to order drinks.

A mixture of R&B and drum 'n' bass boomed from the DJ's decks. It wasn't what she was used to in a club. Give it a chance, she thought, it's still early. Her eyes landed on Pascal who was talking to a waitress (a waitress in a club!). He was still wearing his work clothes. His lack of effort relaxed her a little, though she also noticed a small part of her was irritated by his arrogance.

He sat back down beside her and a moment or

two later a bottle of champagne arrived on a tray. A separate waitress brought a metal stand with an ice bucket. The first waitress poured the drinks, the second one placed the bottle in the ice.

Sissy winced at the taste of the champagne but sipped it anyway. She would have preferred a WKD or shots, or even a beer, but she knew to admit that would be to admit her inexperience, and she most definitely didn't need to advertise that.

The club gradually began to fill, though the dance floor remained stubbornly empty. Men and women sat at separate tables. It was like they'd come in packs. As the night wore on, the men became more boorish and the women found the courage to step onto the dance floor, holding on to each other for balance in their precarious footwear.

The music made talk impossible, particularly as Pascal was preoccupied with some business with one of the men behind the bar. He was up and down all night, each time casting an apologetic glance to Sissy as he left, who was feeling increasingly uncomfortable. The VIP area was positioned to dominate the room. People sat there to be seen. Crossing her Converse-clad feet beneath her, she lifted her freshly filled glass to her lips and wondered how long before she could reasonably make her excuses and leave. She took her phone out to check the time just as Pascal returned, breathless with yet more apologies. His eyes locked onto her phone, and then her, and she immediately felt guilty, though she knew she

169

shouldn't. He lifted the champagne bottle and held it to the light. She was surprised to see it was almost empty, but then the waitress had never been far away, topping up her glass, giving her a friendly smile whenever Pascal stepped away from the table, but it was always just such a small amount, it seemed like nothing.

Waggling the bottle at her, Pascal said, 'I see you've been busy.'

The strangeness of the evening was at last too much for her; his rudeness, her clothes, that club, those people. She stood up intending to leave but immediately fell into the stand holding the ice bucket. Even through the banging music, the clang of metal on the hard floor was loud and out of place.

'Whoops,' Pascal said, catching her arm.

'I like your style, Frenchman,' a male voice said. 'Champagne in one hand, a woman in the other.'

Sissy turned to see one of the men Pascal had been with earlier looking at her. She didn't like him; tall, well-built, too sure of himself. One of those guys who look too clean, who act like their shit doesn't smell. The kind of confident guy who demeans everyone around him just by his presence. She snatched her arm from Pascal's grasp, keener than ever to get out of there, but he let her go too quickly and she stumbled backwards and fell to the floor with a bump. The noise and flashing lights whirled around her aggressively.

Pascal knelt down with a look of concern on his face. She was grateful he wasn't laughing at her and allowed him to pull her up. She leaned against him, dimly aware of his arm around her back, enjoying the sensation of being tucked into him.

'My God, you're so fucking pissed. It's okay. Come with me.'

He led her through a door by the bar to a place where the air was cooler and the violence of the music fell away behind them. Then through another door into a room with a desk and a sofa.

'Beat it,' he told the guys in there, who jumped up and skipped out before Sissy even saw their faces.

'I'm sorry. I'm so drunk,' Sissy mumbled, as he lowered her onto the old leather couch.

'Yes. Yes, you are. And I am far too sober. It is not a fair arrangement but we will sort that out.'

He pulled over an office chair on wheels and sat down opposite her, clearing a space on the small coffee table between them. The lighting was stark compared to the club. Sissy had to blink a few times to get her bearings. The room looked like some sort of ramshackle office, with receipts and invoices pinned to a noticeboard behind the desk. Beside the door was a bookcase full of thick ring-binders. An old-looking music system and a small round table with an array of spirits next to some glass tumblers sat beside the couch.

Pascal reached into his inside coat pocket and Sissy began to giggle. He paused and looked at her, arm half-in, half-out, like a Napoleon impersonator.

'You didn't take your coat off,' she was saying. 'In the club. You kept it on.' She'd no idea why it was so funny but she fell sideways laughing. His straight face only made her laugh harder.

'One moment, actually,' he said, and rose. She stopped laughing long enough to see him take two long strides to the door. He turned a key in the lock and sat back down.

Without looking at her, he took a small clear bag from his inside pocket and placed it on the table. He reached for a CD box, inspected it, wiped it on his sleeve, and inspected it again. Then he opened the bag and reached in with his pinkie finger. Gathering up a small pile of powder, he dropped it onto the CD box. Then, taking a card from his wallet, he separated and chopped the powder into lines and slid the CD case over to her.

'You see how polite I am? I let you go first. Uh, wait. One moment.'

He stretched over to the drinks table and lifted a straw, which he cut in half using scissors from the desk.

'Use this. Cleaner than a note.'

Sissy took the straw and paused, unable to decide how she felt about this turn of events. Her head told her to get out of there, but the sofa was so low and squishy and her body had already demonstrated an unwillingness to do her bidding.

'It will straighten you up,' he said. 'Go on. Just that little one there.'

They all looked the same size to her. What the hell. She leaned over and sniffed, leaving a messy trail which he scraped into another line. Her eyes watered but she was surprised by how easy it was.

Pascal's head was bent over the table now, first one nostril, then the next. He whipped his head back, his fingers flying to his nose to stop any escaping. Then he looked at her with an unnerving focus.

'I expect you're feeling better now.'

When she didn't reply straight away, he slid the CD case back to her.

'Do one more. Do it, do it,' he said, impatiently. She might have said no had she been able to arrange her thoughts in a proper manner. Instead she leaned over and snorted another line.

Pascal was on his feet now, not quite dancing, not quite marching on the spot. He clapped his hands together and announced his work for the evening was over. They should have some fun.

Sissy didn't know how to describe it. She felt very *awake*. The room seemed brighter than before, though as far as she knew no one had changed the lighting. Somehow she had sobered up considerably, though she wouldn't say she felt *straight*, exactly, but she did feel *very in control*, and she thought Pascal's suggestion about *having fun* was a *very fucking good one*.

She followed him back to the club but didn't return to her table, choosing instead to mingle with the disparate groups on the edge of the dance floor. She didn't care any more about how she was dressed, in fact, the women in their short skirts and high heels looked ridiculous, tottering around waiting for some guy to buy them drinks.

Imagine coming out to dance dressed like that, she thought. And the make-up made some of them look like guys in drag. Thick, black eyebrows painted onto foreheads that barely moved at all, hair extensions, manicured nails, fake tans. Sissy saw through it all. People stole sly glances at her, but she didn't mind their whispers. She was real. She was authentic. She felt powerful.

Pascal, despite having announced his work for the evening to be over, was interrupted on a regular basis by the two guys Sissy had seen him with earlier. She assumed he was dealing the same coke he'd given her for free. He had an air of importance, like the whole room wouldn't function unless he was in it. She liked that she was with him. She liked that he kept his long black coat on, wearing it like a robe. He was the king and that made her — well, she didn't exactly know what it made her, but whatever it was, she was confident in that position. She recognised she was subservient to him. It made perfect sense. He was older, he was her boss, and most importantly, for whatever reason, he was acting like he really, really liked her.

They took two more trips to the back room which were fast and furtive, both of them eager to be where the action was, and sometime around 1 a.m. he told her it was time they left. He had a mini-cab collect them from the club's back door. It wasn't so much that she wanted to spend more time with him, but she liked the drugs he had, and besides, she had a lot of questions.

He lived in a one-bed flat somewhere between Hackney and Bethnal Green. The fact they were both East Enders convinced her of their compatibility, and their conversation in the taxi was all about how *real* the East End was and how pretentious the rest of London was in comparison, with the exception of a few pockets south of the river. She agreed with him completely, even though she hadn't been further west than Victoria or seen anything further south than Vauxhall by night.

His flat was entered through a security door and up a flight of steps past a stack of bikes and a child's buggy. Three different locks and they were in. He snapped the light on and her own reflection greeted her in a large mirror facing the door. Her face was surprisingly pale and her eyes red-rimmed. She looked almost ill, which didn't correlate in the slightest with how she felt.

Pascal had disappeared into a room just off the small hallway. She found him already cutting lines onto a rectangular glass coffee table and she experienced a small surge of irritation. The room was blandly male, everything white and cream apart from the black leather two-seat sofa. One wall was decorated with framed posters advertising club nights of times gone past. After the energy of the club, however shit it had been, this flat was an utter comedown.

Pascal tapped the table.

'Come. Yours.'

She bent over and made the line disappear. A bottle of rum appeared on the table beside her, along with two glass tumblers, thick, crystal-cut.

Music came next, a fast drum 'n' bass, and the lights dimmed. Her heart was racing. She took a deep breath and let it out slowly, enjoying the swooshing noise she made. She wondered whether they would have sex. She assumed they would, even though nothing like that had passed between them. There had been opportunities for Pascal to kiss her in the back room of the club, or in the taxi, but he'd shown no interest. Maybe that was the difference between men and boys. They had the ability to maintain purely platonic relationships. Pascal talked a lot. She seemed to be forever waiting for him to draw breath long enough for her to get a word in, and when she did, she noticed how his head moved like a horse chomping at the bit, waiting for his turn.

'Clubs are my passion,' he said. 'Bringing people together, good music, conversation, a party. Nothing else in life is as important, in my opinion.'

'Totally agree one hundred per cent with you there, Pascal. All of us in one room, all bouncing to the same beat, nothing else going on but the DJ lifting us, carrying us. It's fucking awesome, like, I haven't been coming to clubs that long but I don't know how people *live*, like actually fucking *live*, without that, you know what I mean?'

'Your jaw is going crazy. You will break your teeth like that.'

'I know. I can't seem to help it. It just goes round and round.'

'You may want to try one of these.'

He turned to a shelf behind him and took

down a large white bowl containing lollipops in various brightly coloured wrappers.

'Oh my God, this is genius.' The words could hardly come quickly enough. 'I'll have a purple one. My God, I used to have these as a kid. What a flashback.' She unwrapped it, dipped it in the rum he had poured out for her, and put it in her mouth. 'So what's the deal with you then?' she asked. 'A bowl of lollipops in case a bunch of kids come to visit? And that club — you acted like you owned it, but if you own it why are you working at a shitty call centre? No offence, but it *is* pretty shitty. Even I know that and I haven't worked anywhere else, unless you count a Saturday job in a fruit shop.'

'It's a shitty job, but what can I say? There is money in it. In knowledge there is power. A lot of people these days, especially governments and large corporations, they want power. So we find out what people think and pass it on. They pay us to give them the knowledge. It is you at the bottom end who gets the shitty stick. But, to be honest, I find it quite shitty as well. In France I work hard, I study, get good degree. Come over here for MBA and then what? Well, you see me every day. Do I look full of the joys? No, of course not. But club nights, music, promotion. That I love. And there I make easy money. So why the hell not? Life is too short to be miserable.'

'Yes!' Sissy exclaimed. Here lay her expertise and she poured it all out. You never *ever* knew when your time would come, one minute you're fine, the next a hole's been blown into your life and you risk being destroyed by the backdraft. That's why she was so *fucking grateful* to be here, right now, with someone who *really understood her*, who had their priorities straight, because if she had stayed in Glasgow for *one more day* with *those fucking people*, she would have had to just get her hands on a gun and blow her brains out.

'Seriously, you can get a gun in Glasgow? How easy?'

'Probably really fucking easy if you know the right people, not that I do, I don't want you to get the wrong idea, I'm just saying that I might have *had to get to know* the right people, do you know what I'm saying, Pascal, do you?'

'Yes, yes, like me. I could get to know the right people, but like I already said, life's too short. You know all about that. It's really fucking shit. You're too young to deal with that. You must be a very strong person. I admire that.'

She hadn't considered herself to be a strong person but now she realised that, yes, she was. What a long way she had come in the space of a year. Her future was a dazzling one. She would never look back ever again. Never be that person ever again.

They took lines with increasing frequency until it almost seemed one of them was chopping while the other snorted, and yet the bag of powder didn't deplete in any noticeable way.

'It's like the magic porridge pot of cocaine,' she said, but he didn't understand the reference and she didn't bother to explain it. Her eyes were heavy now, her limbs like weighted ropes trying to drag her down, but her heart was racing so fast she thought if she looked in a mirror she would see it thumping in her chest.

Outside, the sun was coming up and there was still one question she hadn't asked him.

'Pascal, why did you ask me to the club?' Even through the armoured wall of cocaine-fuelled confidence, she was nervous to ask.

His head was bent as he rolled their first spliff. He sniffed and licked the paper as he mulled the question over.

'Why wouldn't I?' he said, at last.

They didn't have sex but fell asleep fully clothed around 10 a.m. on his bed. At some point in her sleep, she became vaguely aware of a sensation of something travelling down her body but she couldn't rouse herself to react and whatever it was stopped. Later, travelling home on the bus, she reflected on that moment. Pascal, she decided, was a bit of a gentleman.

★   ★   ★

A figure stood at the brightly lit window, watching her as she came down the street. She kept her head down, pretending not to see him. It was only then she realised she'd been away for almost twenty-four hours. She shook off the guilt that tried to sneak its way in. She was a big girl. He wasn't her keeper.

'Where the hell have you been?' Cam asked, before she had even closed the door behind her.

'What?' she scowled in return. 'I crashed at a mate's.'

'I've been worried about you. You could have called.'

'What are you, my dad? Can I get past, please?'

She pushed past him into the kitchen and poured herself some water.

'Do you know what?' he said, following her in. 'You're so fucking selfish. Did you not even think to get in touch? Let me know you're still alive?'

His words felt like a barrage. She used her thirst to buy herself a few more seconds' thinking time. She sipped slowly on her water, observing his face from behind her glass, so angry and accusatory, and wondered what she'd ever seen in him. He stared back, waiting for a response. Her silence had the diminishing effect of turning his anger into a toddler tantrum.

'Are you not going to answer me then?' he tried again.

'What do you want me to say? I didn't realise I had to be home by a certain time. I thought I'd left that behind me.'

'It's called being considerate, Sissy.'

'It's not as if you called me, is it? Why should I be the one — '

'I've no fucking credit in my phone, have I?' he roared.

'I've been going off my head wondering where you were.'

She laughed at his hypocrisy.

'Did you ever tell me when you'd be back whenever you went out?' she yelled. 'Well, did you? And did I ever ask where you were or who with? No, I didn't and I'll tell you why . . .

because it's none of my business, that's why. Just like my life is none of your business. Just face it, Cam. We're going in different directions.'

'What do you mean?'

'Do I need to spell it out?'

'I think you're going to have to,' he said, quietly.

Uncomfortable with the silence that followed, Sissy had no option but to fill it with noise.

'You sit about all day, every day. You never do anything any more. When's the last time you even changed your clothes? And have you just given up on the idea of getting a job altogether? Are you happy to sit about all day on the PlayStation, smoking away your benefits? We're in London now, Cam. The world moves faster here. You're being left behind. What are you turning into? Oh my God, those fucking dogs, *shut up!*' she yelled, as the regular noise from next door started up. When she turned back to Cam, the hurt on his face made her wince.

'Oh, don't,' she said, in disgust. 'Don't look at me like that. You made me say it. Someone had to. Jesus, you've said it to me often enough.'

'No, I haven't,' he said, shaking his head. 'Not like that. But don't worry. I've heard you. I get it.'

He went to his room and closed the door.

Sissy leaned against the sink, holding her hand to her forehead. She shook with fury and tiredness, and wondered why she felt so bad when in actual fact she hadn't done anything to harm anyone. The barking had settled into a rhythm now, which was almost worse than the initial frenzy because it was impossible to know when it would end.

She took a shower and tried to sleep but her head was full of Pascal. If Cam was angry with her now, how much worse would it be when he discovered she'd spent the night with his ex-boss? But then, she told herself, there was no need to tell him anything. Nothing had happened between them, after all. She could go into work on Monday morning without worrying about any awkwardness. In fact, she looked forward to seeing Pascal, looking him in the eye. She knew a side to him that no one else there did. They were equals.

But then another thought slipped in, a doubtful one. She tried to chase it away and found she had no control over her thoughts at all. They slipped behind her eyes and would not be pinned down. All she wanted to do was sit in silence and not have to answer to anyone ever again. With her head lying against the pillow, she could hear her blood rushing. She focused on it until she fell asleep.

She dreamed she was an astronaut floating in space, viewing the darkness through a round glass helmet. Her hands, encased by large white gloves, seemed not to belong to her. A long steel cable stretched out behind her, attaching her to a huge spaceship. In the distance, to her left, was another astronaut, anonymous in their oversize white suit. They turned and gave her a thumbs up. An intermittent pulse of sound was present. *How strange to have sound in space*, she thought, *perhaps it's just my breath*. It was almost soothing. But then the pulse was suddenly gone, sucked out of the sky, and there was a very deep happening, a seismic shift, and she knew something was very wrong. Her fellow astronaut was closer now and reflected in their helmet was an orange, flickering light. Pulling herself on the cable, she turned to see a huge hole had appeared in the mothership. Everything was ablaze. Even her cable was alight. Even though she knew steel couldn't catch fire, it was happening right there in front of her, the flames dancing closer. The other astronaut was beside her now, tugging on her belt, trying to help, but then there was another noiseless blast and their helmet flew off to reveal Pascal — or was it Cam? — the force from the blast caused their body to spin, and their suit to disintegrate, and then their skin was being ripped off, layer by layer, revealing something so raw and ugly she couldn't bear to look. She turned away, refused to see it, and then all at once she felt so much better, because through the impossible noiseless sound came her father's voice, as rich and fresh and realer than she'd ever known. *Sissy*, he was saying, *Sissy, my Sissy. Hold on tight.*

19

Absent Friends

On Monday morning, she rose early. It was one of those bright mornings that spoke of the possibility of summer, even as breath collected in clouds at street level. Patches of blue filled the spaces between tall buildings, causing commuters to look up and slow down as they emerged mole-like from the underground. Behind them, impatience rippled through those who were still to discover the magic.

The morning commute was one of the few times Sissy's petite stature was a bonus. She nipped in and out of any gap she found, and ran up the left side of the escalators, tutting at anyone foolish enough to stand on the wrong side. She knew which door of the train to board through in order to be nearest the exit at her destination. She belonged to the city, had become part of its life source. She thrived on its cut-throat pace.

London fell away as she entered the foyer of the neglected building she worked in. As usual, the desk was unmanned. She ignored the elevator and took the stairs, two at a time, half-hoping Pascal would be at the top of them, half hoping he wouldn't be in yet and she could slide into work unnoticed. A voice in her head filled her with confidence. She felt close to him, and was made bold by the fact they hadn't had sex. They had truly connected. In a way, the weekend had rendered them equals because he'd allowed her to see past the hostile front he presented at work.

In the deserted staff room she made coffee and wondered if it would be appropriate to bring him one. As he was French, she assumed he'd prefer it black, no sugar. She was pleased with her insight and thought it would impress him.

As she sifted through the mugs looking for one without a chip or crack, she went back and forth on the matter. On the one hand, she didn't want to suggest anything was different in their working relationship, on the other, weren't they friends now, and didn't friends do kind things for one another?

Laying her discomfort aside, she picked out two mugs in the same colour. She made the coffee and walked along the corridor to Pascal's office. It was empty.

With an overflowing mug in each hand, she hovered between his office and the swing door into the call floor, uncertain of her next step, her decision-making process hampered by annoyance at her failure to predict this set of circumstances.

'Good morning, early bird! What brings you in at this time?'

It was Tony. At forty-four, he was the eldest of the managers. He laughed when he saw her holding two coffees.

'Come prepared, eh? Monday morning rocket

fuel. Can't say I blame you. Just don't expect extra pee breaks.'

He held the door open for her, and Sissy, after checking the wall to see which phone she was on, went to her booth and placed both coffees by the monitor. Still ten minutes before she had to begin calls. Her workmates were arriving now, slouching in with their usual grey demeanours. She sipped her coffee and wondered why they were all so . . . dull. There was no other word for it. She'd tried initiating conversation with a few of them but her efforts had fallen flat. No one seemed interested in anyone else. They clocked in, did the work, clocked out. She assumed they must have lives beyond the office where they laughed and enjoyed themselves, but there was no evidence to back up her theory. Most of them were still in their twenties and already had an air of defeat around them. She'd stopped making the effort with them.

Just before nine, she made a trip to the Ladies' and cast a glance into Pascal's office as she passed. Still no sign of him. When she returned to her desk, she kicked herself for not taking the coffee mugs back out with her. Now she would have to look at them all morning.

The clock ticked round with interminable slowness. By mid-afternoon, she accepted he wasn't coming in. She was desperate to ask Tony when Pascal would be back, but it would be odd to do so. She fell into a terrible mood and failed to complete a single survey all day. At five o'clock, instead of going home, she ducked into a pub and slammed a couple of vodkas,

186

ignoring the bar maid's lips, pursed tightly in disapproval.

If you don't want customers on a Monday, then don't open on a Monday, you stupid cow, Sissy thought, even as she noticed she was the only female in the place and was younger than everyone else by at least a couple of decades. A man in a suit leered at her from the end of the bar. He raised his eyebrows and his glass. Question: drink? She slid off the bar stool and back into the early-evening crowds.

The vodka at least made the journey home bearable, though it was clear more would be required to shift her mood. She stopped into the shop at the top of the street for a bottle of wine and a tub of ice cream, and in a fit of spontaneous generosity bought Cam a couple of beers. Getting pissed on a Monday was only acceptable if you did it in company, and besides, they needed a proper catch-up to clear the air between them. She hoped he'd be up for it because the last thing she needed was another argument.

Rik opened the door before she managed to turn her key. With a stab of guilt, she realised she hadn't factored him into her evening's plans, but the expression on his face suggested her plans were being rewritten without her permission.

'What's wrong?' she said from the doorstep.

'You'd better come in,' Rik replied, holding the door open.

The door to Cam's room was ajar. Through it she saw the usual mess. She carried on into the kitchen, placing the carrier bag with the booze and ice cream onto the table. Nothing appeared to be amiss.

'What is it?' she said again, aware of a knot of fear tightening in her stomach — a skill acquired just over a year ago and which was proving to be a regular affliction.

Rik just stared.

'What?' she shouted.

'He's gone,' Rik said at last, with a small shrug and a shake of his head. He spread his hands wide like a magician — now you see it, now you don't.

'What do you mean he's gone? Who are you talking about?'

'Cam. He's gone.'

'But what do you mean 'he's gone'?' she pressed, panic rising.

'Come with me.'

She followed Rik through to the tiny back hallway that led to the garden. He flicked on the outside light and they went outside. A hole stood where once a fence panel had been. It was now possible to walk straight into May and Jimmy's garden, which remained resplendent with dog turd.

'What the fuck?' Sissy said.

'He lifted the panel, went into their garden, nicked the dog. And now he's fucked off. I don't know where. No note, nothing. But I've been in his room and a lot of his stuff's gone, plus the hold-all he brought it down in.'

'But he wouldn't do that . . . ' began Sissy, and then stopped. The proof was here, staring her right in the face, and didn't it seem now, with the benefit of swift hindsight, entirely inevitable?

A yapping started up in their neighbour's house, informing her that Cha-Cha had been left behind.

'He couldn't even take the most annoying one,' Rik sighed.

'Maybe he's just taken him for a walk?' Sissy said. 'Maybe he'll be back in a minute?'

'He'd better not be, for his own sake. Neanderthal Man's already been round reading the riot act. He's been onto the police again.'

'Fuck.'

They both jumped when their neighbour's back door cracked open. Before they could disappear inside, Cha-Cha rushed out and deposited a pee against the opposite fence.

'Poor little fucker,' said Rik. 'Not only does it have to live in a shit-hole, but it's lost its buddy. You have to wonder, don't you? If Cam's such a warrior for doggy social justice, why did he only take one of them? And the better looking one at that. Sorry Cha-Cha. No offence.'

The dog came through the gap and sniffed around their feet.

'It was worse for Bolt,' said Sissy. Her voice sounded far away from her body. 'He's so much bigger. Needs more exercise.'

'Cha-Cha?'

Light spilled out from their neighbours' kitchen, and May appeared at the back door sporting a face puffy from crying, and streaked black with mascara. She called the little dog again, and sniffed and wiped her face with her cardigan sleeve which was pulled over her fist. When she saw Sissy and Rik, she hurried out and scooped up Cha-Cha, scattering some old, dried-up shit in the process.

'Oh baby, my baby,' she murmured to the dog, before raising her eyes to Sissy and Rik. 'I wish you'd never moved here,' she hissed. 'You fucked up everything. You better tell that friend of yours if he shows up round here again, he's dead. Jimmy's fucking beside himself, do you know that? He loves that dog. Adores it. Your mate's in big trouble, even if he goes back to Scotland. Jimmy knows people everywhere. Make sure you tell him that.'

She went back inside, leaving Sissy and Rik shocked by the encounter.

'Do you think he's gone back to Glasgow?' Sissy at last managed to whisper.

'Come on,' he said. 'Help me put this fence panel back.'

They each took an end and lifted it high enough to slot it between the fence posts. Winter had thickened the wood and the panel didn't want to slide into place.

'Fucking typical of Cam,' Rik breathed, using all of his strength to force the panel down. 'Leaving all the hard work for someone else.'

He returned indoors, leaving Sissy alone. For some reason, she was drawn to the section of fence they'd restored. She ran her fingers over it — damp, rough — and thought of their tree in the woods at the back of Cam's flat in Glasgow.

The light went on upstairs in Rik's bedroom, causing her to look at the house properly for the first time since moving in. The bathroom, an afterthought, protruded into the garden, soaking up rainwater from the ground. Dark streaks stained its walls. Sissy was no expert, but she reckoned the whole thing was liable to crumble, sooner or later.

★　★　★

Texts, phone calls, Facebook messages all went unanswered. As the week wore on, Sissy's initial distress turned to anger.

'How fucking dare he?' she asked Rik. 'He knows I'd be worried. How hard would it be to let us know he's safe?'

And then: 'What if he isn't safe? What if something's happened to him? Should we call the police?'

Rik was annoyingly sanguine about Cam's disappearance.

'It was always on the cards. He never sticks at anything. It's just the way he is. He'll be fine. Anyway, I'm quite happy to have a living room, aren't you?'

Once they established the extra rent could be covered between them, Rik went back about his business and didn't mention Cam again.

Things weren't as simple for Sissy, who experienced Cam's loss as a type of capsizing, just as she'd been getting herself steady again. She experienced herself as shrinking, to the point where she began to wonder if she was real.

She placed a photograph of her dad beside a mirror and spent hours studying the similarities between their two faces. Sometimes she held the photo beside her face and tried to imagine they melded into one. Her hair was red, whereas his was more auburn, though they had the same kink running down the left side. She loved that. She couldn't believe she hadn't noticed it when he was alive. Their eyes were the same pale blue. The realisation that she couldn't say with certainty what eye colour her mother had hit her like a warning, but it paled in significance to the alchemy that was her face. Sometimes she looked in the mirror and he was there. A flash, and then gone. It made no sense. She didn't change from day to day, so why was his presence in her reflection such a sporadic one?

They had the same nose, she supposed, especially if time lengthened and thickened it the way she'd heard it would. She willed time to hurry and change it as often as she willed time to slow down because she didn't want the day to come when she couldn't remember his laugh, or the sound of his voice, or the feel of his bristle coming in at the end of the day, or the fact he didn't have freckles, like her. He didn't have her peachy cheeks. He was white, almost blue. Very Scottish, he'd said. The only time he changed colour was when the sun came out, and then he burned red in an instant. They had that in common.

Sissy's gaze fell to his mouth. His lips were thinner than hers. She tilted her head this way and that, thinking about how her skin would slacken as she got older and how her lips would probably turn down at the corner like her mother's. So what is it? Where is he? How are they connected?

Outside, the sun slipped behind cloud and the bedroom was cast in grey, creating a gauze-like effect between herself and the mirror. She leant forward and peered into her own eyes. It's the eyes then. And not just the colour. She lifted the photo, held it to her face, studied it and looked back at herself, over and over, trying to draw him into her. Her pupils expanded. Black holes, she thought. What's in there? He's in there, he's in there. I'll keep looking.

★ ★ ★

Pascal, Pascal, Pascal. She wrote his name over everything. Even Rik noticed.

'Is that not the dickhead Cam had a problem with?'

'Fuck off, Rik. Leave me alone.'

She told herself she had nothing to feel guilty about — Cam hadn't even known about Pascal when he left, after all — but she experienced a sense of disloyalty, nevertheless, which only made her resent Cam in his absence even more.

Pascal was rarely in the office, and it proved tricky to find ways of being alone with him when he was. Sissy was increasingly desperate to talk to him about the night they'd spent together. The longer she left it, the more likely it would fade from memory, or fall into a hazy quagmire of random party nights. Maybe to him it *was* just another random night. She couldn't fail to notice, as he strode around the call floor with his long coat swinging behind him, one hand frequently pushing his hair back from his face, how he barely looked at her. But then he barely looked at anyone unless he had to.

She was on her break with Hazel, the lady with trigger fingers and air freshener. Hazel was an actor in her fifties who did occasional voice-over and theatre work. Her voice was as deep and rough as a chain-smoking man, and very persuasive at getting people to talk.

'I came out this way, sweetie,' she said, if anyone was brave enough to ask. Sissy thought her forty-a-day habit probably helped.

Hazel was buxom, wore heavy eye make-up and her face was etched with lines, particularly around her mouth. She oozed a kind of glamour, albeit a faded, rough-around-the-edges kind. Sissy tried to coincide her breaks with Hazel's because, although they had little in common, she found she enjoyed being in the company of a woman, however briefly.

'I've been meaning to talk to you,' Hazel said, leaning in to take a light from Sissy's cigarette. She stepped back as she inhaled, then blew out a huge cloud of smoke. Her lungs were well-exercised from years on the stage, apparently. Whatever the reason, it was an impressive display.

Sissy waited for her to elaborate.

Hazel swung her head around the corner of the lane they stood in. Seemingly satisfied the coast was clear, she took another draw and tapped the fag while trying to formulate her sentence, which came out as a single word.

'Pascal.'

Sissy stiffened. Deny everything, she told herself, knowing she was already turning red.

'Number one,' said Hazel, 'he's bad news. Not right for you at all. Not right for any woman, I'd wager. Having said that, here comes number two: I'm old and ugly enough to know nothing I say will make a blind bit of difference — who gives a fig what I think, eh? — so in order to curtail the painful sideshow I'm seeing every day, here is number three: I'm going to tell you where you're going wrong.'

Sissy tried to laugh, shake off Hazel's words, but her body rebelled and wouldn't do her bidding. Her face felt like it was on fire.

'Now I know things are different these days, and all you young ones are feminists and whatnot, but, darling, some things are universal. Namely, a man doesn't care for a woman he knows he can have. He wants what he can't have, alright? So my first piece of advice for you is to stop sitting up like a damn dog begging for a biscuit whenever he comes within five metres of you.'

Sissy wished for a hole to open up so she could vanish through it.

'And my next piece of advice is . . . Oh, look, darling, I don't want you to take this the wrong way, and I know everyone wants to feel comfortable and that's important, blah-di-blah . . . but you need to clean yourself up a little. I mean, Christ, what's this you're wearing?'

Stunned, Sissy looked down at her usual jeans and trainer attire.

'I bet you've got a lovely little figure under there, haven't you? But to be honest, darling, with those clothes on, you don't look any different to those awful nerdy boys up there. In fact, Pascal's always so preoccupied, if he does catch you out the side of his eye he probably thinks you're one of them.'

Hazel took another deep draw of her cigarette.

'I don't know what — ' Sissy began, but then Hazel was exhaling again and speaking over her.

'I don't mean come in done up like some dolly bird, my goodness, no. You don't want to be obvious about it. But a skirt would be marvellous. Bit of lipstick, you know. My God, I didn't think anyone needed telling this. It's the ABC of getting on in the world, dear.'

She took a final drag of her cigarette and tamped it out against the wall.

'And number four,' she said, holding the fizzled fag end in front of her face, 'is don't be a litter lout.'

She sashayed to a bin and deposited the cigarette.

Sissy's mind flew back to the women in the club that night, all of them so different from her. She'd never been the type of girl to fret about clothes or hair or make-up. But then, perhaps that was the reason she'd only ever had sex with one person.

She finished her smoke in a series of quick, shallow draws, and darted back upstairs with a new sense of purpose, eager to get back to work. If she moved quickly enough, perhaps she could trick time into speeding this day along.

20

Liars and Scissor Blades

It had been several months since Anne had last seen Susan, a gap of time that was new to both of them, and which burdened Susan with more guilt than usual, a fact which Anne was all too aware of and intended to exploit to the fullest, with no real idea of what she hoped to achieve by doing so.

It was decided that instead of a hotel, Susan should stay at the bungalow. Financially it made sense, though Anne wasn't pleased at the prospect of someone being in her house unsupervised, even if it was her daughter.

'I'll stay in a hotel if you'd rather, Mammy,' Susan sighed. 'I'll get a discount at Jude's, won't I?'

'No, no. You can't put Jude out like that. No, you stay where you like,' was the reply.

They all went, though Anne remained in the car, quietly suspicious that the whole thing was an elaborate ruse to relocate her away from Jude. It was true her wrist had healed, and true that Jude was doing much better these days, but Anne had no intention of going anywhere.

They pulled up in front of the small, brown-brick building and took a moment to take in the air of general neglect which hung over the place.

'What a sight,' said Susan. 'Have you not been keeping an eye on it?'

'Haven't you?' Danny retorted.

'I live two hundred and fifty miles away, Danny,' Susan sighed, as she exited the car. The door snapped shut before he could respond. Anne winced and reached into her handbag for an indigestion tablet, while Danny clamped his lips and shook his head.

'I suppose I should have been keeping an eye on it,' said Jude, eager to diffuse the tension. 'I've had the time. It's just — well, you've never really wanted to come back, have you, Anne?'

With no discernible response, there was nothing for it but to head inside.

The gate creaked and dragged across the stone ground as Jude and Danny followed the path up to Susan, who was waiting by the front door.

'So a gardener's first on the list,' she called, moving aside for Danny, who had the key. He shouldered the door open and knelt down to work his arm around to clear the pile of junk mail that was wedged there.

Inside, a thick layer of dust covered the sill. The SCIAF box that had stood there for as long as anyone could remember, and which had somehow escaped the exodus of holy items to Jude's, gaped at them forlornly. Danny rummaged in his pockets and dropped some change into it.

'Old habits, eh.'

He opened the interior door and a stale, musty smell greeted them. Susan bustled her way past him.

'A cleaner too,' she said, jotting it down. 'I mean, I'll do what I can this weekend, obviously, but it really needs something regular. That's if she plans to keep the place, of course. Any ideas, Jude?'

Something about Susan's tone made Jude pay attention. The hallway was small, and with three adults standing in it, the bungalow felt little more than a doll's house.

'No,' Jude admitted, surprised by the question. 'I've told your mum she's welcome to stay for as long as she likes, of course. But I can easily pop by once a week with a mop and a duster, if you're worried. I don't know why I didn't think of it myself.'

'No, no,' said Danny. 'That's too much. We couldn't ask that.'

'Someone's got to do it,' quipped Susan, as she stepped into the kitchen.

Jude and Danny shared an embarrassed smile.

'She was only supposed to be with you until her wrist got better,' said Danny, with a frown. 'I don't want to feel like we're taking advantage.'

'I don't mind,' Jude offered. 'It's family, after all.'

She thought she saw him flinch, then quickly recover himself. His face arranged itself into a smile, though it didn't travel as far as his eyes.

'Of course you are,' he said, placing a heavy hand on her shoulder. His eyes caught hers. They were grave and somehow reassuring and intimidating all at once. Then he nodded, affirming something for himself only, and stepped away into the living room.

Jude's relief at having avoided a potentially emotional moment was tempered by the realisation that the only room left for her to inspect was the bedroom. Bedrooms were private places. Surely it would be more appropriate for either Susan or Danny, or better still, Anne herself, to deal with it. Sounds of industry came from the other rooms, pots and pans clanging in the kitchen, windows being heaved open in the living room, leaving her no option but to enter the bedroom, which faced the back of the house and was cast in darkness by the drawn curtains. She pulled them open and weak sunshine spilled in. Really, everything was in an organised state, she needn't have worried, but Susan should at least have fresh bedding, so she slid back the wardrobe doors until she found a pile of sheets and duvet covers folded neatly on a shelf, and selected the newest-looking set.

'Oh, damn.' Danny's voice carried through from the living room, and then Susan's immediately after, 'What did you do?'

Jude stepped out to see Danny holding the broken pieces of a picture frame.

'Nothing,' he said, forever the defensive little brother. 'It was already like that.'

Susan took it from him and shook the shards of glass onto the telephone table. She retrieved the photograph from between the sharp edges of the damaged frame and held it out for Jude to see.

'I put this in a frame for her last time I was here,' she said. 'Sure, she'll be disappointed by this. I wonder why she didn't take it with her to yours, Jude. I'll pop it on the side here, don't let me forget. We'll get her a new frame easy enough.'

Susan and Danny returned to their tasks, but Jude was drawn to the grainy, black and white photograph. A petite, dark-eyed Anne smiled laughingly out at her, her delight on this, the happiest day of her life, communicated itself loud and clear through the years. Slim and tiny beside Patrick, who was serious and handsome in his wedding suit, Anne wore a plain, floor-length white gown, which Jude remembered being told had been made from parachute silk, as so many gowns and christening robes were back then.

Jude missed her father-in-law. His reserved placidity had provided something of an oasis in an otherwise noisy family. She had often found herself sitting alongside him at family parties, while the others dominated with songs and loud conversation. She hadn't considered them great friends, but allies of a sort. Sometimes she thought her relationship with Peter was a mirror to Anne and Patrick's. Knowing the older couple had held together through the years, despite such differences in outlook and personality, had given her hope. Patrick's death had left her feeling unexpectedly alone. Peter, Susan and Danny, despite their grief, had rallied for Anne, arranging themselves around her like scaffolding, making it difficult to see in, reminding her of her outsider status, despite her providing the family's first grandchild.

She ran the hoover over the carpets, and

between the three of them the bungalow was spruced up in under an hour. While Susan unpacked her bag and Danny checked the garage, Jude took the photograph to Anne, who blanched when presented with it. Jude assured her they would find another frame in no time.

'How is it in there?' Anne asked, nodding to the house without looking at it, sitting as stiff and ram-rod straight as an aged ballerina.

'It's fine,' Jude said, slipping the picture into her bag. 'I changed the bed and cleaned the bathroom — not that it needed it,' she added, hurriedly, knowing Anne would be mortified had she left any mess behind. 'Susan gave the kitchen a wipe, and Danny opened the window for a bit of fresh air. There's a lot of junk mail, but that's to be expected. Nothing to worry about, honestly.'

Anne nodded and returned herself to the view straight ahead of her. Jude had a sense she was seeing something other than the tidy lawns of the inoffensive cul-de-sac.

That evening, everyone, including Emma and Lucy, gathered at Jude's. Jude felt a pang as her nieces breezed in and kissed her airily. The lightness of their lips, their soft cheeks against her own — she wanted to catch it and somehow preserve it. They ordered Chinese takeaway and watched a talent show on television. They drank wine and enjoyed Emma's derisive commentary on the state of television these days. Susan was unusually quiet and, when the opportunity arose, Jude cornered her in the kitchen.

'Is everything all right?'

Susan's expression immediately confirmed that everything was not all right. She gripped Jude's arm, leaned forward and whispered, 'She's mad.'

'What do you mean?' asked Jude, frightened by Susan's intensity. 'Who's mad?'

'My mother, Jude. My mother's fucking mad.'

Susan opened her eyes so wide, Jude could see the pink fleshy rim that would normally be tucked out of sight. She began to shake, all of her, her head, chin and arms. She loosed her fingers around Jude's arm and looked around, as if searching for someone else to pass the news of her mother's madness on to.

Reminded of the drunks she occasionally had to manage at work, Jude nodded. Stay calm, she thought, be reassuring, don't do anything to enflame the circumstances. 'Okay,' she said, soothingly. 'Take a few breaths. Whatever it is, we'll work it out, okay?'

A peal of teenage mirth emanated from the living room.

'I can't,' said Susan, taking a step back. 'I can't talk about it with her just down the hall. But I don't know what to do. Jesus.'

Jude continued to nod and soothe, nod and soothe, and, after agreeing they could talk about it later, Susan began to gradually calm.

'Now when you're ready, we'll go back through together.'

Susan nodded and drank some water from the tap.

'Scottish water,' she said, with a weak smile. 'Can't beat it.'

Jude began to relax a little now they were back on familiar ground.

'How's Manchester?' she asked. 'The boys getting on all right?'

After finding her in the garden at Peter's fortieth crying over Phil's latest transgression, Jude had learned the hard way to keep her enquiries into Susan's life focused on the children.

'I can't just leave him,' Susan had said with derision.

'Of course you can. You're a grown woman with a job and a family. I bet your mum would love to have you and the boys back in Glasgow.'

What had been intended as positive support had prompted a fresh outpouring of misery and it all came tumbling out. Anne knew the marriage was in trouble but was unsympathetic. Marriage was a sacrament. A life-long commitment. The Donnellys had never shirked the work of God and they never would.

Jude was horror-struck and urged Susan to think for herself. 'It's not the 1950s, for goodness' sake. Your mum'll get over it.'

'You make it sound so easy,' Susan sneered. 'What would you know about it?'

The words stung. After all, it was true Jude was completely free from the same kind of parental obligations, but she didn't consider it to be the blessing Susan did. She bit her tongue and dug a little deeper to find sympathy for her sister-in-law, who would not be moved from her decision to stay in an increasingly loveless marriage. She'd made her bed and would lie in it, as her mother would say, and as long as she did, she could be sure of her mother's approval, or if not approval, then at least she would avoid incurring her wrath.

'The boys are fine,' Susan said, picking up a bottle of wine and pushing past Jude before there was space to ask about her philandering husband.

As the evening wore on, Susan's belligerence grew. At first it manifested in her being unusually interested in and helpful towards everyone apart from Anne: did they enjoy their food, need another drink, was school okay, was work? Jude felt powerless to stop it. The only thing she could think to do was drink more quickly — a trick she'd learned over the course of her relationship with Peter — and if she failed in her attempt to keep Susan relatively sober, at least she herself would be tipsy enough to withstand the fall-out.

If Anne noticed the drama unfolding around her, she gave no sign. At ten o'clock she announced she was going to bed.

'Are you all right, Mammy?' Danny asked. Anne had always been a night owl so her early retiral, especially when in the company of her children and grandchildren, was unusual.

'Aye, she's grand, aren't you, Mammy?' Susan said, before Anne could respond. 'Are you away to bed, Mammy? Are you?'

'Help me up, Danny, will you? There's a good boy,' Anne said, extending her arm. Danny leapt forward and helped his mother to stand. Emma and Lucy stood and hovered just behind.

'Ah, isn't that sweet, Jude?' said Susan, though there was nothing sweet about her tone. 'Is that you, Mammy? Off to bed.'

Without acknowledging Susan in any way, Anne made her way across the living room floor on the arm of her son.

'Off to bed to dream of my *daddy*,' Susan said, in a provocative sing-song.

It was such an odd thing to say, and such an odd way to say it, that the little group paused in their journey and turned, to Susan, who looked back at them as though she'd been caught with her hand in their pockets. Anne's face was stone, Danny's made of confusion, and Emma and Lucy's curiously expressionless. Jude remained on the sofa, the wine glass on her lips a feeble buffer.

After what felt like an impossibly long silence, Anne looked down the length of her nose and said, coldly, 'Go to bed, Susan,' then left, still on Danny's arm. Emma and Lucy followed.

The room seemed to breathe out. Susan refilled her glass and Jude drained hers.

'What the hell was that?' whispered Danny, when he returned, having left his daughters upstairs to fuss around their grandmother.

Susan's mouth tightened with the effort of pulling her bag over from its spot on the floor. Rummaging inside, she located a plastic carrier bag and threw it down. It landed heavily on the coffee table.

'What's this?' asked Danny, picking it up.

'I found it at the back of her wardrobe,' said Susan, her face dark with anger.

Danny opened it up and looked in.

'What the hell?' he said, pouring the contents onto the table.

From the bag came a cavalcade of paper which caught the air and slid messily among the empty Chinese food cartons.

It wasn't until she leaned forward that Jude realised the bundle of papers were family photographs. She recognised Anne, older than in the wedding picture from earlier, and slightly tired-looking now, with a young boy by her side who, she realised with a pang, must be Peter. He looked to be around nine or ten years old. Picking it up, she looked for signs of the man he would become, but the child's questioning eyes suggested a vulnerability rarely seen in the adult Peter.

Her gaze wandered to the sturdy baby on Anne's lap — Susan, presumably — sitting with a serious expression and petted lip, and behind them was an aproned torso, but its head was missing. Thrown by the picture's odd composition, it took Jude a few seconds to realise the photograph had been torn. 'That's a shame,' she began to say, but she was distracted by Danny falling to his knees, and raking through the pictures like a dog after a rabbit.

'Don't bother,' Susan said, and something in the way she said it gave Jude the sensation of entering a new place or time, or returning from some place she would have preferred to remain. 'They're all the same. Dad's been cut out of all them.'

Wordlessly, they sifted through a range of black and white, sepia-toned, Kodak multicoloured moments. Here was Susan's sixth birthday, Danny's Holy Communion, Peter's confirmation, the day Patrick bought that white Renault, the old shop in Govan. What connected them all was the missing person. A series of rips and cuts had reduced Patrick to nothing more than a jigsaw of limbs, a dismemberment of memories. Some of the pictures had holes stabbed through them, as if the clean slice of a scissor blade wasn't effective enough for the job.

'I told you she was mad,' Susan said to the back of Danny's head as he let the images fall through his fingers. 'She should be locked up.'

'Not helpful, Susan,' Danny said. 'What makes you think it was her? It could have been an accident.'

But the precision with which the photographs had been destroyed was evident.

'It's like she's decapitated him. Killed him,' Susan said, her voice shaking now. 'Why? Why would she do that?'

'Has she shown any signs of anything?' asked Danny.

They turned to Jude with the earnestness of small children. 'Dementia, you mean? Alzheimer's, that kind of thing?' she replied, uncertainly.

Danny winced.

'God, no. She'll outlive us all,' Jude laughed, and wondered why she was laughing when the situation was far from funny.

'Jude,' said Susan. 'You're the one who spends most time with her. We're relying on you to let us know if anything's wrong, you know. We're trusting you.'

When Susan first started teaching, she worked

hard to disguise her nerves and exert authority. She worked so hard at it, there came a point where her teacher persona refused to stay in the classroom. It followed her home, inserting itself into all of her adult relationships. For most people, Susan's patronising tone was merely annoying, but for Jude it was a reminder of all the different teachers in all those different schools who had treated her as a special case, lavishing too much praise when she was good, and too many serious talks when she wasn't. Jude's learned response to that certain teacher-voice was mortification.

'There's been no sign of anything like this,' she said.

Susan and Danny continued to stare.

'Honestly, I would have told you,' she said, blushing, wondering why she felt like a liar.

'What are we going to do?' Susan asked Danny. He sighed and collapsed onto his backside, taking a fistful of photos with him and stuffing them back into the bag.

'Why does she hate Dad so much? And our childhood,' Susan continued, her voice wavering. 'Was it all a lie? The whole time we were growing up . . . Did she hate him all those years?'

'Of course she didn't. Now shut up!' Danny snapped.

Emma and Lucy came in.

'Is everything all right?' asked Emma.

'What are those?' said Lucy, reaching for a photo.

'Nothing!' Jude jumped up and placed herself between the girls and the worst of the spill. 'Give us a hand tidying these plates, will you, girls?'

'Sure, Auntie Jude.'

They began to tidy the mess left over from the meal, while Susan and Danny gathered the broken pieces of their childhood. Everyone was aware of the girls' eyes wandering from the plates and empty food cartons, but they didn't ask any more questions about it, and that suited everyone fine.

21

Unfamiliar Passion

The unframed wedding photo remained intact on Anne's bedside table. Emma and Lucy had cooed over it when they'd taken her upstairs. She looked at it now and wondered what to do with it, mystified as to why she'd let this one survive the cull. Perhaps it was the innocence of it. Perhaps it was because she couldn't quite believe the fear she saw in the picture now, hiding behind their smiles but announced loudly in their eyes. Perhaps it was simply because she had felt such hope on that day.

She'd always liked the look of him. A tall, slim man who wore his hair unfashionably long, despite his mother's protests. Because he was tall, he habitually stooped, which caused his fringe to flap over his eyes. He'd spent a year at Blair's, studying for the priesthood, but returned home for reasons that were unclear. To still the whispering neighbourhood, Mrs Donnelly let it be known that Mr Donnelly was ailing. Praise be to the Lord, who had sent their only child home in the nick of time. Patrick took over the shop, allowing his mother more time to care for her husband, whose mind was no longer so sharp.

With the Donnellys taking a step back, Anne had worried for her job. Patrick was the new boss and anyone, apart from his own mother it seemed, could see he wasn't up to it. So before he could run the place into the ground, she'd set about spotting problems before they arose and dealt with them in such a way that Patrick could claim responsibility. She assumed stocktaking duties as well as cashier work and accounting, all the while working to keep Patrick involved. She'd seen it after the war — men returning to find their roles usurped by the women, and how useless they'd felt, and what harm that sometimes led to — and she didn't want to run that risk with him, lest word got back to Mrs Donnelly that he wasn't happy with her. Patrick, for his part, had been impressed by Anne's quiet capability. He understood she was showing him the ropes and was grateful, though he remained mystified as to her motivations.

Under Anne's supervision, the business grew. Mrs Donnelly was delighted. Even Father Murphy made a point of dropping by to congratulate Anne.

'Made yourself indispensable, I hear,' he said with a wink. 'Clever lass.'

What was intended as a compliment communicated as a warning for Anne. Father Murphy might as well have added, 'They'll not get rid of you now'. A reminder of her precarious position in the world.

Before long, Mrs Donnelly was telling everyone what a great team her son and Anne made, and soon it felt like the whole neighbourhood was in on the act. It became a running gag:

'When are you two making it official?'

'Ah, go on, Patrick. Make an honest woman of her.'

Gradually their relationship was gossiped into existence and could not be refuted. She was twenty-five and, according to some, had missed the boat. Patrick was regarded as an odd fish by most, and so, generally, the entire neighbourhood was quite tickled by their pairing.

Instead of dancing, Patrick liked to take walks. Anne considered him to be a gentleman, quite different from the few dates she'd had to fight off at the bottom of closes. Restrained, respectful, he barely dared to hold her hand. It was this quality more than any other that Anne admired. She took it as a sign of good breeding. For the first time in her life she surrendered herself to desirous notions. Her days were filled with thoughts of his gentle hands, dirty from cash and groceries, running across her skin. She developed a fascination for the flexing of his forearms as he carried boxes in and out of the shop.

'I've never known a woman blush at the sight of a man rolling up his shirt-sleeves,' murmured Mrs Donnelly, much to Anne's mortification. As for Patrick, he kept his head down and she assumed it was because he, like her, could barely contain himself. For the first time in her life, she began to feel the possibility of a worthwhile future. She was marrying up. Once she had that ring on her finger, she would be secure. She didn't yet dare to dream of the family she longed for, though it hovered on the edge of her subconscious; the sense of belonging, the unconditional love she'd been missing her whole life at last within reach.

If there was an actual proposal, Anne didn't remember it now, but somehow or other they ended up standing opposite each other at the foot of the aisle. Perfectly, she reached the groom just as the organ music ended. Her dress was of parachute silk. For the first and only time in her life, she experienced elegance. She lowered her head and raised her veil, took a deep breath, and looked into the eyes of her husband-to-be.

A slick of sweat coated his brow and chin. He was pale. No smile. His lips were dry and his eyes wider than a toddler's unexpectedly plucked from the arms of his mother.

He reached out and grabbed Anne's hands so suddenly she jumped in fright and dropped her bouquet of hand-stitched daisies. Father Murphy cracked a joke and the congregation laughed, but Patrick kept hold of Anne so tightly she thought her fingers might break.

'Anne,' he whispered. It was more of a croak, really. His brow was furrowed, his gaze so terribly serious that Anne felt a jolt of alarm. She dismissed it as excitement, a thrill caused by Patrick's unfamiliar passion. His tongue swept his lips, which she noticed now were white and cracked. Painful-looking. He tugged on her hands then, trying to shake some important message into her. She was ready to listen, she really was, but when he spoke, all he said was, 'I feel sick.'

And then they were married.

He was never cruel to her. Not intentionally. She was convinced of that and clung to it as a life buoy in rough seas. He rarely, if ever, raised his voice. And if her circumstances had been different, perhaps she would have asked more questions before jumping in.

She longed for and dreaded her wedding night in equal measure, and so when their wedding guests formed the bridal arch for the new couple's exit to married life, she ran through it with trepidation and glee, having changed from her long dress into her honeymoon suit of skirt and blazer, even though shop business removed any possibility of an actual honeymoon.

They walked hand-in-hand through Govan's damp streets until they reached Patrick's parents' house, where they would all live together. Mr and Mrs Donnelly had given up the big bed for their son and his new wife. It was only right, Mrs Donnelly said, and besides, Mr Donnelly's health was such that he needed to be downstairs for reasons of practicality.

Patrick turned the key and stepped back to allow Anne through. She held back, doubtfully.

'Ah, okay,' he said, and hoisting her in his arms he carried her over the doorstep into the narrow hallway. The only light was a dim glow from the moon. When he placed her on her feet again, Anne kept her hands placed around Patrick's neck, which was not easy given their respective heights. She had to tiptoe and almost stretch further than her new suit would permit her.

The distance between them, and the hallway's darkness, colluded to hide his face, which is why she was so startled when he stepped back from her and, ignoring the stairs which led tantalisingly to their bedroom, walked through the living room to the kitchen at the back.

'I'm parched,' he called. 'Cup of tea?'

Her brief confusion was banished as her sharp mind leapt to make sense of her new role. A smile slowly spread across her face as she realised he was being considerate. This was her cue to ready herself for him and clearly he didn't want to embarrass her while she changed.

She took the stairs as elegantly as befitted a married woman, though really she wanted to tear up them, two steps at a time. By the time she reached the top, she thought she would burst.

She couldn't recall ever feeling so awash with emotion: fear, excitement, joy. Perhaps they would be blessed and make a baby that very night.

She pushed open the door to Mr and Mrs Donnelly's bedroom. Our bedroom, she reminded herself, and almost fell into giggles as she realised it still *was* Mr and Mrs Donnelly's bedroom.

'Mrs Donnelly,' she tried. It suited her.

The bed was a normal double, but to Anne, who had only ever slept in a small single, it was gigantic, its significance beyond measure. She stared at it for a few seconds, then hurriedly stepped out of her clothes into a white chiffon nightdress which had been gifted to her by her old landlady. She checked her reflection and licked and sniffed her hand to make sure her breath was fresh, tugged back the covers of the bed and climbed in.

Her eyes wandered the room. She felt rude,

even though there was no one to witness, and it was her room now anyway. She wondered what would be an acceptable waiting period before clearing the old furniture out and bringing the new in. The moss green curtains weren't to her taste at all. She chastised herself for being ungracious and settled herself down to wait for her husband, casting her arms above her head in what she hoped was an alluring manner.

As the minutes ticked by, her initial excitement gave way to irritation. She reminded herself to be patient. After all, they had the rest of their lives together. She strained to hear his footfall on the stairs but the only sound was resounding silence, which somehow seemed louder than anything else she'd heard all day. Soon, irritation turned to anger, but she contained it, not wishing to ruin their first night as husband and wife.

When at last she did hear him begin to make his way up, she was so annoyed she decided to punish him by pretending to be asleep, though she remembered to leave her arms arranged above her head. He entered the room quietly, pausing for a moment by the door before making his way round to the empty side of the bed. She heard him unknot his tie and the soft swish of arms departing sleeves. It was an effort not to open her eyes, especially when she heard the tinny clink of his belt buckle. Without realising, her breathing had become shallow and erratic.

Her body rolled slightly as his weight shifted the mattress. She sighed and stretched and feigned surprise to see him.

'Hush now, stay asleep,' he whispered. He kissed her forehead before lying down to face the window, curled up tightly, away from his bride.

Anne stared into the darkness, nursing her humiliation until first light began its creep through the patchy curtains, casting a soft green glow. At last she fell asleep, having made sense of her rejection by acknowledging how tired they'd both been after such a long day.

They had the rest of their lives, after all, she reminded herself again.

Having eschewed the trappings of femininity for so long, Anne now found herself buying lipsticks and sheer stockings, and having her hair set weekly. For the first time, she examined her figure and found she was pleased with her trim shape. In short, she fell upon all the wily tricks she'd gleaned in her years with Nettie, at which she'd always turned her nose up. Now they served as a lifeline, her only means of hope.

Patrick came to bed later each night, leaving Anne to fall asleep alone, which she did, always careful to leave one bare leg exposed enticingly above the bed clothes, ever in hope of awakening his repressed carnal instincts.

Only the fact that he wasn't altogether cold with her made life bearable. There were soft words, chaste kisses, to which Anne responded with enthusiasm, but he always excused himself and walked away, leaving her frustrated and tearful.

At church, while the congregation prayed for redemption, she prayed for her marriage to ascend from ratified to consummated. Until sex occurred, Patrick could move for annulment at any time. However unlikely that may be, it was a notion that grew alongside her desire to be loved and possessed by him, pinned down and anchored, made finally secure.

The summer after they married brought a two-week heatwave that saw households sleeping with open windows and scant coverings over the beds. Upon waking early one morning with her nightdress sticky with sweat, Anne was bewildered by an unfamiliar stirring beneath the sheets above Patrick. At first glance it might have been a mouse, but as the last vestiges of sleep departed, comprehension dawned. A fearful union of disgust and fascination compelled her out of the bed and round to Patrick's side. He was on his back, frowning even in sleep. Beads of sweat dotted his brow and his head was tipped back slightly so that his mouth hung open, tongue glistening within. Gently, she knelt by his side and took a peek beneath the covers. With a gasp, she immediately dropped them again. Then she pulled them straight back so she was looking at all of him.

Without stopping to think, she untied the pyjama cord and the fabric of his trousers fell away. Then she eased her fingers beneath him and began to tug the trousers down, lifting one hip, then the other. A little moan came from Patrick but he remained asleep. With no idea of what she was doing, she took his penis between her hands and began to gently stroke it. He jerked and stiffened even more, which she took as encouragement. Another groan escaped from him but his eyes remained closed.

Keeping one hand on him, she lifted her nightdress and climbed onto the bed, manoeuvring herself on top, one knee on either side of his narrow hips. She shifted until he was right at her, but he wouldn't go in. Balancing herself with one hand on the mattress, she reached for him and tried to fumble him in. It seemed their bodies couldn't reach agreement.

She moved again, squatting this time, at which point Patrick opened his eyes. Panicked, she lifted herself and gulped a deep breath, just as a child about to dive under water might do.

'Anne,' he said, voice croaky from sleep, alarm spreading across his features. 'What are you . . . ?'

Before he could say any more, she plunged herself down on him. They both cried out. It was over in seconds.

Afterwards he pushed her off him and dressed hurriedly. Then he turned to her and said, 'Don't do that again,' and disappeared downstairs before they could talk about it. His words meant nothing to Anne, who reclined in the bed, breathless and triumphant. There'd be no stopping her now.

★   ★   ★

Jude was woken by a crash. She leapt out of bed and ran the short distance to Sissy's bedroom where Anne slept.

'Anne?'

She knocked on the door and pushed it open.

220

The bedside lamp lay on the floor, casting a light across the beige carpet. Above it, sitting in shadow on the bed, was Anne. Jude was relieved to see her.

'I heard a noise,' she said, coming towards her. 'Are you all right? What's wrong?'

Anne made a low moan and rocked back and forth, cradling herself, trying to soothe herself back to sleep. It wasn't until Jude kneeled down and felt something dig into her knee that she noticed the brown plastic beads of Anne's rosary strewn across the bed and carpet.

'Are you ill?' Jude asked, hesitant to touch her in case she was in pain.

'He won't leave me alone.'

Jude immediately remembered Danny's earlier worry about Alzheimer's and dementia and felt a jolt of alarm.

'Who won't?' she asked, softly, taking Anne's hand.

Anne snatched her hand back. 'Get away from me,' she cried. She threw her arms out, causing Jude to startle and fall backwards. Only then did the fog seem to clear from Anne's vision. She rested her head on her shoulder and squeezed her eyes tight shut, flexing her fingers, as though chasing away the remnants of a bad dream. Jude could only watch and wait until at last Anne took a deep breath and shook her head.

'Are you all right, dear? I don't know what came over me.'

Jude scrabbled forward and pulled herself up to sit beside Anne.

'I'm fine. But you? Did you have a bad dream?'

Whether it was the lateness of the hour, or the strange light given off by the toppled lamp, or simply the desperation of having kept it bottled up inside her for years, Anne sensed an opening, an opportunity for lightness akin to offloading to a priest in the confessional box.

'He should never have married me,' she said, and then wondered if she'd really said it at all. She looked at Jude for confirmation, surprised by her own plain-speaking. Jude's face had a guarded, cynical expression. It was infuriating.

'He shouldn't have married me,' she said again, louder this time. She wanted the message to get through. How she enjoyed the truth of those naughty words, free in the world at last.

'He shouldn't,' she said again, marvelling at this new voice coming from her body. What was she doing? 'He should never have married me,' she said again, forceful this time. A wave of suppressed anger spilled over with the words.

She repeated it again and again, for her own benefit as well as Jude's, confirming something she had known for years but which had lain buried, just beyond reach of her understanding.

'He never loved me. He never did.'

She was rocking again, that self-soothing motion that Jude had interrupted.

'I don't think I've been loved in my whole life.'

'Oh, come on now,' Jude said, a little more forcefully than she intended. It was a ludicrous statement, but there was no denying Anne's distress. Adopting a softer tone, she added, 'You've had three children. Of course you've been loved.'

The rocking continued, but Anne looked straight ahead of her and spoke with determination.

'Ah, yes,' she sneered. 'The *children*. They loved me all right. They loved me because if they didn't, who would take care of them? That's not *love*. That's self-preservation. I'm talking about real, unconditional love. Being loved just for *me*.' Her eyes narrowed and gleamed in the half-light. 'Loved enough not to be abandoned. Loved enough not to need a priest to find me a home, loved not because I can save a business, or because someone needs a . . . a *disguise*. Loved. Just *loved*.'

She curled into herself, her mouth opening wide in a painful, silent cry.

With no idea of what to say, Jude wrapped her arm gently around Anne's shoulders, and rocked with her to calmness.

Soon afterwards, they went downstairs and Jude made tea. They sat at the kitchen table, and for a while the only sound between them was the clinking of a teaspoon as it stirred sugar into a china cup, Jude having decided that Anne deserved her tea served properly.

She sipped, and began.

'Aunt Margaret wasn't my auntie at all. She was just a woman from the church who had a daughter and no husband. When Father Murphy dropped me off that night, she couldn't say no. Her card was too badly marked already. Not two ha'pennies to rub together either. My father gave a bit now and then, but not enough, you know? Everyone was poor back then. I always felt like an intruder, like I had to prove my worth. Could never get too settled. I expect you know what that's like.'

Jude nodded, not because she agreed, but because she didn't want to stem the flow of conversation.

'I didn't complain though,' Anne said. 'I stuck in. Did everything I was supposed to. I was a good girl, I was. Top of my class in everything, but it was never good enough. The teachers said I should have stayed on, but Margaret only had eyes for her daughter. As it should be, of course. Nettie. Pretty wee thing, thick as a plank, Lord forgive me, it's true. Still, Nettie and I were close enough as long as I minded my place.'

'And then they emigrated,' Jude murmured. 'That must have been hard for you.'

'You didn't think like that back then. You just got on with it. At least I had a job.'

'The shop in Govan.'

'Aye, the shop in Govan.'

'Where you met Patrick.'

'Aye.'

Silence.

'Susan found the photographs,' Jude ventured. 'In the bungalow. All ripped up. You must have been very angry with him.'

'God forgive me, it wasn't even his fault.'

Jude was bursting with questions. She'd never seen this version of her mother-in-law before. At long last she'd been admitted to the inner sanctum. To speak out of place would be a sacrilegious act. But Anne had an air of surrender about her now, and all Jude had to do was listen.

'Did you ever hear about the time the shop flooded?'

Jude shook her head. Anne ran the curved edge of her spoon over the surface of her tea, making a figure eight, while she thought of the best place to start her story.

'It rained for months. No one could remember anything like it. Father said we should be lining the animals up in pairs in case Noah turned up. Eventually the river burst its banks, spilled into the streets. Well, the gutters couldn't cope, could they? People were being evacuated from their homes, right, left and centre. I said to Patrick we should move the stock from the cellar up into the shop, but he wouldn't listen. We had sandbags, you see. And somehow our sandbags would succeed where everybody else's failed. Stupid man.' She gave a small shake of her head, her husband's ineptitude still a source of exasperation even after all these years. 'The only reason I listened to him was I had the three children by that point. I had enough to do without arguing with him as well. And then, of course, we got a knock on the door one night. A drunk fella on his way home from the pub had seen the water pouring in over the cellar hatch. Off you go, I told him. Sort it out yourself. I told you this would happen, I said.'

'That sounds reasonable enough,' Jude smiled, when Anne paused to sip her tea.

'Once he was gone, I thought, I can't trust him to sort that on his own. So I rapped on my neighbour's door and asked her to mind the children. I put on my boots and my coat over my

225

nightdress, and took an umbrella and walked through the dark to the shop.'

She paused again. Despite Anne's grave manner, Jude had the sensation of being fed titbits. For the first time in their relationship, she was desperate to hear what her mother-in-law had to say next.

'When I got there, the hatch to the cellar was shut. I'd have expected it to be open so the water could be bailed, but there was no sign of activity. I thought maybe the drunk had exaggerated, maybe even imagined it. I went in through the shop door, which was open. The sandbags had been moved so I knew Patrick was in there. I was angry he hadn't put them back, so I did, even though they were sodden. The shop floor was dry. Everything was normal and I was relieved by that, but then I heard movement down in the cellar and I thought that must be where the damage was. The drunk had said the water was pouring in through the hatch, after all, even though it had seemed clear when I arrived, so I went over, picking up the mop as I went, cursing Patrick for not having it down there already, and I opened the door to the cellar.'

Anne had barely lifted her gaze from her tea cup while she'd been speaking. Now she pressed her lips tightly together, glanced up at Jude, took a drink and winced.

'This has gone cold. Is there more?'

Jude immediately lifted the teapot and poured, a small river trickled down from the spout. Anne spooned a sugar in and stirred for what felt like a maddeningly long time. When she could bear it

226

no longer, Jude asked, 'And how was the cellar?'

Tears rimmed Anne's eyes for a moment, then broke loose, rivulets running down her gnarled face as she leaned forward and hissed, 'It was *disgusting.*'

22

Breach

Anne's secret was a ball of electricity that glowed and pulsed between the two women, connecting and repelling them at the same time. Having laid bare what she considered to be the ugly truth of her existence, Anne could hardly speak a word to Jude, though she found her presence to be a comfort, a knowledgeable shadow, accepting, unquestioning.

The revelation of Patrick's sexuality was profoundly moving for Jude, who viewed the situation from a perspective Anne could not. Jude wondered, but dared not ask, if he'd always had lovers, or if the incident in the shop cellar was an isolated one. She thought of her gentle, unassuming father-in-law, and realised what she'd interpreted as reserve was actually deep sadness. Despite her sympathy for Anne, she secretly hoped he'd found happiness of a sort somewhere. The alternative was too tragic to contemplate.

'He should never have married me,' Anne had said, humiliated by the certainty that if he'd been born fifty years later, he never would have.

Jude found Anne's lingering disgust difficult, but saw no merit in tackling the homophobia that poured from the old lady's lips now. Instead she assured her that of course Patrick had loved her; hadn't he been a good father, hadn't he provided well for the family? And if he hadn't loved her, why did he stay with her once homosexuality became decriminalised? It was a weak argument, but the only one Jude could find.

'You make it sound like I should be grateful,' Anne sneered.

Everything about her was a sneer now. Honesty had removed the need for further pretence, and years' worth of poison spilled out in vast torrents that Jude sometimes struggled to keep up with.

'And all this nonsense in the papers about sex offences and la la la. Ridiculous.'

Putting aside the possibility of Alzheimer's, a spectre which frequently arose as an explanation for Anne's disjointed conversation, Jude gradually began to piece together an idea of Anne and Patrick's life together.

'What I went through to get those children. He should be so lucky.'

The emerging picture was a harrowing one, and there was no possibility of lightening the load by telling Susan and Danny the truth. Their relationship with the church was not as steadfast as their mother's, but they were too far steeped in Catholic teachings for Jude to contemplate opening the conversation. Thankfully, Susan's distance and Danny's fleeting visits made keeping the secret an easier task than it otherwise might have been, though that too became a bone of contention, as Anne had no inclination to reign herself in around Jude any longer, letting loose her darkest thoughts regarding her children. Susan was a bore, a born martyr, subjugating herself at every turn, no self-respect. Danny was a gumption-less sap whose every breath apologised for his existence. When all was said and done, Peter was the only one of her children she could be proud of.

Jude clamped a hand over her mouth when she heard this because, despite his bravado, Peter had never lost the guilt of disappointing his mother when he dropped out of law to pursue happiness in music. Her rage sparked unexpectedly to life, and then smouldered until it became a blaze that threatened to consume her. She wanted to scream at Anne, hurl abuses at her for all the years she'd watched Peter prostrate himself at his mother's feet in an effort to win her approval, only to be rebuffed with talk of Danny, who, according to Anne, was always doing so well, even when his marriage was falling to pieces. Back then it had been poor Danny, such a kind soul, a diligent worker, far too easily taken advantage of. There was nothing for Peter to do but agree, painfully aware that Anne played them off against each other, but loving her no less for it. After a while, Jude learned not to pass comment.

'Jude, she's my mother,' he'd sigh, words that not only ended the conversation, but alerted her to the fact she'd crossed the line by questioning the sanctity of the mother-child relationship. After all, it was a relationship she had limited experience of, despite having a daughter of her own.

230

The sanctity of the mother-child relationship did not appear to be of concern to Anne, who took every opportunity to remind her of Sissy's failings.

'She deserted you just like Susan did with me. We're the same, you and I,' Anne said. 'Sacrificed everything for our families and now look at us. Left alone. Abandoned. Do they ever give us a thought?'

Jude, whose capacity for confrontation had always been weak, accepted what Anne said, even began to believe it. She resolved herself to honour Peter by being as patient and sympathetic to his mother as possible, no matter how unpleasant she became. As for rescuing her relationship with Sissy, it wasn't difficult to imagine she was better off without them.

★ ★ ★

It was only when driving to work that Jude found space to think. Without understanding how, her life had become a series of carrying out services for other people. Whether at home with Anne, or at work with Aleks, she drifted from task to task, each job a welcome distraction from the growing realisation that her life's purpose had eluded her, that every day was just another blip on the way to oblivion. Sometimes she felt she was doing okay. Her drinking was back within sensible parameters. She took her antidepressants like a good patient. They allowed her to function, though sometimes she felt a glass wall stood between her and reality. She could look through

231

it and see how bad everything was, but it didn't cripple her. No one would know from looking at her that she was an empty shell, a husk of a human being.

Even Aleks had taken a step back, at first out of respect for her loss, but in time she sensed his impatience and accepted his retreat as inevitable. She wondered if his withdrawal was a calculated move on his part, designed to worry her back into his arms, but she experienced all of this from a distance, as though it were occurring in someone else's life. She couldn't bring herself to react.

They'd gone several months working in the same office, operating with a heightened veneer of professionalism, when at last one afternoon Aleks snapped.

'I cannot do this any longer,' he said.

Jude looked up from the spreadsheet she was working on, eyebrows slightly raised, giving the impression she was surprised to discover she wasn't alone.

'Is everything alright?' she asked, assuming his problem was a work-based one she could help with.

'No! Everything is not alright!'

He pushed himself back from his desk and swung his chair round to face her. It was only then she realised he'd lost weight. His face was gaunt, and dark circles ringed his eyes. Despite this, she still felt a soft calm wash over her as she looked at him. He cared for her. He was a safe place in the world. She wanted to go to him but old habits kept her seated. His eyes beseeched her to understand, she knew what was required, but she couldn't breach that glass wall that went everywhere before her these days.

'Okay, okay,' he said, rubbing his face in frustration. 'You're going to make me say it.'

She had the sensation of being in a car without any brakes, hurtling to the top of a hill with no idea what lay on the other side. She wanted to stop everything but had no means of doing so.

'I need to know where we are, Jude. I've been patient, haven't I? You know how I feel about you. I want to give us a try. But you — I've no idea where you are. One minute you're going to leave him, then all of a sudden he's dead — I'm sorry to be blunt — I know it's complicated for you and you've been through so much, but I think I've been as understanding as anyone could hope to be. I've been straightforward, and tried to give you all the space you need. But it's time now, Jude. If there's no future here, I need to know.'

She didn't know what was holding her back. The door was open. All she had to do was walk through. It was the easiest thing in the world. But hadn't she always taken the easiest route? Done what she could to avoid conflict, allowed herself to be swept along with Peter, going so far as to have a baby she wasn't sure she wanted? And look where that road had taken her. She loved her daughter, but couldn't parent her, and now there was another lost soul in the world trying to make it on her own. She struggled to find the words, hoped he'd know by looking how grateful she was to him for everything — and

233

how sorry she was that it had to be this way.

Finally, she could only shake her head. His eyes, so dark and full of concern, pinned her to a different future, a future she knew wasn't hers.

He came round to her side of the desk. Stretched his arm out, gently touched her shoulder, at all times implicit in his gaze was the question: *Is this all right? Am I allowed?*

For a moment, she teetered between two worlds.

'I'm sorry,' she said.

Her body was rigid with the effort of not crying. He came closer to her, bent his head to hers. She closed her eyes and felt his warmth radiate towards her. His hand slipped behind her neck. Her skin jumped beneath his fingers. It was so long since she'd been touched. She tilted her head back and he found her lips. Wrapping their arms around each other, they kissed as though they'd waited their entire lives for this moment. Hope and relief and gratitude flowed between them until Jude realised she was being pulled into something that had the power to obliterate everything else, or more specifically, something which she could *use* to obliterate everything else. With a cry, she pulled herself away and moved swiftly behind her desk.

'I can't do it,' she whispered, unable to meet his eye. 'I can't. There's always just this *guilt*. Betrayal. He's gone. I know, it doesn't make sense. But I can't get past it. I'm sorry.'

It wasn't the whole story but it was one she knew he would understand.

Aleks' lips tightened as he absorbed the

information. Hadn't he known it would go this way? But still, he was furious. Such an unfair fight. Who could compete with a dead man?

Fury quickly gave way to nausea, or at least something he attributed to nausea. The sinking, dragging sensation he felt in his core was unfamiliar. He had no words for that.

'I understand,' he told her. 'Don't worry about it. Everything is fine here.'

'Maybe we could have a drink some time? Just as friends?' She hated herself for saying it, and cowered when she saw the anger in his eyes.

'You can't have everything, Jude. Let's just leave things now. Okay?'

And then he was gone. It was the right thing to do. He'd get over it. They both would. Already she felt inexplicably lighter.

For a long time now, she'd been waiting for the phone to ring, to hear Sissy's voice. Anne had told her she'd come running once the money was cut off, but instead there was only a silence that grew longer and darker with every passing day. She'd wrestled with it, until out of the silence emerged one indisputable fact: more than love, more than grief, there was a yearning.

23

Ma Cherie

Sissy thought she had never been so happy. She had taken Hazel's advice and it had worked. She now found that adulthood suited her exceptionally well, especially now she'd moved on from all the losers in her life. She was flying. She'd earned a promotion to floor supervisor at work, and on top of that, she was desirable. Pascal was proof of that. At weekends, she accompanied him to whichever club he was attached to, and because he was working, it made sense for her to work too.

'It's easy, low-risk work,' he told her. 'It would be supremely helpful to me.'

'But I'm here anyway,' she said, embarrassed to take wages from her new boyfriend. 'I don't mind doing it for free.'

Pascal cupped her face and looked at her tenderly. 'Don't give yourself away for free, *ma cherie*. Learn to value yourself. I insist on paying you.'

And so she became his drop-off girl, delivering little bags of pills or wraps of powder around the club, or sometimes in taxis to clubs elsewhere. When taxis proved unreliable, Pascal paid for driving lessons and said he would hire her a car when she passed her test. She felt like his queen. Security got to know her and ushered her past the queues. She was important. Wherever she went, people fell over themselves to greet her. Her arrival heralded good times. She was glad to be of assistance, knowing the produce she delivered would ensure its consumers hours of ecstatic enlightenment. She was making the world a better place, and to think it was all thanks to Hazel.

'Nothing to do with me, darling,' Hazel said, through a typically extravagant cloud of smoke.

'Really,' Sissy insisted. 'You were so right. A pair of heels and a skirt and look at me now. Floor supervisor before all those people who were here before me.'

'I think shagging the boss may have helped, don't you?'

Hazel stubbed her cigarette out against the wall.

'Jesus,' said Sissy. 'What's the point in offering advice to someone if you're just gonna be sniffy with them when it works?'

Hazel dropped the fag end in the bin and turned to give Sissy the benefit of her middle finger.

'Fuck's sake,' muttered Sissy, stamping hers out underfoot. She'd been careful not to gloat about her success on the call floor, but she'd considered Hazel mature enough to handle an honest conversation, and frankly, there was no one else she could confide in.

'Shagging the boss'. It sounded so seedy and made her feel cheap. She'd love to tell Hazel that shagging was the smallest part of it. In fact, shagging was barely in it at all. Their relationship was deeper than that. It was based on mutual respect and caring. Pascal had opened up a whole new way of being for her and she would support him however she could. She'd learned he was prone to low moods and needed space to process his feelings. She worried he relied on too many stimulants to get through the day but he laughed at her.

'Stimulant? What is that? Coffee is a stimulant!' and then he'd wrap his arm around her waist and pull her to him and kiss the top of her head. 'I am much, much older than you are, therefore far wiser. Do not question me, grasshopper.' He'd tickle her until she begged him to stop and afterwards she'd forget to worry for a little while.

As she climbed the stairs back to the office, she wondered how to make it up with Hazel. Apart from Pascal, she was the only person in the entire workplace who had ever shown any interest in Sissy's life. It felt important to have her on side.

'Were you looking for extra shifts?' she asked, just as Hazel was taking her seat.

'Always.'

Sissy nodded. 'I'll see what I can do for you. Shouldn't be a problem.'

She lingered, but Hazel's gratitude was barely worth the wait. A muttered 'thanks' and she was back on the phone, dialling the next number.

Sissy wasn't on the phones this morning. She was tasked with drawing up rotas, assigning employees to various projects, monitoring calls and employee check-in times. Apart from a few extra pounds, promotion only meant a different type of mind-numbing work and the opportunity to make enemies.

'Hey,' she called across the room to a spotty guy in a grey sweatshirt. 'Yeah, you,' she said, when he turned round. 'You were five minutes late back from break. I'm taking it off your lunch, okay?'

The guy barely acknowledged her, just turned back round to his monitor. She felt eyes on her.

'They will not like you,' Pascal had said. 'You must not care. Don't be a child about it, Sissy. It's an adult's job.'

So she swallowed her discomfort and stalked the floor searching for slackers. It's what she was paid to do, after all. She was privileged to have this status cast upon her, she reminded herself, thinking of how far she'd come in a relatively short space of time. Sometimes she wondered about Cam and whether he was all right. She assumed he'd made it back to Glasgow. She pictured him hanging out at all their old haunts: the benches by the garage, Rory's boathouse, the cafes. She couldn't imagine him in any other setting. When her fondness became difficult, it morphed into anger and reduced him to a pitiful character from her past. He'd probably even put Bolt into a shelter by now, having discovered how much attention a dog requires. That was Cam all over. Some people just don't grow up, she thought. Thank God she was moving in the right direction.

24

A Stranger on the Other Side of the Glass

It was years since Jude's last trip to London — a midweek jaunt for her birthday. Peter had organised tickets for *Phantom of the Opera*, having sent a young Sissy to stay with his mother. Sissy must have been seven or eight. It was the only time they'd gone anywhere without her. How giddy they'd been to have a taste of freedom again.

She'd never travelled down on her own though, and she was nervous about navigating her way around. She remembered how intense she'd found the crowds, how much she'd relied on Peter to steer her through. As the train pulled into King's Cross, she steeled herself for the experience.

She was right to. The instant she set foot off the train, she felt she could be swallowed up and lost forever on that platform alone. She didn't expect to be staying long so she'd packed lightly. All she had was a single rucksack and a small satchel draped across her body, into which she'd had the foresight to pack a couple of family photographs. Even if Sissy didn't want to see her, she'd definitely want something of Peter.

She allowed herself to be carried by the crowd through the ticket barrier to the main concourse. She was looking for the Victoria Line, but when she saw a sign for taxis, she immediately changed her mind.

The journey passed in silence, for which she was grateful. However, with nothing to occupy her except her own thoughts, she grew increasingly anxious. What if Sissy turned her away? How would she cope with that? She began to regret her decision to come. Perhaps it was better to live on in ignorance after all.

But that was her teenage voice talking, her scared voice. She wasn't the child any longer. The important thing was to make sure Sissy was okay. That she wasn't about to throw her entire life off a metaphorical cliff. That she hadn't already done that.

The view from the taxi alarmed her further. How could there be so much homelessness in this day and age? It had been bad before but nothing like this. How could it have gotten so much worse? What did Sissy make of it? Did it tarnish her? Was she still positive about life?

And the people — so many different types of people. How was it possible they all existed alongside each other in such close proximity?

Eighteen is too damn young to be an adult, she thought.

By the time the cab reached Walthamstow, Jude had a newfound respect for her daughter. Whatever the reasons, however she had arrived at the decision, coming down to London had been a bold choice. Staying down, even bolder. Jude had never been that brave.

She asked the driver to drop her at the top of Sissy's road. She wanted the last few seconds to compose her thoughts, or perhaps she was just postponing the moment of truth.

So this is where her daughter had been living. Good for her.

An old lady came out of one of the doors ahead. Jude smiled and received a curt nod in return. As she approached, the lady shuffled down the short path carrying a plastic bag full of rice which she upended onto the curb. It was immediately set upon by a noisy flock of seagulls.

Seagulls in London, Jude thought. Everyone wants a piece of the action.

She counted the numbers until she came to a green door half-way down the street. Looking up at it, she experienced a moment of elation. No unsightly cling film on the inside of the windows for warmth, no steel bar across the door. It was a proper house, respectable. Quickly, she chastised herself. When had she grown so old?

She stepped up the tiny path and rapped smartly on the door. No more thinking. She heard movement inside, saw a shadow on the other side of the glass. She fixed a smile on her face, but when the door opened it revealed no one she knew.

'Can I help you?' the young man said.

Flustered, Jude stepped back and checked the number.

'Maybe I'm at the wrong house ... I'm looking for my daughter?'

Another voice carried through — 'Who is it?' — and a face appeared. At last she was back on familiar ground.

'Rik! How are you?'

It wasn't that he seemed displeased to see her, but she could sense he wasn't happy.

'Jude!' said Rik. 'What a surprise. Are you all right? Would you like to come in?'

He shuffled the other man out of the way and opened the door wide.

'Come in, come in. Noah, put the kettle on, there's a love.'

He brought her into the living room and sat her down on the couch. He'd developed a passion for interior design of late. New items arrived weekly: cushions, lampshades, rugs, fairy lights, mirrors, cactus plants. A massive chandelier hung from the tiny ceiling. Jude couldn't help smiling at the clash of styles.

'So this is where you've been,' she said, taking it all in.

He stood in the centre of the room and gestured nervously. 'It isn't finished yet.'

'It looks great,' Jude said. 'Really great.'

He smiled, gratefully.

'Ah. Oh. This is my boyfriend,' he said, as the other man came in carrying a mug of tea. 'Noah, this is Jude. Sissy's mum.'

'I'm sorry, I don't know how you take it,' he said, handing the tea over. 'I took a guess. Just milk?'

'That's perfect, thank you. Aren't you having one?'

A look of panic crossed his face and he looked to Rik for guidance. Jude took a sip to hide her amusement. They clearly weren't used to entertaining. Their nerves were endearing.

'I'm sorry,' she said. 'I should have called but — '

'Yes, yes,' Rik said. 'I'll have a coffee. Go on then.' He practically shooed Noah out of the room.

'So how have you been?' he said, taking a seat on the other sofa.

She wasn't sure how honest she should be. The last time she'd seen Rik, he'd been a child.

'Not bad,' she decided. 'And you? Are you enjoying London? You seem to be doing all right for yourself.'

'Yes,' he nodded, his eyes drawn to the window by the noise of a passing moped. 'I've been promoted at work, so that's nice. More pennies. I mean, the job is *dull as sin*,' he rolled his eyes, 'but I *love* London. Work's work, you know?'

Noah arrived with the coffee. Looking at him properly, Jude could see he appeared to be a few years older than Rik, slightly podgy with a dark stubble. Not the type she imagined Rik would go for. But then, he was so young. Too young to have a type. She resisted the urge to tell him she hoped he was being careful. There was no point. Hearts were made to be broken.

A swell of emotion caught her by surprise. She tried to hide it behind her mug but spilled tea on herself in the process. She apologised for the mess and Rik showed her to the bathroom so she could clean up.

She gripped the sink and stared into the mirror. She had to get her nerves under control before she saw Sissy. She splashed her face and

244

practised her breathing. After a few moments, she felt calm enough to face them again. They were waiting for her in the kitchen.

'So, Sissy's not in, I take it? Typical. Where is she then?'

A nervous look passed from Rik to Noah.

'Jude,' Rik said. 'Sissy doesn't live here any more.'

'What?' Jude said, as she felt the room tip sideways.

'She moved out a few months ago,' Rik was saying. 'I thought you knew.'

'Months ago? What?' she said again.

'She's going to fall!' a voice called, and a pair of hands grasped her.

'Sit down,' Noah said. 'Look, here, at the table. I'll make more tea.'

When she was safely deposited in a chair, Noah filled the kettle. The water came out in a rush. Somewhere a dog began to yap. It was too much. Her mind was flooded.

Rik sat opposite her and took her hand between his. Here was something solid to hold on to. Something to blame.

No, they hadn't had an argument, as such. Well, actually, there had been several, but there was no single issue that had pushed her over the edge. After Cam left, they'd grown apart. She was seeing someone — a guy she worked with — and had a different set of friends. Different interests. Meanwhile, Rik had fallen in love and Noah had moved in. Seemingly that had been the last straw. He was sorry, but he hadn't expected her to be so jealous that he'd found someone. He'd thought she might be happy for him.

Jude listened to it all with a growing sense of foreboding. Poor, poor Sissy. It had happened all over again. She'd lost someone she loved and then had to deal with a stranger in her midst. Not that Anne was a stranger, of course, but she had made their home seem strange in the strangest of times. Jude suddenly understood why Sissy had left, and with the arrival of this understanding she felt the awakening of a wildness, a primitive, urgent need to bring her daughter home and keep her close.

'Where is she? She must have left a forwarding address?'

'You could get her on Facebook,' Rik suggested, pulling his laptop towards him. He pressed a couple of keys and swivelled it so Jude could see. 'That's her page.'

Jude leaned into the screen, disbelieving the images before her. Sissy, her sweet, tomboyish, fun-loving girl had seemingly morphed into a party girl. High heels, tiny shorts, impossible cleavage.

'Her hair . . . ' breathed Jude.

'Extensions,' said Rik. 'Honestly. She went full-scale diva on me.'

Jude clicked through the pictures. Sissy in the middle of the crowd; Sissy with her tongue out and some type of pill balanced on the tip; Sissy kneeling at some stranger's crotch, looking suggestively at the camera; Sissy, with long tumbling red locks falling around her bare shoulders, one finger poised provocatively

246

between brightly painted lips; Sissy, with her back to the camera, being held by a dark, long-haired man, he grinning straight down the lens with one hand tucked in the back of her skirt.

'That's the boyfriend,' Rik said.

Jude peered into the screen. He was older, but how much older was difficult to say. Instantly she despised him. Arrogance oozed: the tilt of his head and jut of his chin, the twist in his smile, and worst of all, the complicity between him and the photographer as he fondled her daughter.

Noah placed a fresh mug of tea before her. Without meaning to, her eyes scoured the room for alcohol. She was relieved not to find any. One less battle to have. She curled her hand around the mug, and when it began to burn her hand, she held it tighter. She thought she might vomit.

'It doesn't seem so long ago she was in a school uniform,' she said. She knew how trite and predictable she must sound but she didn't care.

'Do you have an address for her?' she asked again. Please let him have an address I can go to, she thought. Please don't let me have to write to that girl, a complete stranger.

'Nah,' said Rik. 'She's somewhere in Hackney though. So not far away.' He nodded encouragingly.

Christ, young people are so bloody stupid, she thought. She gritted her teeth and pulled the laptop towards her.

'All right then,' she said, grimly. 'How do I do this?'

With Rik and Noah's help, she composed a short message and sent it off. Once it was gone, she felt helpless. Almost immediately, Rik announced it had been received and read. Hope soared.

'How can you tell?' she asked, sitting up straight.

'It tells you. Look, there.'

They waited expectantly for a reply. When it didn't materialise, Jude sent another: *I'm in London. Your old house. I need to see you, Sissy. PLEASE.*

They watched the screen avidly. The notification came through informing them the message had been read.

'She's writing, she's writing,' cried Rik, wondering how he'd suddenly come to be so invested in this relationship.

Jude heard his excitement and took it as encouragement. The reply arrived: *GO AWAY.*

Jude slumped back in her chair. Rik's smile froze on his face. Noah remained by the kitchen sink wondering if he should offer more tea, possibly with sugar because he recalled his nan saying that was good for shock.

'What do I do now?' Jude looked up at Rik, whose confusion was so apparent she immediately felt bad for asking.

'Um. Mobile?' he offered, realising as he said it that Jude must have surely already taken the obvious approach.

'Not unless you've got a new number for her? It just goes dead.'

He shook his head. 'Same number as always. I

haven't used it in a while.'

'What the hell happened down here? Where's Cam?'

Rik filled her in on the main details, leaving out the more salacious aspects of their early time in London. 'And then I met Noah. I thought she'd be pleased we could split the rent three ways again at least, but she didn't like it, did she?'

'No, no, she didn't really,' Noah agreed. 'I'm a good housemate,' he said to Jude. 'House-trained and everything.'

His limp joke made no dent in the mood.

'Oh my love,' Jude murmured, staring at the long-haired party girl on the screen. 'It happened again, didn't it?'

Rik and Noah exchanged worried glances. Jude reached forward and stroked Sissy's face. Then she looked up at Noah and said, 'You pushed her out. You didn't mean to, but you pushed her out.'

Instinctively, Rik and Noah knew not to object to Jude's words, however hurtful they were. In fact, they'd done everything they could to accommodate Sissy but, despite this, her moods had only grown darker. The only time they truly relaxed in their own home was the weekend when she went to party at whatever club night her boyfriend was promoting. Through the week, they were forced to tiptoe around the house, so as to avoid incurring her wrath, which was ironic, as they considered themselves highly evolved members of the species, whereas she had become nothing more than a lout, leaving a messy trail wherever she went.

'I don't know what to do now,' Jude said again. 'I just don't know.'

No one knew what she should do. Rik felt particularly helpless. As the person who'd known Jude and Sissy longest, he felt he ought to offer some solution. At last he announced she must stay with them, at least for the night. Ignoring Noah's panicked expression, Rik gave Jude's shoulders a squeeze.

'Maybe she'll have a change of heart overnight,' he smiled.

She patted his hand in gratitude. How the world moves on when the child becomes protector of the adult. She hadn't expected the day to arrive so quickly.

There was no trace of Sissy left in her bedroom, though at least the bed remained. A faint scent in the air suggested it had been repainted recently. She knew it was unreasonable of her to feel offended that Rik had moved on so easily. It wasn't unusual for friendships forged in school to fall away. She was irritated he knew so little about Sissy's life, however. Unable to even say where she worked, other than somewhere close to Liverpool Street. Just as quickly, she forgave him. He wasn't Sissy's mother. Why should he know if she didn't?

Next day, with nothing more than 'Hackney' to go on, Jude took the train to Bethnal Green and wandered the streets in search of Sissy. She couldn't contemplate the possibility of not finding her. Sissy would come out of a corner shop, carrying a pint of milk, or she'd be on her way home from work, or en route to a bar, and when she laid eyes on Jude all her resistance would fall away. Finding her was the only obstacle and it was completely surmountable. They were mother and daughter. Natural law would lead them to each other.

By the third day Jude was desperate. The dank, crumbling streets and constant blare of traffic, the hostility of strangers, the sheer futility of trying to find one person among millions. She felt permanently grubby and her feet ached. She could do with a drink but she didn't want her grasp on reality to dilute in any way. She needed her daughter. That's all she needed.

She took respite in a cafe that gave the appearance of having had a great deal of money spent on it in order to look old and shabby. An older couple, perhaps in their sixties, came in and sat at the table next to hers. The man asked his wife if she needed to go to the bathroom before they ordered 'so we don't have to shift these tables again'.

'No,' she replied, firmly. 'I'll go after we've ordered.'

'Righto, righto,' he said, in a placatory tone. He picked up the menu and read aloud, suggesting they might have this, or that, reminding her he'd already had two eggs that morning. When the waitress came to take their order, he did the talking, acting as a middle man between she and his wife — *Do you want this? Or that?* He negotiated a double shot Americano but emphasised it had to be in a small cup, the implication being his wife's bladder was not up to the task of holding the contents of a large cup.

Jude wondered if he realised how loudly he was speaking. His wife didn't look at him but appeared to stare at some indeterminate object lying somewhere behind the waitress. All that caffeine buzzing around her system. Maybe that's how she gets her kicks, Jude mused. Maybe she needs it just to maintain a conversation with her overbearing husband.

He excused himself and went to the bathroom. His wife didn't alter her gaze in any way. Jude thought she detected a delicate kind of sadness; it was there in her perfectly tidy honey-coloured hair, her cardigan, her rounded shoulders. She seemed out of place for the area.

He returned and their food arrived. They ate; she in dainty little bites, never once looking up from her plate, he in great chunks which he chewed while watching her. Without meaning to, Jude weaved their life story. It consisted of boredom and oppression and, she thought, could only culminate in them hating each other.

It came time for Jude to leave. Her body was tired, but she wouldn't find Sissy in here. As she gathered herself to leave, she noticed beneath the couple's table that the man continually rubbed his foot against his wife's calf. It was such an unexpected intimacy that she gasped. She felt like a small child at the theatre when the curtain is pulled back to reveal the hidden world behind. Their discreet exercise in love, or perhaps just forty years of gentle habit, hit her with force. She paid her bill hurriedly and burst out of the cafe onto the street where she doubled up and retched. Her breath came rapid and deep, and then she was sobbing, great hoarse sobs that wracked her body. All around her the writhing powerhouse of London continued its grind and everywhere within it, nowhere to be seen, was Sissy.

25

Uncharacteristic Consideration

Jude explained it to Anne as a wall of sea that rose from the concrete and smashed over her. Anne listened quietly, patiently, and when Jude finished she still said nothing.

Instead, she laid a hand on Jude's knee and patted it. After a moment or two, she took out her rosary and began to pray. When Anne asked with uncharacteristic consideration whether she should go on, Jude said yes, please.

A space opened up between them which left room for conversations that had never happened before.

'As a child,' said Jude, 'I thought all I had to do was hold on till I was an adult and then all the fear would go away. And for a while it did, but . . . lately, it feels like I'm just . . . I don't know . . . kind of loose? Like there's nothing holding me together. And I'm getting looser every day. There's nothing holding me down. I could just float away. I could disappear and no one would care. Not even me.'

'Oh, now, stop that at once. People would care. I would care! Sissy would care! Oh, she's having a tantrum just now but she'd care all right, mark my words. She doesn't know how lucky she is to have a mother who cares. To have a mother at all. Excuse me.'

Anne dug up her sleeve for a handkerchief. There was always a handkerchief up there, Jude realised. Anne blew her nose and continued, her voice harsher now.

'That's the way of it, of course. Spoiled children. How could they be anything else? Take my lot, for instance. I'm just a burden to the two that's left.'

And so the conversations became circular healing rituals of prayer and sympathy, where they each found strength in the other and consolidated their beliefs. Anne in particular was very proud of bringing Jude to the Lord, and was convinced there was some higher purpose in her daughter-in-law's misery. She approached Jude's conversion with a fervour that succeeded in masking the other problem in her life. But only for a short while.

Ever since she'd told Jude the truth about Patrick, a portal appeared to have opened up within her, through which all pain and memory poured through. It was impossible to distinguish one from the other. Reluctant to burden Jude with even more to worry about, she kept to herself all the aches and spasms her digestive tract threw at her, turning instead to the Internet for advice. From there she found a website ready to furnish her with a wide array of pills and potions, though sometimes she thought the amount of mixing and matching of products was doing her more harm than good. She consoled herself with her life-long belief that time and God heals everything.

What she really needed was a doctor, but the

mere idea of walking to the surgery made her want to lie down. There was no question of asking for a home visit — precious resources had to be preserved for those who needed them. She could ask Jude to drive her, of course, but it was difficult to find the right moment, especially as Jude had to work so much these days since that Aleks fella had moved on. Besides, despite having left pills lying around for weeks, Jude had asked Anne only once if she was feeling all right, and had accepted the reply — 'Just a bit of indigestion, dear' — more readily than one would have hoped.

So she was back to square one. True, it was a years old problem, but now she was old she didn't seem to have the same tolerance for it. But what did she expect? She was approaching her eightieth year, after all. Indigestion tablets weren't miracle workers. Only God provided miracles. However, she didn't like to ask Him for favours for herself. It seemed so shallow and wrong.

In the end it was an ambulance job.

She was wakened one night by a pain in her abdomen so severe it took her breath away. Her groans disturbed Jude, who immediately called the emergency services.

'I just needed my pills,' Anne chastised later. 'All this fuss over nothing.'

Jude accepted the chastisement and made no reference to Anne's frightening consumption of Entonox in the ambulance, or the way her teeth ground the mouthpiece, or how her knuckles turned white because she gripped it so tightly, frightened someone might try to take it from her.

Doctors and nurses came and went, questions were asked, the answers noted, and then the same questions were asked again a little while later.

'I've already told you all this. I want to go home.'

But there was no going home.

'How long have you had that yellow in your eyes?' someone asked.

Jude sat up and leaned over to check Anne's eyes, but Anne closed them and turned her head away.

'Any ideas?' the nurse asked Jude, who could only shake her head and apologise for her ignorance.

Tests, tests, tests.

Danny arrived, a stricken look on his face.

'Ma! Are you all right?'

'Oh, who called *you* . . . ' came the withering reply.

Tests, and tests and more tests.

Susan arrived a few days later and was greeted with a judgemental, 'Oh, you *made* it then.'

'It's not uncommon for people to lash out at those they need the most. Try not to take it personally,' a nurse advised.

Susan stayed for the weekend, and Danny came every day after work. Jude took the week off.

'It's easier for me,' she told Danny. He nodded his agreement before he left. As she watched him make his way down the corridor, she considered how foolish it was to think a child might do the right thing for their mother.

She stayed with Anne for hours every day for some reason she appeared to have been granted a dispensation beyond normal visiting hours, and while Anne slept, Jude kept a vigil over her.

26

The Helper

'I have to go to Manchester. Business,' said Pascal.

'Were you going to tell me?'

They stood in the flat's narrow hallway, she blocking his way, having just arrived back from work to discover him on the way out, carrying a suitcase. For a moment she'd thought he was throwing her out.

Pascal dragged one hand through his hair and tossed his head back impatiently. He put the suitcase down and brought the palms of his hands together.

'I am an adult,' he said. 'And you are an adult. Yes?'

He left a silence in which Sissy was compelled to nod her head.

'Good! So . . . ' He spoke in a very clear and clipped manner so there could be no misunderstanding. 'I have a business which means that every now and then something comes up which requires me to *be a fucking businessman!*' His voice soared towards the end of the sentence and his face came in close to hers, twisted and furious. She immediately reddened and, much to her shame, felt tears fill up her eyes.

'I'm sorry, I'm sorry,' he sighed, pulling her into him. She forced her head sideways so she

259

could breathe. 'I'm sorry. It is very stressful. Idiots up there to deal with.'

The agency had for some time been looking to set up a separate office in Manchester.

'I thought it was going well,' Sissy sniffed. He sighed and leaned back against the wall.

'It is, it is.' He wiped a hand across his face and shook his head. Suddenly his whole body slumped and he looked straight at her. 'Such fucking idiots, I swear,' he whispered. 'I have to do everything my damn self. That's why I am so glad I have you. You, I can trust. You will keep everything running for me while I am gone, yes?'

'Of course,' she said, in a small voice.

He kissed her on top of her head and squeezed round her, dragging his suitcase. 'You're such a good girl. I don't know what I'd do without you.'

'But Pascal . . . '

He sighed and looked upward. 'Yes?'

'When will you be back?'

'I will email. Or call, even. Listen,' he said, laying a hand on her shoulder. 'I still need you to be at the club this weekend. My boys will look after you, all right?'

'So you're going to be away all week?'

'Jesus, I feel like I am talking with my mother. Look, I may be back in a week, I may not. Work will dictate. Now, do you think you can handle things here or do I need to make another arrangement?'

She shook her head vigorously. 'No, no, I'll be fine here.'

'Good. Oh, there's my taxi. I have to go.'

He disappeared down the stairs, leaving her

wondering what exactly she was in charge of.

She went in to work the next day and managed to catch Tony before her shift began.

'He said what exactly?' Tony frowned.

'Just that . . . you know . . . I was to keep things running. I wasn't sure what he meant.'

Tony laughed. 'I think we'll cope without the magical Pascal for a few days, Sissy, but thanks all the same.'

Her face a fiery red, she muttered a thank you and went to her booth, trying to nurse a smidgeon of gratitude that at least Tony clearly anticipated Pascal's imminent return.

Friday arrived and, with no call or email from Pascal, Sissy was forced to go to the club by herself. It was a new venture so she took it seriously. The admin had been done, hundreds of emails and texts sent, flyers posted, DJs and dancers booked. A good buzz was rolling on social media. All that remained was to ensure the customers had the night of their lives. She couldn't quite believe that Pascal would be absent this evening, but then she thought of how he trusted her and she felt better.

She arrived early and hooked up with the two guys she'd seen that first night, who were Pascal's regular runners. One was Jason, tall, smartly dressed, arrogant; the other a little guy everyone called Fame. He was scruffy, skinny and edgy, never still, and his eyes constantly scanned his environment.

'Paranoid,' Pascal had said. 'That's good in his line of work.'

Jason was the front man in Pascal's absence.

He dealt directly with the club owner and delegated to his team, which this evening consisted only of Sissy and Fame.

'Where's everyone else?' asked Sissy. Normally Pascal ran a team of seven or eight, all of them with their own contact list. Together they guaranteed whichever club they worked for a high turn out, and a lucrative base for Pascal's 'product supply business', as he called it.

'At Rumba's,' he said, referring to a massive club in the West End. He glanced up from the list of names he was scanning. 'We're just trying this one out tonight. Pascal wants to see if we can handle two on the same night. Let's show him we can, yeah?'

He left to hand over the completed list to the door staff.

'That means I'm your boss,' Fame told her with a cheeky grin, flashing a gold front tooth.

'Fuck off are you,' she replied, while they waited for Jason. Sissy thought Pascal was short-sighted to have someone on his team who looked as dodgy as Fame, but then what did she know? She kept quiet and avoided him whenever possible, which normally wasn't difficult. Tonight looked to be a different matter.

'All right, you two,' said Jason on his return. This place is gonna be jumping and it's your job to make sure it stays that way. Sissy, I want you to stay close to Fame, all right? Let him take the lead. If you sell everything, you can refresh your supply from him.'

Fame shot her a toothy grin that caused her to scowl. 'Cheers, boss,' he said. 'I won't let you down.' He stepped sideways to throw his arm around Sissy. 'And I'll keep an eye on this one, don't you worry.'

She gave Jason her best grin. A bad atmosphere helped no one.

The club began to fill with familiar faces, and plenty who Sissy didn't recognise, though many of them greeted her like a best friend. Regardless, she met them all with the same hyped enthusiasm, long-lost friends all. Here was the guy who hit on her every time he saw her; she hugged him and squeezed his cheeks because he always brought at least half a dozen friends. He'd be easy enough to lose in the crowd later, but it paid to make him feel special. Here came the lonely brunette who would pay Sissy repeat visits as the night went on, each time with an apology and a request for just one more pill. Here was the C-list celebrity who always brought an entourage and required close attention. So many different types of punter, each of them Sissy's responsibility for the evening.

She moved between groups, and for the first time couldn't catch a lift from their playful vibes. She was reminded of that first night she'd been out with Pascal when she'd felt so dowdy and out of touch with everyone else. She'd sorted herself out since then — heels, hair, eyes, lips — but she felt like an imposter as she flitted from table to table, her face making all the right expressions, but doing nothing to dispel the hollowness inside. The room continued to fill, people spilling in from outside, the space between them growing smaller. At the same time, the DJ's tunes dug a little deeper, taking the dancers further into his world; signalling the journey to come, though he wasn't ready to take the brakes off yet. Other than the DJ, she and her little team of Jason and Fame were the most important people in the room. The way she saw it, neither could do their job properly without the other. They were all in it together.

It was shaping up to be an underwhelming evening until Jason became aware of another dealer in the room. Fulfilling his legal obligation, he alerted management to their presence. Once their product had been confiscated, they were escorted from the premises and the flow of Sissy's business intensified. Before long, she had to locate Fame for more pills and powder.

'It's a fucking gold mine in here,' he yelled, bouncing with the beat. She wondered how he had time to dance when she was being hauled into various groups for chat and deliveries. She signalled that she wanted more product and he nodded and headed to the side. She sighed and followed him. Why he had to make such a song and dance about it, she didn't know. He passed her a bag of twenty pills and ten wraps of cocaine, which she slid into a slim purse attached around her waist before disappearing back into the crush.

By midnight, the tunes had kicked in and the crowd soared. Word came that the line outside went round the block. Jason and Fame announced the evening an unparalleled success. Normally she would be high with them but she couldn't get on it. She remembered Pascal's instruction to keep things running and wondered if he'd be pleased with her. Working the club without his presence in the background was a big deal. She needed to prove she was reliable, make him proud of her. He hadn't called all week, and only responded to one of her texts. His silence had taken on greater significance with each passing hour, despite her efforts to minimise her reaction to it. He's busy, she thought. He's stressed. Don't give him more to worry about.

The crowd heaved and surged once more, transported to an impossibly high plane by the ramped up beat. Lasers cut across the darkness, beams of light guiding people home, back to source, the origins of their existence.

Sissy observed it with sullen detachment. The walls were lined with old beat up sofas on which various couples reclined, stroking and kissing each other, blind to the audience in the room.

A pale, sweaty face emerged from the darkness, shouted in her ear, and a swift exchange of cash and drugs was made. They kept on coming, the excited faces of the early evening now given over to expressions of grim focus, each of them intent on crawling their way back to the high they'd involuntarily vacated.

Soon her stash had gone and she had a pile of notes she wanted rid of, possession of money being a larger source of anxiety than anything else. It wasn't difficult to imagine being robbed for money, whereas the drugs made everyone roll over and beg. She stole her way through the room until she found Jason behind the bar making the blonde bartender laugh. He came towards her with a frown on his face.

'I told you to deal with Fame.'

'Yeah, for refills. You didn't tell me to give him the cash.'

She pointed to the belt around her waist. With a curt nod, he opened his palm to receive and, with hands kept low behind the bar, she passed the money over.

'That's it, I'm done,' she said. 'I'm going home.'

He gave a quizzical look. 'You sick?'

'Uh, yeah,' she said. 'I'll see you.'

His attention was already back with the blonde.

Maybe she *was* sick, she thought, as she went to collect her coat. Either way, she couldn't get out of there fast enough. It wasn't until the cool London air wrapped around her that she realised how oppressive the club had felt. She slipped her heels off and walked barefoot until she found a cab office.

In the cab she flipped her phone over and over, resisting the urge to text Pascal. To call was out of the question — too demanding, too needy — but a text could be tended to when the recipient was ready. The phone found its way to her pocket. She wouldn't be rash. She'd decide when she got home.

She gave the driver thirty for a twenty-one-pound fare and told him to keep the change. Her street was quiet, no sign of the chaos currently occurring in dark little bubbles across London. As she approached the door to their flat, she heard music. With a sudden flare of excitement, she hurriedly opened the door and walked through, checking the bedroom as she passed. Pascal was in the living room, bent over the table. He inhaled the powder and threw his head back, eyes alighting on Sissy in the doorway.

'*Ma cherie*,' he said, standing immediately and opening his arms wide.

'Pascal,' she cried, and rushed forward to accept his embrace. 'Why didn't you tell me you'd be here?'

He kissed her on each cheek, then reverted to his position by the table. He hoovered up a second line then, after offering the straw to Sissy who refused it, scooped her up in his arms and carried her through to the bedroom. She squealed and laughed and he said he was a cave man and threw her onto the bed.

His kisses were hard and impossible to respond to. In between kisses he called her names, bitch, whore, but it was borne of passion so she didn't object. When he paused to unbuckle himself, she quickly struggled out of her top. She tried to pull him back down to her, but instead he turned her over and tugged at her underwear until it gave way. Then she felt him at her but she wasn't ready and he couldn't get in. He jabbed away, cursing in French. Sissy stared at the headboard, willing it to happen, but with each attempt he felt softer. Her humiliation grew as she waited for the inevitable.

'Ah, fucking *merde*!'

The bed shifted as he stood up, leaving her on all fours with her head hanging down, looking at

267

her hands. The sound of his buckle as he fastened himself up quickly so she couldn't see was her cue to fall onto her side.

'I'm sorry,' she said. He batted her off with his arm, refusing to look at her. 'We should talk about this, Pascal.'

'Fuck it,' he said, as he left the room. 'I'm taking a shower.'

'Pascal, it doesn't matter,' she called after him, only to be answered by the slam of the bathroom door and the sound of water raining into the plastic bath tub.

★   ★   ★

Next day, they woke in the early afternoon and went for brunch in one of the local cafes. He bought a broadsheet which he read at the table, emerging from behind it now and then to sip his coffee. She nursed her hot chocolate and gazed through the frosted glass window, trying to imagine what the people beyond it might look like.

Pascal told her he had to be back and forth between Manchester and London for the foreseeable future, so if Sissy had trouble with that she should let him know. It was only fair.

Of course she didn't have trouble with that. What was she, a child?

He couldn't be distracted with a stream of texts or nonbusiness related emails. All his focus had to be on his businesses. He was doing it for her. Did she understand?

Of course she understood, though she didn't

voice her surprise. She didn't realise he considered them to be a long-term thing. But yes, she understood. She was grateful and only wanted to help in whatever way she could.

She was his eyes on the club front. He trusted Jason but it would be useful for her to keep a watchful eye.

Anything he wanted, she told him. Anything at all.

★ ★ ★

He wanted her to attend two extra club nights through the week, so she did, and somehow managed into her day job as well, too tired to care any more about what Hazel might think of her, or what she could be telling other people. She patrolled the call floor in a zombified state, no longer noticing if people were late back from breaks, or took too many toilet breaks. When Tony pulled her up for being late herself, she shrugged and walked past him. Somewhere in the muddled depths of her mind she rationalised that Pascal was equal with Tony, and as Pascal was the one making her late, they had no right to expect the usual standard of work from her.

One day she nipped out to have a smoke and found Hazel leaning against the wall in their usual spot down the lane. Hazel turned her back as Sissy approached, which Sissy reacted to with a wave of paranoia. It was only as she got closer she realised Hazel was crying. Automatically, she opened her arms and wrapped them around the older woman, half expecting to be shrugged off, but Hazel allowed herself to be held.

'Thanks,' said Hazel, awkwardly extricating herself after a moment or two. She sniffed and wiped her face with the end of her cardigan sleeve.

'Do you want to talk about it?' asked Sissy, doubtfully.

Hazel screwed her face up and shook her head.

'It's silly,' she said. 'Nothing important.'

'It looks important,' Sissy said. 'Important enough to be crying over.'

Hazel shook her head even more vigorously. 'It's nothing. I don't want you to get the wrong idea. It's just my little grandson's first birthday. My boy, he lives in Cornwall, you know?'

Sissy nodded. She'd heard all about Hazel's son, the carpenter with a surfboard, Hazel's pride and joy.

'It's just, I can't get down there as often as I'd like. They sent me a picture, look.'

Hazel lifted her phone to show Hazel a handsome, smiling man holding a laughing blonde baby.

'He's gorgeous,' Sissy obliged. 'The baby, I mean. I mean your son's alright too but . . . '

Hazel laughed. 'That's okay, I understand. I'm just having a moment, really, Sissy. I miss them, that's all.'

'Why don't you go down and see them then?' asked Sissy.

Hazel's face tightened and she sighed. 'Why do we not do anything, love? Money. I can't afford to take the time off. My voice-over stuff's been pretty quiet of late. Hey ho. That's the way it is sometimes. It'll change. It always does.'

She gazed down at the photograph. 'I don't know what's wrong with me. I'm used to this sort of thing. I'll see him eventually, once I get a few pennies put by.'

'Of course you will,' Sissy said. 'You'll get down there in no time. I've been putting you down for extra shifts.'

'I know you have, darling. I'm grateful. Anyway, time for me to get back up. Could do without a lecture from Tony today.' She gave Sissy a warm, genuine smile. 'Thanks for listening, treasure. That was really helpful.'

Sissy watched her walk away, feeling a bloom of pride. She wished she could do more, and then realised she could. She hurried down to the main road and found a cash-point, where she withdrew £350.

Powered by the conviction of doing good, she ran back to the office and breathlessly put the money down in front of Hazel, who was in the middle of a call. Hazel broke off her sentence and looked from the cash up to Sissy in slack-jawed wonder.

Sissy laid her hand on Hazel's shoulder.

'It's a gift,' she whispered. 'Don't say anything about it.'

For the rest of the afternoon she was buoyant. Even Tony commented on her improved mood, and word went round that Sissy was sharp again on anyone late back from break.

Hazel cornered her in the crowded staff room at the end of the shift, just as everyone was collecting their bags and coats. Seemingly oblivious to her audience, she brandished the money in Sissy's face.

'What the hell's this? I'm not a charity case, you know.'

'I know you're not,' Sissy replied, stunned by Hazel's aggression. Over Hazel's shoulder she saw people look at them.

'So you can keep your money, Little Miss High and Mighty.'

Hazel shoved the money into Sissy's chest. The notes fluttered around her and scattered across the floor. Sissy fell immediately to her knees and began to gather them up.

'I was only trying to help,' she called, but Hazel had gone. Sniggers came from a group in the corner.

'What you all looking at?' she scowled, feeling heat rise across her cheeks. Everyone returned to the business of readying themselves to leave. She scurried around, picking notes up from between bad-smelling trainers — trainers which were on the feet of people who made no move to help her; people who were beneath her, dull people who were doing nothing with their lives.

'Fuck off,' she told them. 'Go on, get out.'

Somebody tried to cover their laugh with a cough.

'Fuck off, I said!' she cried. 'Go on. Get out, get out, get out!'

An explosion of laughter and they sauntered away, leaving Sissy on her knees, clutching her money messily between two shaking hands.

She didn't know what she had done wrong, or

why people could be so touchy about money, something which, after all, was only a social construct, according to her dad. Surely it was abundantly clear that she could afford to give it away? Maybe Hazel thought she was showing off about her wealth. Sissy dismissed this thought almost as soon as it arrived. She wasn't wealthy, after all, she was only lucky enough to be living rent-free. Something Hazel would no doubt disapprove of.

The longer she thought about it, the more she began to wonder why she'd tried to help Hazel in the first place. After all, she'd been nothing but cynical and opinionated about her relationship with Pascal, she barely said thank you for the extra shifts Sissy organised, and now she'd publicly humiliated her.

That night back at the flat, and after the best part of a bottle of wine, Sissy decided it would be acceptable, given the circumstances, to call Pascal. If she could just hear his voice, she would feel better.

She dialled him, expecting it to go to straight to voicemail, but he picked up almost straight away and her heart soared. He wanted to talk to her. There was a slight pause, and then a female said, 'Hello?'

Sissy immediately felt sick.

'Yes, can I help you?' the voice said, with a hint of impatience.

'Sorry, wrong number,' Sissy mumbled, and ended the call.

She gripped the phone in both hands and paced up and down the small living room in agony, instantly regretting her decision to hang up. Not only had she forfeited the opportunity to find out who the strange voice belonged to, but Pascal would think she was an idiot for reacting so badly.

She jumped when her own phone rang. The screen told her it was Pascal. That was a good sign, surely. He wasn't trying to hide anything. She accepted the call, feeling her inner chaos subside already.

'Hi,' she whispered. Why was she whispering? Be normal, for God's sake. She sank into the corner of the sofa and waited for his response.

There came a sigh.

'Pascal?'

A throat clearing.

'Pascal, is that you?'

'Yes. Yes, it's me.'

The sound of his voice, so rich and mildly accented, seemed such a comfort. She had a sensation of almost folding in on herself.

'It's you,' she murmured, almost laughing now at the panic she'd found herself in seconds before.

'I told you not to call,' he said. His voice had a warm, regretful air that didn't tally with his words. It confused her. 'I told you,' he repeated. 'I said do not call. You were warned.'

A cold, paralysing dread crept over her.

Another sigh travelled down the phone to her ear.

'You are a silly girl, Sissy. A silly girl.'

She was left clutching the phone to her ear, straining to hear anything at all in the silence on the line. At some point, long after midnight, she left the phone there and went into the bedroom. From beneath the bed, she pulled out her suitcase. Inside was a zipped compartment. She opened it and took out the letter to her father. She still couldn't bring herself to read the contents. It felt odd to have a letter that would never be read, but she clutched it to her and tried to find comfort in this small connection, knowing that somehow or other it would have to be delivered sometime.

27

Sapphires in the Gloom

She didn't go into work the next day. Instead, she scrolled through Facebook and decided to message Rik. He replied almost instantly, bright and breezy like they'd seen each other only yesterday. When in reality it had been months. Without telling him about Pascal, and without asking about Noah, she agreed to meet him in their old regular in Vauxhall that weekend. It felt strange to be going backwards. Strangely good.

She made tea and toast and scoured the Internet for anything interesting. She googled Pascal and the company name and found where he was in Manchester.

At least he hadn't been lying about that.

She closed the laptop and returned to bed, and followed the same routine for the rest of the week. Occasionally she dialled into her voicemail and listened to Tony grow ever more irate as he wondered where she was. She didn't care. She'd done her best for everyone. She was done now.

On Friday night, Rik greeted her outside the club with an affectionate bear hug. Noah stood behind him, smiling nervously. She couldn't bring herself to be overly friendly — he was still an intruder between she and Rik — but she kissed his cheek and allowed the queue's fledgling carnival spirit to lift her a little.

It had been so long since she'd come to a club just to party. In a way she felt fresh to it. Rik gave her a pill. She hugged him then, seizing him by the arms, looked him straight in the eye and said, 'I love you. Right? I'm telling you now before this kicks in. I mean it. Okay?'

Rik grinned and kissed her forehead. 'I know you do.'

Inside, the music lifted and carried them back to a time of friendship, a time when all their possibilities were endless and bound to unfold beautifully before them. It was almost like the old days, although Noah made a poor substitute for Cam. Still, she grabbed his hand, and Rik's, and didn't look often in Noah's direction.

Pascal intruded on her thoughts, but she experienced the pain as an ache of some exquisiteness. As she moved to the tune of relentless drums and whistles, she was suffused with gratitude for all he'd taught her. He was flawed, they were all flawed, but the music was there to save them, catch them, hold them, show them the light, bring them home.

★ ★ ★

The toilets were full of guys in deep conversation, or perhaps negotiation. Sissy slouched against the wall as she neared the front of the queue, eyeing the outfits. Mostly it was tight jeans and no shirt, but occasionally someone had made an effort. She particularly admired one guy's headdress with giant yellow feathers. He bent over as he leaned into the mirror while reapplying his turquoise eyeshadow, his buttocks like small hard melons.

'No staring, rudey!' he winked. She smiled but didn't bother to compliment him. She needed another pill but thought she'd be fine waiting till she'd peed. She should have got it before coming in, given it a chance to sink in while she waited. The queues in the ladies toilets of gay clubs were the longest she'd encountered. She suspected few were there to piss. A door would open and two or sometimes three men came out, only to be replaced by similar. She'd resigned herself long ago to sharing with all the men in the place, though she'd never solved the mystery of how so many large bodies could fit into such a small space. Behind her there came a minor disturbance with raised male voices and apologetic female ones. Two girls jostled their way to her.

'Pretend we're with you,' one begged.

'Please, I'm gonna burst,' said her friend.

Sissy made space for them in front of her, enjoying the sound of their Irish accents.

'Thanks. We thought we were the only girls in here.'

'We didn't even know it was a gay club. We're a pair of fucking bumpkins, honestly. Hello, I'm Maura and this is Katie. We're just over for the weekend. Do you live here? Do you come here all the time? We don't have anything like this at home, do we, Katie?'

'No, but it's fecking great. Nobody hits on you all night. Unless. I'm sorry. Are you gay?'

Sissy laughed. 'No, you're safe with me.'

Another cubicle emptied. Katie grabbed Sissy. 'Come on in with us. You must have been waiting ages.'

They squeezed into the tiny space, the two Irish girls giggling. 'Race you!' Then came a commotion of elbows and hips until the one called Maura took her seat and sighed.

'Oh Jesus, thank Christ for that,' she said, letting it go.

'You're Scottish, right?' said Katie. 'I recognised your accent. Are you on holiday?'

'No. I live here.' Instant respect from the tourists. Sissy was proud of that.

'I'm so fecking jealous. Maura, hurry up, will you? I'm gonna pee my pants.'

They switched round. Katie letting out an even more dramatic sigh than Maura as she went. Sissy felt an instant wave of affection for them. They seemed so young. She felt protective. When it was her turn to pee, she noticed them whispering to each other.

'What?' she grinned, enjoying the stretch of her face, the heaviness of her eyes.

'Nothing,' said Maura.

'Wait until you're finished,' said Katie. 'You know you can rub your tailbone if you're having trouble. Look, like this.'

Katie reached behind Sissy and began to massage her.

'Eh, do you mind telling me what you think you're doing?' said Sissy, not because she objected but because she ought to be the one in charge.

'Honest, it works a treat. I do this on my wee

sister all the time,' said Katie. There was a conspiratorial silence while Katie massaged the spot and then through the hubbub of the outside world came the unmistakable sound of water hitting water. 'See? Didn't I tell you?'

Sissy was awestruck. 'Oh, my God, you made me pee! That's like magic!'

Katie accepted the compliment graciously.

'What age is your wee sister?' Sissy asked, embracing herself and rocking back and forth.

'She's only three. She's gorgeous, isn't she, Maura?'

'Aye. A wee diamond.'

Sissy remained on the toilet marvelling at her new friends. She told them she loved them, gave herself a shake and pulled her jeans up. 'Right. Now you have to tell me what you were whispering about.'

They shared a shy smile. Sissy's tummy made a little flip and a heat spread across her face as a possible future emerged before her. She'd never considered it before, but weren't they so beautiful?

'Turn around,' Maura said.

Sissy hesitated, then turned her back to them and leaned against the cubicle partition. A soft hand brushed her hair to the side; the delicacy of her touch made her gasp.

'Jesus, Katie. Feel her hair. Gorgeous.'

Katie moved up against her. Both girls took a portion of her hair and stroked it. Katie dipped her head into Sissy's neck. 'Smells amazing.'

An involuntary groan almost escaped from Sissy's throat as four hands stroked her hair, a cascade of caresses running from the tip of her head to where the fake curls stopped just above her waist.

'Feels nice, doesn't it?' one of them said.

'Tell you a secret,' the other said. 'We've taken E.'

My God, they're just little babies, Sissy thought.

'Turn round now. Give us your arm.'

Sissy turned to find Katie smiling at her. She looked delighted. Well, no wonder, Sissy thought, with that head of dark curls and those ice blue eyes, not to mention the smattering of freckles across her nose.

'You have a constellation on your face,' Sissy said, moved by the wonder of her.

Maura took her arm. 'Wait till you feel this.' She began to lightly stroke Sissy's arm.

The partition wall began to shake, and a rhythmic humping sound came from the other side. Katie looked concerned and Sissy immediately wanted to soothe her. She stretched her free hand out to cradle Katie's face. 'It's okay,' she said. 'That's normal for here. My God, your skin feels like a . . . like a pelt, or something. The sort of thing a man would go hunting for.'

Katie and Maura burst into giggles.

'I'm serious,' Sissy said. 'Do you two know how beautiful you are?'

The girls exchanged a shy glance. Maura's fingers continued to trace a swirling pattern on Sissy's arm. It felt so good.

'Go on,' Sissy said to Maura. 'Kiss her.'

It just felt like the right thing to do. They were

unique, independent people. They weren't part of the outside world with its petty rules and obligations. Here, everyone understood each other. 'Kiss her,' she said again. 'It'll feel amazing.'

Maura looked doubtfully at Katie. Sissy put her hand on the back of Maura's head and pushed her towards Katie. 'It's okay,' Sissy said, enjoying her mastery over years' worth of indoctrination. 'You're allowed.'

The alarm on Katie's face was immediate and unmistakable and was Sissy's first clue that perhaps she'd misjudged the situation.

'What you doing, man? You told us you weren't gay,' Maura said, ducking backwards.

'I'm not. But there's nothing wrong with being gay,' she replied, confused by their hostility.

'I never said there was,' Maura replied. 'But *we're* not.'

Sissy was suddenly aware of an oppressive dark cloud of shame hovering right above her.

'Well, what the fuck was all that about then?' she asked.

'We were just trying to give you a massage,' Katie said in a quiet voice. 'We like how it feels.'

'Oh Jesus, you're bloody children,' Sissy told them, scratching at the hairs on her arm which now prickled like a rash. She rubbed vigorously, trying to distract herself from her mood's crash-landing.

Shouldering Katie aside, she pulled the door back and left them behind. The guy with the yellow feathered headpiece continued to admire himself in the mirror, rolling his hips and pouting. Sissy brushed against him as she headed for the door — *hey careful, bitch* — she flipped him the finger. They meant nothing, these micro-aggressions. Everyone knew what was important. She made her way through clusters of over-wrought clubbers who populated the corridor between the dance room and toilets, trying to shake off the memory of Katie's worried face. She focused on the sensation of cutting through the air, aware of every new shape made as she filled up her space, intent on bringing back her rush. She slammed the swing doors open into the main room and gasped in the hot, salty air. Stalking the edge of the dance floor, she found Rik entangled with Noah. She grabbed him by the shoulder and yelled into his ear.

'I need another pill.'

He broke off the kiss. His eyes roved over her head, pupils as huge and black as the universe. Moisture glistened across his forehead and above his lip. She slapped his arm.

'I'm here. Look at me.'

'None left,' he shouted.

'What? How's that possible?'

He shrugged and fell back into Noah's waiting arms.

She weaved through the room. Bodies were clumsy and sweaty now, banging into her as she went. The bass was too loud, like a sonic boom blasting over and over, it reverberated in her stomach, making her nauseous. The air was tinged with aggression, the men more muscly than before. They looked at her with disdain, confirming everything she felt about herself. No crowd-surfing now.

A mass of energy caught her eye. A constant trickle of people moving in and out of the darkened area under the stairs made her think of bees in a hive. She edged closer, mimicking the focus with which everyone came and went. No party atmosphere here, only the serious business of getting high.

'Can I help you, darlin'?' The voice was so close, she had the impression of feeling, rather than hearing, the words. She turned and was momentarily confused by the familiar pale face of Fame grinning at her, his gold tooth appearing black as a sapphire in the club's gloom. He wore a chequered black and orange pork pie hat with a cream-coloured baseball jacket, the sleeves pulled up to his elbows. A gold chain hung round his neck and rested on top of the white vest beneath.

He wrapped his arms around her waist and pulled her towards him.

'Fancy seeing you here.' He bent to kiss her but she gripped his upper arms and pushed back.

'You working?' she shouted.

He cast his eye disparagingly around the room.

'What else would I be here for?' he sneered.

'Got any pills?'

He looked at her warily.

'They're just for me. I'm not working.'

'How many?'

She handed him money and loitered while he

collected her order. He returned and slipped her a small bag which she opened straight away, retrieving a pill and swallowing it.

She was aware of Fame taking her hand and saying something in her ear, but he was too quiet and she had to ask him twice to repeat himself. Then something scratched her palm. She looked down to see a neatly folded twenty-pound note kept in place by his thumb. He was speaking again and this time it made sense.

'You wanna get with me?'

Laughter exploded out of her. She didn't mean to offend, but he walked away with his shoulders rolled forward, his head low. For the first time she felt something for Fame that wasn't rooted in disgust. She was struck by his vulnerability — it must be lonely work being a straight dealer in a gay club. She made a mental note to check in with him later but for now she had to dance.

She turned to enter the heaving mass of bodies, a thousand souls casting themselves around to the rhythm of the DJ's beat. She searched for a way to enter, to find her space and begin her journey to the centre of the universe, but whenever she saw a way forward, bodies would close together and reject her advances, cutting off her route. She looked around for the last person who had been decent to her. There he was, leaning against the wall, keeping watch over the deals being struck beneath the stairs. He was small and wiry and had an aura of don't fuck with me about him, but all she remembered was his loneliness, and all she could feel was how lonely she was too. He noticed her looking and ramped his 'I don't give a fuck'-ness up a notch. It was all the invitation she needed.

28

Woman

'Yeah, yeah, but what's your actual name?' she said.

'You know my name. What you give me such a hard time for?'

'I'm giving you a hard time because no one on this earth calls their beautiful newborn baby Fame, that's why.'

'Aw, you think I was a beautiful baby. You're right. I was. I mean look at me now. I'm proper fit. Feel that.' She did — despite his skinniness, Fame was ripped. 'I must have been the most gorgeous baby they'd ever seen.'

'Babies aren't born like that. Don't try telling me you don't spend most days in the gym. Do you even have a job anyway?'

'Yeah, I've got a job. You know I do. You've seen me do it.'

'So, you're just a dealer? It's not just something on the side that supplements your proper job?'

'No, it *ain't* just something on the side that *supplements* my proper job. It's my job, innit. Don't use big words with me, woman. I ain't impressed.'

She liked that he called her woman. She *was* a woman. She rolled onto her tummy and snorted the next line, though really, why did they call it snorting? That sounded like something a pig would do, noisy, messy, whereas the powder slid neatly up her nostrils. It *glided*.

'I'm not trying to impress you. Ow, don't,' she said in response to him slapping her backside.

'Don't tell me what to do,' he said, stretching into the space she vacated. 'I be king of my own place.'

'You be king of Pascal's place, mate, only when he ain't around,' she said, mimicking his London accent.

She was up now, prowling Fame's living room, stepping over ashtrays and bottles and used condoms. 'Where's my fucking clothes?'

'Don't be giving me no back-chat, princess,' said Fame. 'Not when I bring you back to mine and give you all what I've got.'

She paused and turned to him, a look of exaggerated incredulity on her face.

'All what you've got?' she said, punctuating her mockery with a forward motion of her head, much like a chicken. '*All what you've got?* You're fucking kidding me. And English is your first language? What a fucking joke.'

'At least I am fucking English,' he snickered. 'What are you? Some Scots bitch moving into my country, my bed, taking all my fucking drugs. Don't think I haven't noticed. People in glass houses, mate. You ain't in no position to judge me.'

He chopped out some more lines while she continued to stalk the room.

'What you looking for anyway?'

'My clothes,' she sighed. 'Where are they?'

A rush of tiredness stole over her. She wrapped her arms around herself and began to shiver. Weak sunlight streamed in through the venetian blind and sloped across her body. Hundreds of tiny hairs stood erect on her skin. Casting her eye around, she could only see his jeans and shirt lying where they fell a few hours earlier. Confused, she reached for a cigarette and poured more beer. Fame sat bolt upright, sniffing deeply, making sure everything went as far in as possible. Then he stood.

'Don't you be worrying about your clothes. You don't need them just now.'

He placed one hand gently on her shoulder, pushing her down.

'My clothes — '

'You don't. Need them.'

★　★　★

At some point, maybe days later, her clothes appeared again. She left him kneeling on the floor rolling a joint, nodding along to whatever music was streaming through his headphones.

She followed the flow of people to the tube but resisted being swept down the stairs and stood blocking the way, aware she was committing the ultimate London crime but unable to move her feet forward. Move, she told herself. Get on a train. Go home. But there was no home. Commuters streamed around her, elbows and bags jabbing as they passed. There was no home. No place to go. No one waiting. No point to anything.

She had money in the bank, but it wouldn't last forever. Even so, she wasn't inclined to go into work, or look for another job. She also knew it was likely Pascal would ask her to leave the flat when he returned. Even if he didn't, she couldn't stay there if she had any self-respect.

There had to be some of that somewhere.

She spent the days between Fridays travelling around museums, something she hadn't done since her parents had taken her to the big galleries in Glasgow. Memories of silly poses with dinosaur skeletons and stuffed apes overshadowed the serious portraits she stared at now, trying to locate the genius that warranted their public admiration years after their creators had died.

Walking down a narrow street on the edge of Soho, she was surprised by the sound of live music coming from a dingy-looking bar. It was late afternoon and most of the bars were quiet, preparing for the imminent onslaught of drinkers from the abundance of local media offices.

Stained-glass windows marred her view and for some reason her feet wouldn't carry her through the blue-painted door. Instead she leaned against a black railing and enjoyed the old-school sounds of the bodhran and fiddle.

Her phone beeped. It was a text from Fame telling her Jason wanted her to work on Saturday night. She deleted it without replying. Another text came through telling her he was throwing a party at his flat on Friday night if she wanted to hook up. She had no intention of going, of course, but at least it was something.

29

Wild

The party consisted of eight or so people crammed into Fame's tiny living room, all of them greedily focused on the coffee table where the powder was. The music was low, a secondary consideration, and the mood jagged and insular. This was all completely obvious to Sissy, who stood observing the group from the living room's doorway.

In a way, they reminded her of the losers from the call centre.

All she had to do was walk over to Fame's laptop and change the music, but why should she? Let them spend their time scurrying around in a mediocre high. If they didn't appreciate the magical power of music, then they didn't deserve to crest any waves.

Fame stood at the window talking to a tall, slim girl, while he rolled a smoke. At one point, his hand dipped into her mane of hair and flicked it from her neck. She tilted her head back and laughed, and put her hand out to take a pill from him before slipping it in her mouth. Their little secret.

Sissy walked over and squeezed herself between them.

'Hello there, motherfucker,' she grinned, highly amused by her own outrageous greeting.

'Where's mine then?'

Fame raised his eyebrows, roll-up hanging off his bottom lip. He lit up and inhaled deeply before replying.

'Sissy, this is Joanna. Have you two met?'

Sissy turned her attention to the blonde. Fucking *Joanna*.

'Nice to meet you,' she said, and turned back to Fame with her hand cupped for treasure. It arrived in the form of two white pills. She was pleased. She would have settled for one.

'Would you like some of my water?' Joanna offered, but Sissy shook her head and took a swig of beer to wash them down.

'I was just saying,' Joanna said, her voice languid and mellifluous. 'I was just saying about the trees.' She indicated their view out the window to the street below. 'The trees are so lovely. All the colours. I love autumn, I really do.'

Fame grinned. A goofy sort of half-laugh escaped him as he agreed that he, too, loved autumn.

'A time of change, innit,' he said. 'A time of possibility.'

Joanna nodded profusely. 'Totally,' she said. 'Totally.'

'Oh, bullshit,' said Sissy.

They turned to her, expressions of shock and hurt on their faces, like she'd just lobbed rocks onto their sandcastles.

'Fucking autumn,' Sissy scathed. 'Who could love autumn? Only an idiot. You want to talk about the colours? The yellows and browns, the oranges and reds? Did you not stop to think that

293

everything's just *dying?*'

'Fuck off, Sissy,' said Fame, uncertainly. Joanna looked worried, which spurred Sissy on. 'Think about it. Someone punches you, you get a bruise. It goes all the colours of autumn, doesn't it?'

Joanna nodded, beginning to smile at what she perceived to be a poetic analogy.

'But actually it's just damaged skin.'

The smile dropped and Fame rolled his eyes.

'Think of — I don't know — a fucking *broccoli,*' Sissy continued, with equal amounts of conviction and relish. 'You buy it in the supermarket and it's gorgeous and green and lush, right? Then you forget all about it and discover it a week later at the back of your fridge and it's turning yellow. You don't then fucking think, oh, how lovely, how fucking *autumnal* is my broccoli, do you? No. You think, fuck this, that's too manky to eat. Into the bin it goes. One-fifty wasted or whatever. Autumn is the year DYING, you stupid fucks. It's a fucking miserable time. And there's those eejits who pay thousands to go on holiday to see it actually happening in, I don't know, Maine or California or somewhere. It's happening on your fucking doorstep, eejits. Like, right under your skin. All of us. Dying all the time.'

Somehow she'd been derailed from her original point, but it didn't matter. She was just as passionate about this one.

'You're cheery, aren't you?' Joanna quipped, sending a sly glance to Fame which enraged Sissy further.

'A fucking realist is what I am. Sometimes I feel I'm the only one. Look at you lot all crashed out and swimming in bliss. You don't know, you don't *know*.'

How to understand the truth of everything.

'I look at all these people around me, all of them milling around, going to the pub after work, or the shops at the weekend, all of them just wittering away, frittering away their time, and I remember what my dad said, all right? He said people are *stupid*.'

She allowed a short pause for the profundity of the statement to sink in.

'I'll admit, I thought he was out of order at the time for saying that, but what did I know? He was right. I wish . . . you know what I wish? I swear, what I wouldn't give to sit down with him now, adult to adult, and tell him how fucking *wise* he was. I'd give him all the respect I didn't give him when I was a kid. I mean, think about it, right? Look at it from his point of view. To die when your kid's just seventeen is shite. You've had all those years of sleepless nights, your freedom gone, thousands of shitty nappies, having to be super patient as all the meals you've cooked get moaned about or chucked on the floor or whatever — I mean, wee kids are hard work. And then they grow up into cheeky fucking teenagers and all they bring you is stress because they're *so much fucking smarter than you*, you know? And you're just an old man, a joke to them, and then puberty leaves and their hormones finally calm the fuck down and they turn into something resembling an actual halfway decent fucking person, and then just as they're about to leave home, go to uni, get a job, whatever, begin their own life outside of the home, and just as you're about to get your own life back — wham. A fucking blood clot strikes you down. What a fucking fucker. Do you hear me? Do you know what I'm saying?'

No one was listening. Fame and Joanna had melted away to join the main group. It enraged her. Such stupid fuckers all hunched over, look at them, not a shred of dignity between them, all scrabbling for the next joint, line, whatever. What did they know of life? Most of them were older than she was and had no idea of what was really important, or how swiftly their circumstances could change; how the world can pit itself against you in a single second. They had no idea of what it is to endure heartbreak, to be abandoned by those who should look after you, and somehow emerge stronger, find the will to rise above it all. All they cared about was their next high. Their ignorance was disgusting.

Approaching the table, she elbowed her way in and took the rolled-up note from between Fame's fingers.

'What the fuck?' he said, but by then she was hoovering up what was meant for him. 'That was fucking mine!'

She tossed her head back and wiped her nose with the knuckles of her free hand. She threw the note onto the table and stood up.

'Hey, watch it, man,' said somebody, aggrieved at having to move back to let her through.

The room crackled with hostility but she didn't care. She stepped over pairs of legs, lifting jackets and bags, searching.

'I can never find anything in this place!'

'What are you doing?' Fame asked, as he followed her around the room. 'This is not your fucking stuff, so why don't you put it back.'

She shoved a jacket into his chest. She didn't want his stuff. He was stupid to think so. He barely warranted acknowledgement. She stepped round him, making sure her shoulder gave him a good thud as she did so.

She went through the other rooms, the hallway, the kitchen; Fame's irritating presence behind her the whole way, his voice bleating on. In the kitchen, she poured herself a large measure of rum and sipped it slowly, eyeballing Fame, daring him to utter a wrong word, make a wrong move.

He loitered by the kitchen door, unsure of his next move. Behind him Sissy saw his mates regroup, like a flock of birds resettling after a scare. She knew he wanted to be with them. She enjoyed that she had pulled him away, but what was growing inside her was a feeling to dwarf all others; a sense of being too big for this shit life. Too powerful. Too wild. Too good. If she were to tip her head back and roar, a thousand lions wouldn't be louder.

She found what she was looking for glinting in the bowl on the bedside table. Her hand swooped in and picked them up. Somehow they arranged themselves to dangle provocatively on her middle finger, which she held up before her.

297

'What you doing, you stupid cow? You ain't fit to drive.'

'Don't tell me what I can and can't do.'

All her life people had told her what to do. Why had she let them? Why had it taken all this time to realise she was her own boss? That she owed no one anything? That she knew more about everything than the rest of them put together? It didn't matter. She knew it now. She was ascending, emerging fantastically into the world, like a phoenix. Her history was falling away and everything new awaited her.

Fame stepped forward and swiped for the keys, but she sidestepped him and he tumbled onto the bed with its wrinkled duvet and cum-stained sheets. Just looking at them made her want to peel her skin off. Instead, she made a dash for the front door and ran down the stairs, laughing, or screaming, at the words he hurled after her.

'Sissy! That's my motor! Sissy! Don't you dare! Sissy! Leave my motor alone!'

* * *

It wasn't until she put the key in the ignition that she realised where she was going. A voice so small it was almost a memory warned her against it, but she didn't want to listen. The night's beauty rushed upon her. Even the moon seemed aware. It hung back, distant and humble; it paled into nothing compared with the artificial blaze of a sleeping city. The roads lay open and empty. The whole of London had been gifted to her.

She drove with a razor-sharp focus, obeying the speed limit and guiding the car over speed bumps the way a mother's hand might caress a baby's head. Ha. Her inner poetry was potent. She'd conquered London. Nothing of interest here any more. Soon she picked up signs for the M1, and as she pointed the car north, at last the monster inside burst forward and took full control. Jealousy was in charge now. Jealousy and anger and hurt. At last she was brave enough to destroy everything. She imagined she even looked different. How could she not? But she didn't doubt that Pascal would still recognise her.

The motorway was a silken tunnel lined with cones of luminosity, crowned with such amber gems she might have been in Aladdin's cave. A necklace of white lights guided her. Two roads: one sweeping forward, one trailing back.

Her foot pressed the floor and she and the car shot through darkness like a comet, music their companion, transporting them into space, or sea, or just there, on that road with a sprinkling of other vehicles, all of them lonely crusaders riding the witching hour.

Far-off lights made her think of local civilisations, the sheer optimism of human settlements, the fragility of lives in flux. Nothing was permanent, everything that existed was fleeting; the whole world was beauty in transit. Blue and white road signs emerged from the blackness like angels. Her jaw fell open as she approached an orange box by the side of the road. It had a black telephone sticker on it. The idea that out there in all that dark, she could pick up a phone and hear a helpful human voice at the other end — well, it was so magnificent it almost made her want to die with happiness.

★ ★ ★

For some unknown reason, the music appeared to have stopped. Suddenly a car rose up in front of her and she slammed on the brake.

I'm not going to make it, I'm not going to make it.

Her arms went rigid between her shoulder and the wheel. As she bore down hard, she could see the vehicle in front had two passengers.

At last, she stopped with centimetres to spare.

Heart thudding, she expected the driver of the car in front to get out and scream at her. She'd almost killed them. She stared into their rear-view mirror. It was impossible they were unaware of her existence.

After what felt like an eternity, they moved off.

She sat at the roundabout for many minutes, shaking and trying to steady her breath. Paranoia scrambled to warn her she'd been sitting too long, probably attracting attention in hidden traffic cameras.

She let the window down and cold air rushed in. In the distance, the sun sent its first yellow tendrils to yawn delicately over the land.

30

Old New Beginnings

Pascal had been okay in the end. He'd taken one look at the car, its interior covered in vomit, and brought her into his office, no questions asked. She slept on the floor beneath his window and he covered her with his leather coat. She found the smell of it comforting, but when she woke up she knew she was done with him.

She gave him the keys to the car and he promised to return it to Fame within the week. He said he would take care of the valet and send her belongings when she sent him an address.

From there she took a train to Glasgow and found a room in a flat on the south side. She shared with two others. Professionals. Quiet. Ideal. The last thing she needed was more party people in her life.

She'd never noticed before how the air can be different from city to city. Glasgow was colder, fresher. There was something to it, a familiarity that came from being born and raised in a place. The sun set where it should, cast off the colours it always had. Why they should look so different in Glasgow she didn't know, but she accepted it and knew it was right, just as she knew the clouds hanging low overhead were right, and the sound of the rain was right, whether it came as a drizzle or flood. In London, she hadn't been aware of anything amiss in the shape of the world, but Glasgow had a tinge of something that was so uniquely to do with home, and childhood; a sense of belonging, even though there had been no fanfare to welcome her home because as yet no one knew she was back.

She took the red tourist bus from George Square and wondered how she could have grown up to know so little about her own city.

Alighting near the university, she couldn't fail to think of Grammy and another of her well-worn tales:

'The Headmaster came to our door and told Aunt Margaret I should be going to university. 'No, no,' says Margaret. 'That's not for the likes of us. We can't afford that.' The Headmaster's eyes looked like they would pop out of his head. 'You won't need money,' he told her. 'That one will get scholarships!' But Margaret was firm. 'No, no,' she says. 'I need her working and that's that.' All I could think was how she's ruined my life. Ruined my life then caught the boat to Australia. In some ways it was thank God for your grandfather.'

She always blew a little puff of air from her lips at this point, which gave the impression she found it funny but not enough to laugh fully. She always shook her head too, as if she couldn't believe what she was hearing, even though they were her own words from her own mouth.

Sissy had only the vaguest memory of her grandfather. She had gathered the impression over the years of a quiet man living in the shadow of a Goliath woman. Even her father

302

hadn't spoken very much about him. Was that odd, she wondered, and would her own father disappear from conversations now he wasn't here? In fact, she realised with a jolt, it had already happened. Whether she'd intended to or not, Sissy had arranged matters so there was no one to talk to. In the middle of Kelvingrove Park, she felt a surge of nausea as she contemplated the fact she'd become complicit in his eradication.

Finding a bench, she sat and waited for the sickness to pass. A crocodile of children clattered noisily past her, accompanied by two carers. Sissy looked past them up to the Gothic spires of the university building. So high, so imposing. Despite her grandmother's stories, Sissy had never been attracted to it. 'Not for everyone,' her father said. It had always been a source of tension, so she'd filed it away as something not worth thinking about. Now, sitting on that bench, her head full of ghosts, she felt the stirrings of something else deep inside her.

★ ★ ★

She took a job answering calls and emails from disgruntled rail passengers, of which it transpired there were many. For Sissy, the new routine was a breeze after the hostility she'd endured on calls in her previous job. She handed out apologies with cash and vouchers and enjoyed hearing the change in the customer's voice before they hung up. Her supervisor told her she was too generous, but as grateful emails poured in congratulating her on excellent customer service it became easy to disregard the warnings, especially as prospectuses for various universities arrived through the post. Hungry for change, Sissy spent evenings poring over them, dreaming of a day in the future when she could go to see her mother with apologies bolstered by tales of achievement.

One day she took a train and a bus to the north-west part of Glasgow she'd grown up in. She walked past her old school, went to the places she, Cam, and Rik had hung out in. She had lunch in their favourite cafe and from there walked to the park. Her breath ran ahead of her in billowy clouds. The trees were mostly bare and the paths strangely quiet.

She took the curved path behind the rhododendron bushes, and as the pond came into view she scanned for the boathouse in which they'd spent many a truanting afternoon. At first she thought it had been removed, but then she saw it lying on its side, head first in the pond, no doubt pushed over by cider fuelled teenagers. Walking over, her suspicions were confirmed by the presence of empty bottles lying in the long grass.

She sighed and took a seat on the bench, which at least remained intact, albeit with a few new layers of graffiti. There was no sign of her name, or anyone she knew in amongst it. The cold seeped through her jeans and numbed her backside, so she got up again and began to walk.

The park had the odd quality of being altogether familiar, yet entirely new to her. She realised she'd never really looked at it before. The intricacy of the chipped gold angels encircling the water fountain struck her as a kind of miracle in their down-at-heel setting. Swings wrapped two and three times around their metal frame carried a double sadness; not only were they unusable and, no doubt, the source of disappointment to small children and tired parents, but they whispered of underwhelming weekends, days and nights of teenage wanderings, wild souls with nowhere to go, nowhere to be.

A few drops of rain blew in and Sissy turned towards the exit, keen to be on a bus before the weather changed. Behind her she heard a scurry of footprints and a voice called, 'Here, boy!'

Suddenly a dog wound itself around her legs, causing her to almost topple over.

'Sorry!' the owner called.

Sissy bent to scruff the dog behind its ear and it jumped up at her, its pink tongue lolling out the side of its mouth. She looked into the dog's eyes, one green, one blue, and her heart lurched.

'Come on, boy,' the voice said from behind her. 'Sorry about this.'

She remained kneeling as Cam grabbed Bolt by the collar and clipped his lead. For a moment she thought he would walk away, but then he did a double take and stared, and she realised her long hair had momentarily disguised her.

Slowly, she pushed herself to standing, caught red-handed, though up until that moment she hadn't realised she'd been hiding. Bolt jumped on his lead and Cam pulled him into line. He looked back at Sissy, mouth agape. In the absence of any other plan, she accepted his scrutiny while doing some of her own.

Was it possible he'd grown taller? It certainly seemed so, though his style hadn't changed. His track suit and trainers were as grubby now as they had been when he was twelve. A rush of affection mingled with guilt for being so shallow.

'How are you, Cam?'

It sounded so trite and formal.

He continued to stare at her, and began to slowly shake his head. Then, just as she was wondering how to extricate herself from the situation, he dived forward and picked her up in a fantastic bear hug. Sissy, he was saying, Sissy, Sissy, Sissy, and then her face was wet, whether from the rain which was coming down heavily now, or from something else, she couldn't say, but she hugged him back, and then somehow they were jumping up and down, even though they were still hugging, and what made them laugh more than anything was the fact of the dog barking and jumping until they all fell to the ground, tangled up together in a jubilant mess.

31

After Midnight

Cam arrived late for his shift at the hotel breathless from running, and distracted with knowledge, or more specifically, the worry of what to do with his knowledge.

He and Sissy had walked round the park, playing with Bolt, avoiding serious conversation, but when the rain had soaked them they had gone to their old cafe to warm up. They ordered hot chocolate and chips, which they fed to Bolt in a bid to keep him quiet beneath their table, and tried to unravel what had gone wrong in London.

'I was a dick,' he said.

'I was a bitch,' she said.

'Rik was a twat,' Cam said, 'Let's blame him.'

They laughed at the nonsense of the statement. Sissy explained about the new boyfriend and how she'd had to move out when he came along. When Cam asked why, she only sighed and shook her head.

'I was a dick,' she said. Cam snorted into his hot chocolate. She smiled.

'I don't know,' she said. 'I felt a bit . . . pushed out. It felt a bit like when Grammy moved in with me and mum.' She shrugged. 'It just pushed my buttons, I guess.'

Her eyes had watered and she'd stared down

into her cup until he lunged for another topic.

'I can't get over the hair!' he cried, sounding false even to himself. 'It looks awesome. What made you do that?'

She'd blushed and lifted the ends. 'It's all fake. I don't like it. I'm going to have it taken out soon.'

'Well, I think it looks nice either way,' he'd said, and lifted his cup and clinked it against hers.

She'd told him all about her plans, which universities she was looking at, and he'd told her he had a job in catering, which wasn't the whole truth, and enough of a lie to be ashamed of. He didn't even know why he'd lied, only that it wasn't the time to be truthful. They'd talked for hours until Cam had realised the time and dashed to work.

'Of all the nights to be late, Cam!' Jude said, as she emerged from the function suite laden with plates.

'I know, I know, I'm sorry,' he replied, skipping past her with his hands up, guilty as charged. 'I'll hang my coat up and be straight there.' But she'd already disappeared into the kitchen, allowing a cacophony of banging pans and beeping machines to escape through the swing doors.

When he'd returned from London, he'd been given short shrift by his mum and stepdad.

'It's not you. It's the dog,' his mum said.

Cam knew it was neither he nor the dog that was the issue, but rather his stepfather.

'Put him in a shelter,' his mum had said.

'Someone'll take him.'

The suggestion boiled his blood. He could just as easily imagine her saying the same thing about him.

He'd spent weeks sleeping rough, mostly in the boathouse until a bunch of little shits kicked it over one night. Then he'd taken to the street and that was where Jude had found him. She'd taken him back with her and fed him and let him wash and then he'd slept for a week. She didn't complain once about Bolt, who was smelly and had forgotten the basics of being a house dog.

Jude had always been decent to him. He owed her a great deal, though he knew she would deny it. She never lorded anything over him. Which was why he wasn't comfortable not telling her about Sissy.

All evening he mulled it over, spilling drinks, dropping glasses.

'Pull it together, will you,' Jude hissed, uncharacteristically harsh. She immediately apologised. 'It's just this party. I want it to go well. I know the family . . . '

Her whole demeanour changed as a man in a grey suit carrying a small baby approached them.

'Aleks! I was hoping you'd say hello! I hope everything is as you'd expect? Oh, is this your daughter? How lovely.'

Cam made to return to the suite but Jude called him back.

'No, no, come over here, Cam! I want you to meet Aleks.'

Unused to such formalities, Cam shook the

man's hand, which wasn't easy to do because of the baby.

'Aleks used to run this place,' Jude said, lightly, peering down at the baby. 'I think he's back to make sure I haven't run it into the ground.'

The man smiled stiffly, his focus towards Cam because Jude would not look up. 'I know that would never happen,' he said.

'Aleks, this is Cam,' Jude said. 'He's my best worker. Soon, I think he'll be my second-in-command.' She looked up briefly and gave a glassy smile. 'Just like I was to you. Oh, she really is lovely,' she said, looking swiftly down again. 'You must be so proud.'

Cam was stunned by the casual way Jude had seemed to promote him. He hadn't expected it and his mind was instantly alive with possibility. Certainly the place was populated with half-wits who needed telling what to do all the time, but he'd never imagined being their boss. The idea was a tempting one.

'Shall I get back to our guests?' he asked Jude, with what he hoped was an air of polite maturity. Now he saw the prize, he was ready to play the game.

She nodded and he bowed slightly and retreated.

'Well, it was lovely seeing you,' he heard her tell the man. 'I'm so glad you decided to have the christening party here, but I'm afraid I have some paperwork to settle so . . . '

'Jude,' the man said, in a low voice. Cam's ears pricked up, always alert for trouble. He busied himself behind the reception desk, ready to step in, but Jude seemed to have it under control.

'Ah, excuse me. Busy, busy,' she smiled, and turned away. For the briefest moment she appeared to hesitate, but then she nodded her head once, and walked determinedly away.

★ ★ ★

It was after midnight and the hotel was quiet. The last of the party-goers had malingered around the bar until they'd been asked to leave. It was always the same, no matter if it was a funeral, wedding or as in this case, a christening — there was always someone who wanted that extra drink.

Jude could have been home hours ago. Normally, she would be. She didn't understand the need to hang around for this one, or why, even now when everyone had left, she was still behind her desk, shuffling papers. In fact, she could have taken the whole day off and avoided Aleks altogether — someone else could have stepped in adequately enough — but she was curious, she supposed, to see The Happy Man, as she'd come to think of him. Also, there were other venues he could have used. He was making a point. Look at me, he was saying. See how happy I am without you.

To accept his punishment was the least she could do.

Also, she really, really wanted to see him.

At last she understood why she'd stayed late. If she was at home she would be having a drink right now. No matter how many bottles were in the hotel, she would never touch them while at work. At home, she allowed herself an occasional glass of wine, but only if she was sure there was no part of her that *needed* it. Anne's watchful presence normally helped in that regard, but now she was in hospital it was all up to Jude. The constant second-guessing of herself was exhausting.

Inside her desk was a little brown box with a rosary set Anne had given her. A lifeline to the Holy Mother, she'd called it. Use it to pull yourself closer to the Holy Mother of God, Mother of Christ, Mother most pure, the Queen of Families. She took it out and began to thread the beads through her fingers.

A knock on the door. Hurriedly, she put the beads back in their box, knowing even as she did so that it was probably a sin to be embarrassed about them.

Cam's head appeared around the door. 'Hi, Jude.'

Surprised to see him, she called him in. 'You're not night shift, are you?' she said, turning to check the rota on the wall beside her.

'No, I . . . I've been waiting to speak to you but I . . . I didn't know if I should or not. I've been hanging around a bit. Trying to decide.'

Cam had such a hard front, when he let it down everyone paid attention. Immediately concerned, Jude began moving files to the floor and told him to sit. A tidy desk was akin to laying a red carpet. 'Is everything all right?'

He nodded, though his ashen face suggested otherwise.

She wasn't scared or made nervous by whatever he was about to impart. Though she was fond of him, there was enough distance between them to insulate her from damage. His news could only have minimum impact on her life, unless he were to quit. That would be a pain, but not insurmountable.

He breathed in and brought his hands together at the same time.

'I saw Sissy,' he said on the out-breath, laying his hands on the desk. He'd done it. It was out there now, no going back. She could do what she wanted with it.

Jude didn't know what to do with the information. She felt pinned to her chair, trapped by the weight of the ball he'd just passed her. When she spoke, her voice sounded strangled and distant.

'She's in Glasgow?'

He nodded. 'I saw her today.'

She pushed her chair away and stood up.

'I don't know where she lives,' Cam said, quickly. 'I mean, she said she's sharing a flat on the south side somewhere but . . . '

Jude landed back in her chair with a thud.

'She *lives* here?'

He nodded again.

'She *lives* here and she hasn't *told* me?' Jude said, incredulous. Somehow London was an understandable distraction, but to be on her doorstep and not tell her was truly insulting. Any relief at learning her daughter was safe was quickly quashed by anger.

Cam ran his hands down his thighs and gripped his knees. 'I thought you'd be happy,' he said.

'Happy?' Jude exclaimed. 'What's happy?'

She stood and grabbed her coat from the stand in the corner, desperate to be out of the room. This was more than she could cope with, and actually, there was nothing to be done about it anyway. So Sissy was in Glasgow. She still didn't need her mother. Nothing had changed. He shouldn't have told her. Everything had been just fine until he'd walked into the room.

'Did she say where in the south side?' she asked, before she left.

'Somewhere near Shawlands.'

She cruised the streets, wondering which closed door led to her daughter, searching windows for a sign of her. The roads were deserted, as she'd known they would be. At last, when the futility of the operation was clear, she turned the car home.

The house was in darkness apart from the electric candle Anne liked to keep running beside the Virgin Mary. Jude collapsed onto the sofa, one hand covering her eyes. The coffee table was strewn with medicine she'd recovered from Anne's bedside drawer — painkillers, digestive aids, laxatives, herbal tinctures — and she couldn't look at any of it without being reminded of how much she'd failed Anne in recent months. How much she'd failed everyone.

The bottles called to her from the kitchen. She had never seen the point in throwing them out, because she didn't have an actual *problem*, she just needed to exercise a little more self-control, but now she strode through and took them down. One by one she emptied them into the sink, and as the last of it drained away she felt the beginnings of a strange kind of peace settle within her.

32

The Difference

Cam felt bad. Sissy had asked him not to tell Jude she was back. It wasn't that she didn't want to see her — it was more that she wanted to see her when the time was right.

'I messed up everything, Cam. Threw everything away. And my cousins are doing so well! I can't bear the thought of going back like this. My tail between my legs. I need to have something to show for it. To make up for everything. I want her to be proud. You understand that, don't you?'

So he'd promised. And then he'd broken that promise. And now Jude was mad.

He felt more than bad.

He felt frightened.

It wasn't his intention to stir up trouble, but he didn't see how he could work with Jude, knowing as he did how worried she was about Sissy, and not tell her where she was.

But he hadn't expected it to go down the way it had.

He kept it from Sissy. After everything they'd been through, their friendship was climbing back onto solid ground. He couldn't bear to wreck it.

So they continued to meet up, she continued sharing anecdotes from work (she was getting *such* great feedback from the customers!), and her excitement about the future she was planning. He in return continued to lie about where he worked.

In this way, they grew to love each other again.

He told Jude he hadn't seen or heard from Sissy since that first day, and was surprised by how readily she'd accepted it. She never asked. Meanwhile, he grew increasingly anxious that Sissy's grandmother may die before she even discovered she was ill. He resolved to tell her everything, but the right moment was never at hand. He longed for the little bubble he'd created to never pop.

One day, Sissy confessed she had been fired from her job.

'Who the hell gets fired from their job for *being too nice?*'

'I do, apparently,' Sissy shrugged.

Cam hooted. They were in Sissy's room surrounded by books and application forms.

'It's not funny, Cam. If you think about it, it's really fucking worrying. What does it say about the world we live in? Where are we headed? I mean, as a species? Seriously, we're fucked. It was only vouchers and a few quid. They can well afford it. They just don't care if their customers get good service or not.'

'You should go to the papers.'

Sissy shook her head. 'I'm done with it. Look, I've decided which course to do.'

She passed a University of Glasgow prospectus to him.

'Social work?' said Cam, trying and failing to keep the surprise from his voice.

'Yeah, so? I want to help people.'

'I know, but do you want to help *those* people? Trust me, I know what I'm talking about. You'll get no thanks.'

She stretched and helped herself to another biscuit.

'*You'll* get no thanks if you don't shut up, Mr Negative. Anyway, I need to do college first. And I need another job, so if you hear of anything, let me know.'

Cam almost told her they needed help at the hotel while Jude looked after Sissy's gran.

'I really think you should see your mum, you know,' he said.

Sissy's face paled. 'We talked about this already.'

'I know,' he struggled to assemble his argument. 'It's just . . . what if something goes wrong. You know? What if there's no time to fix things?'

She nibbled the biscuit. Her appetite had disappeared and now she just felt queasy.

'What if things can't be fixed?' she said, after a moment.

'Don't be daft! She's your mum, for God's sake. She loves you.'

'Like your mum loves you?' She instantly regretted it. 'I'm sorry. I don't mean to be a bitch.'

'No, no,' Cam said, holding his hands in the air. 'It's fine, really.'

He picked up the prospectus and hurled it onto the bed.

'You know what?' he said, eyes blazing. 'It's

not fine. Not fucking fine, at all. No, my mother might not be the best woman in the world, and neither might yours. Do you know what the difference is?'

She shook her head.

'The difference is my mum never gave a shit for anyone but herself and that dick of a boyfriend. Whereas you? You had it all, Sissy. I don't get why you can't see that. Yeah sure, your dad died and it was awful and it all went off the rails a bit, but — she's been trying to get in touch with you, hasn't she? You told me that yourself. All the way down to London for you and all for nothing. And now you're in Glasgow, in *Glasgow* for fuck's sake! The *same fucking city!* And you still haven't contacted her! Jesus. Give the woman a break, will you? She lost her husband when you lost your dad, you know?'

Sissy blinked rapidly, trying to make sense of Cam's assault. The only response she could think of was, 'They weren't married.'

Cam stood up. 'Oh for fuck's sake.' He picked up his jacket. 'Grow the fuck up, Sissy.'

He slammed the door behind him, causing the papers on the floor to skit across the room.

She immediately followed him, but instead of calling after him down the stairs, she ran to the bathroom and vomited.

★　★　★

Five tests in a McDonald's toilet confirmed it. She banged her fist against the wall. *Damn, damn, damn.*

319

'Are you okay in there?' a voice asked.

'I'm okay, sorry. I'm just pregnant.'

'Oh!' The voice was happy with that news. 'Congratulations, hen!'

She'd known, of course, but instead of facing up to it like an adult, she'd buried herself like an idiot in her work, chucking vouchers and pounds at people like she was God. Like if she was good enough, someone would come and take all her problems away.

Three months late. It could only be Pascal or Fame's. Most likely Fame's, but there was no way to be sure. Normally they used condoms but sometimes she'd been so wasted she only become aware afterwards that they hadn't. Anyway, she was damned if she was telling either of them.

She went to the doctor who arranged for her to see a midwife who asked her a range of questions, including: Have you ever used illegal drugs?

Sissy opened her mouth to lie, found she couldn't, and broke down in tears instead.

'Have I damaged it?'

The midwife handed her a tissue and waited for her to calm down.

'It's generally ongoing substance abuse that we worry about, Sissy. A few mad nights before you find out isn't going to do anything.' She returned to her questionnaire. 'Now, unless you tell me you're planning on partying like that throughout your pregnancy, I'm just going to tick the box here that says No to that question, all right? Don't want some judgemental jobsworth giving you a hard time about it further down the road.'

The woman's unqualified kindness was so overwhelming, she almost didn't say that she might not want to keep it.

'Well, that's all right too. You've got time to decide, but in the meantime I think we need these tests done, don't you?'

Sissy nodded and accepted another tissue.

'I can't believe I've been so stupid,' she said, in a small voice. 'I'm not like that, honestly.'

'Nobody's like that, Sissy. Whatever *that* means. Nobody's like that at all, so don't beat yourself up.'

She ran to the Internet and googled sexually transmitted diseases. For days her mind buzzed with worst-case scenarios. Sometimes she stood before the mirror, sticking her tummy out to see what she would look like if she went ahead. The midwife had said it was only the size of a sprout, but already she could see the change. What she'd thought was weight gain due to not clubbing any more was actually her body preparing to be a mother. She was softening, expanding, accommodating — doing everything a mother should do. It was happening with or without her.

The same midwife called a few days later. Everything was clear, she was healthy. Sissy felt this woman to be something of a guardian angel.

'Don't thank me,' her voice came down the line. 'Just look after yourself, okay?'

All she had to do now was decide. She thought of the mothers she knew: her own, obviously, her grandmother and Aunt Susan. There was Lauren too, of course, but she was a distant figure, polluted by the opinions of others.

None of them were what you'd call adverts for parenthood, not that they'd made a giant mess out of it, but, she realised with a pang, none of them were happy. Weren't children supposed to make you happy?

She thought of Rik's mum, Mrs Sutton, who had always been subject to everyone's derogatory opinions. *Too quiet, so indulgent, such a mollycoddler.* But Rik still called home and gladly went back for Christmas.

So it could be done.

However, it was clear she could never go back like this: pregnant, a single mother, unsure of who the father even was.

She eyed the prospectuses and application forms which she'd tidied away into a corner of her bedroom.

It had to be one thing, or another, and time was running out.

33

Tightly-bound Roses

She hadn't been to the cemetery since the day of the funeral. It had grown so much it almost appeared to be a different place entirely. Of course people continued to die. Why hadn't she realised?

She headed in what she thought was the right general direction, using the giant crucifix at the top of the central path as a marker.

She wandered among the graves, clutching the photo of the gravestone that had been sent through the post by her grandmother. It had been a strange thing to receive, but impossible to throw away. She hadn't anticipated ever being grateful to have it.

A weathered-looking man on a quad bike stopped close by.

'Who you looking for?' he asked, in a matter-of-fact way.

'Peter Donnelly?' she said, almost laughing at the idea this man could know where, among the legions of dead, her father was. She showed him the photograph.

He nodded and got off the bike, beckoning her to follow. He pointed to a section of high-up ground.

'On the left,' he said, king of his domain, and headed back to his bike.

Gravel crunched beneath her feet as she walked slowly up the hill towards one stone which was taller than all the others.

Petty thoughts accompanied her, swooping into her head swiftly, automatically. Imagine making status a priority even in death, she thought. Typical Donnelly behaviour. But she was grateful too, she noticed. Her dad should have something special. As she got closer, she was relieved to see it wasn't ostentatious. It was dignified. A Celtic cross hewn from grey marble. It had been chosen well.

She stepped onto the grass, maintaining what she hoped was a respectful distance from the stone. Having thought about this visit for some time, she now found herself wondering why she'd come at all. Then she remembered the letter.

Through the gaps between graves, she saw an old man a few rows ahead of her, sitting alone on a bench, talking away to invisible company. Far on her left was a couple in their twenties, tidying a patch of ground brightly decorated with windmills and teddy bears. Her father's gravestone had a hole for flowers, but the hole was empty. Something else to be angry with Jude about.

'Will you stop it!' she cried, catching herself and those nearby by surprise. These negative thoughts trickled in regularly. She wanted to move on, not remain trapped in her past. Strange that moving on had necessitated a return home. A few months ago, she couldn't have guessed it.

The roses she'd brought from the supermarket

didn't want to come free of their cellophaned, cellotaped binding. Using her teeth, she worked them loose and they fell in a heap onto the ground.

Flustered, she gathered them up, pricking her hands on the thorns. The stems were far too long to sit neatly in the space left in the gravestone but the thorns prevented her snapping them to a more suitable length. Annoyed with herself, she arranged them as best she could in a lean-to fashion, sure that the first puff of wind would carry them away.

The wrapping began to roll down the hill. She picked it up and looked for a bin. Only then did she notice the view.

'Wow,' she whispered.

Like a great grey sea, Glasgow glittered beneath a milky sky, the curved aperture of which embraced everything in Sissy's sight: a purple patchwork of hills in the distance, motorways snaking through the city, lines of cars shooting like darts in a never-ending flow of near misses; blinking lights on high-rise buildings, countless church spires and glinting windows, plumes of smoke rolling out from tall chimneys before settling in drifts, and running through it all large swathes of greenery flourishing against all odds.

She had missed this entirely on the day of the funeral. Tears pricked her eyes. It was almost perfection.

She put the rubbish in a nearby bin a little further up the hill. On the walk back to the grave she noticed something stuck in a small gap between the stone and ground. It was a plastic rose, peach in colour, its stem bent in half. Picking it up, she recognised it as coming from her grandmother's house. There had been a basket of them that Sissy played with as a child, rearranging them over and over until the styrofoam block that housed them was rendered useless by the repeated stabbing of the roses' sharp ends.

Mud and moss coated the fake rose. Reaching into her bag, she pulled out a bottle of water and an old tissue and began to clean it. As the dirt fell away, Sissy experienced a sense of usefulness that she hadn't felt in a long time.

She placed the rose deep down among the real ones, and remembered how much her mother disliked plastic flowers. Surprising then, that Grammy had been allowed to leave it there. But then memories surfaced of those days after the funeral, when Anne had moved into the house and taken over everything. It was a mistake to believe her mother had control over anything.

Those thoughts again, spoiling everything.

Still kneeling beside the flowers, she bowed her head and tried to bring back the sense of purpose she'd felt only seconds before. Her father's name was etched in gold onto the marble. Peter Donnelly. Loving father, husband, son.

Even though they'd never married.

Everything was lies.

Those thoughts again.

She took out her father's letter and looked from it to the gravestone. Much like the photograph of his grave, the letter was something she couldn't throw away but had no desire to keep. She'd had an idea she could bury it in the soil around him, but the ground was solid and she hadn't had the foresight to bring anything to dig with.

Footsteps came up behind her. Keeping her head low, she pretended to pray as she waited for them to pass. Their approach on the gravelled path was slow but grew steadily. At last they stopped right behind her and she was forced to look up.

The sun was only partially blocked by the figure standing over her. The escaping rays blinded her. She raised the hand holding the letter to shield her eyes, and even then she didn't trust what she saw.

★ ★ ★

They greeted each other almost as strangers. No kiss, no hug, barely a polite smile, but both experienced immense relief at being in the other's presence at last. A coming home, of sorts.

It was strange, Jude thought, how they both cried yet remained apart. Perhaps she should do something, reach out to console her daughter, but she was frightened to touch her lest she disturb her and cause her to run off.

Instead she knelt down, careful to stay at the foot of the grave. The sunlight and her artificial mane of hair gave Sissy an otherworldly quality. Having spent the past several nights by Anne's bedside, Jude half-wondered if she'd fallen asleep and was dreaming.

But the tears coursing down the sun-dappled face were too real for it to be a dream. She stared, captivated by the blue of her daughter's eyes, her puckered lips and trembling chin, and in that moment she experienced again every bumped head and scraped knee, every bad dream and playground fight, and then she found she was on all fours crawling towards her, and she was crying too, and then they embraced and cried together, the way they should have done all that long time ago.

Dad,

I'm so sorry that you've gone. I can't really believe it. Gone. You're gone. I could write it all the way to the bottom of the page and it still wouldn't feel true.

I don't know what it is I want to say to you, except I love you. Thank you for being the best dad ever — even though that does mean I'm going to miss you for my whole life!

So thanks for that!

It isn't fair, Dad. I'm so sorry for you (and for me too, but let's face it you're the one who really counts here!)

You're so young.

And Mum's so young too. Too young to be a widow. I hope you don't mind if she finds someone else. She deserves to be happy. But I think it will take a long time.

I promise we'll never forget you, Dad.

My daddy.
Love you to forever and back,
Sissy xxx

Together, they ripped the letter into tiny pieces and tucked them into the gap the plastic rose had been caught in.

'Your grandmother was never happy with how they mounted this stone,' said Jude.

'I know,' Sissy said, as they walked back down the hill. 'She told me.'

34

The Silver Thread of Wildness

The family had gathered. Susan and Phil and the boys, Danny and the girls, even Lauren had made an appearance. Tall, beautiful, compassionate, she'd kissed Danny's cheek and held his hand in the waiting room, she on one side, Emma and Lucy on the other.

Susan rested her head on Phillip's shoulder, her two eldest boys locked into a game on their phones. Andrew, the youngest, loitered within sight beyond the door, hoping to catch a conversation with someone new. No passer-by was safe from Andrew. Of the three brothers, he was the most exhausting. Always pushing boundaries, breaking rules. Introducing himself to complete strangers, no matter how many times he was warned not to talk to strangers.

'But what if they're really interesting?' he would cry, frustrated by the prosaic protections adults tried to foist upon him. He hurled himself upon people like a crashing wave, washing part of them away with every syllable he spoke. Determined, relentless, effective — wonderful qualities for an adult, Susan told herself repeatedly.

An auxiliary came in and mopped the floor around them.

'Some lad you've got out there,' he said.

Anxiety fluttered to Susan's throat. What had he been saying this time?

'It's great to have the kids in a place like this,' the man confided. 'Gives everyone a lift.'

Susan relaxed again, as far as she were able. Waiting.

Andrew had disappeared from view. She gave him a moment to come back and then went to check on him. She found him deep in conversation with a young woman with long red hair. It wasn't until she noticed Jude standing a few feet away that she realised who it was.

Sissy would have gladly subjected herself to her precocious little cousin's questions all day long if it would have spared her the gauntlet of her family's gaze, but it seemed some sort of silent message had been transmitted. One by one they filed through the swing doors to say hello and act as if they had seen her only yesterday. As though all this time they'd been connected by a silver thread.

'I hear you gave up the acting,' she said to Emma.

'Of course,' laughed Emma, derisively. 'I was never serious about *that*.'

Lucy opened her eyes wide, a warning to Sissy to drop the subject.

Trust *me*, Sissy thought. Great start.

'*Andrew, will you come over here and sit down!*' Susan's sharp voice filled the air.

The little boy stopped whatever had caused the offence and ran to his mother's side with his face ablaze. He sat down beside her, popped his thumb in his mouth and nestled in.

Sissy felt an arm come around her shoulder. The soft, strange, familiar arm of her mother.

'Shall we go and see her?' she said.

★　★　★

Once the diagnosis arrived, Anne had surrendered herself with remarkable ease. First of all came the separation of mind from body, which she supposed was the sensible way of going about it, given the amount of pain she was in.

The spasms, when they came, drove away everything else. Sometimes she remembered the miracle button, but other times she needed help.

'You shouldn't be in pain,' Jude said. 'You press here. See? Like this.'

And her body would be suffused with relief. She would feel herself float off, like a seed on the wind, destined to land on fertile grounds and begin life all over again. In those moments she uttered deep sighs of contentment, but gradually the sound of her seemed to come as though from outside. It distracted her and she had to struggle to stay focused on the flight.

Here was Patrick.

No, no, no.

Trapped between two worlds, and no friends on either.

She thought she was drowning and remembered a time when the city flooded. Water got everywhere, seeped into the shop, spoiled the stock. All those men Patrick brought in to bale. They worked all through the night, hands touching, arms rippling, eyes full of intention, all of them fighting nature in the moonlight.

Oh, but here was Peter, her newborn. The rock upon which she would build everything, so difficult to come by and never destined to be kept. Her prize and her punishment, all rolled into one.

Falling.

When she landed back in the room it was bright and noisy and too full of strangers. She flailed for her beads, felt a gentle hand encircle hers, heard a sweet voice say, 'Grammy.'

'Pancreatic,' said a different voice. Familiar. Can't place it. It was something to do with her but she was just a little bit caught up at the moment.

Grammy, I'm here. I love you. I always loved you.

I'm here too, Anne. I love you too. You are loved, you are loved.

She was swimming through the flood. She had no idea where she was going, or what was up or down. It was all right. It was just the way of it, that's all. So many possible routes and destinations but no way of knowing anything about them. She felt she'd done this before though. In fact, she had the distinct impression she had always been here, doing this. Everything else was a dream. It wasn't frightening to swim in the air, or in the darkness. It just was. She was free and natural. She soared with the grace of angels. All she had to do was follow the silver thread and she would come to the right place. It was here somewhere.

It was here

and here,

and here,

Sissy and Jude travelled together back to the waiting room. For the moment, only they knew the secret of the life lost, and the one still to come. Jude took Sissy's hand, which was almost identical to her own. Their fingers entwined and everything they'd ever been or would ever be was sealed between them. Baby girl, daughter. Mother, grandmother. Friend, foe. Woman, child.

They reached the swing doors and paused to observe their family through the glass. Everyone was leaning forward to see Susan's wildest boy perform a magic trick. Each of them appeared to be absurdly happy.

Acknowledgements

Thank you for reading *Wildest of All*. Now you've finished the book, I'd like to mention my own grandmother who had a similar start in life to Anne. Her mother died when she wasn't much more than a baby, and the family was split up. She went to live with an 'Aunt Margaret' while her brothers went to an orphanage. I believe they were successful in tracking each other down, unlike in *Wildest*. Beyond that, Anne's story is fiction. My nana, as I called her, was a profound influence on me when I was growing up. She was tiny in stature, but a giantess when it came to doling out love and encouragement. She took me to my first writer's group when I must have been aged around ten. I owe her a great deal and miss her hugely.

In writing *Wildest of All*, I prevailed upon the talent of and generosity of many people, not least John Kernaghan and Laurie Cairns who provided me with a much-needed hideaway in Brighton where I finished writing the book. Special thanks to Robin Laing, Diane Thornton, and Lee Morgan for many things but most especially for being my research partners in the world of club nights, to Fin and Vince Laing — my research partners in the murky world of mothering, and to Joyce Henderson and Deborah Colvin for keeping me right in East London. Thanks also to Amber Louise Lynch for providing the inspiration for Sissy's job in Glasgow, Martin St. John and Carl Drake for being my Metropolitan Police consultants, Stephanie Stubbs for her counsel on corporate law, and to Tania Cheston, Vicki Feaver, Amanda McLean, Hilary Hiram, Samantha McShane, Thelma Good, Siobhan Staples, Nick Boreham, Bethany Anderson, Sarah Ward, and Sheila Millar, who all at one point or another offered valuable advice and insight into the development of this book.

I'm also grateful beyond measure to Lauren Parsons and the entire team at Legend Press for their patience and belief in me, and for steering me in the right direction, and to Donald Winchester, who took a chance on me, and always says the right thing in emails.